NEMESIS

ANTI-BELLE
BOOK 3

SKYE MCDONALD

Anti-Belle Books

JOIN THE COMMUNITY!

Click here for a free story when you join Skye's newsletter community!

MORE BOOKS TO BINGE

The Connecticut Commodores Series

Book 1: Scoreless

Book 2: Scored On

Book 3: In the Crease

The Anti-Belle Series

Prequel: The Not So Nice Girl

Book 1: Not Suitable for Work

Book 2: Off the Record

Book 3: Nemesis

Book 4: Just Your Type

Book 5: What Happens At the Beach

As Sarah Skye

The Unlikely Pairings Series

"Inside every rude girl, there is a girl with a soft heart who trusted everyone once upon a time."
-Unknown

This book is for her.

Author's Note/Content Warning

Welcome to my favorite Anti-Belle!

This book contains profanity, whiskey-drinking, and steamy scenes aplenty. You know, the good stuff.

It also contains a m/f fight scene that may be intense for sensitive readers. As ever, this is a work of fiction. Read at your discretion, darlings.

.

1

LIV

"Hey gorgeous, are you from Tennessee? 'Cause you're the only ten I see."

"Wow, really, that's the line you're leading with?" I shimmied to the beat of the music and laughed at the dude. Corny or not, he was cute, and this was a hell of a party. It wasn't every day that little old me got invited to a VIP event. Pretty awesome way to kick off another fiery Nashville summer.

The guy grinned and put his hands on my waist. We danced together, but I resisted when he tried to bring my hips against his. "Aw, come on baby, don't be shy."

His white-capped teeth went well with the white silk shirt he wore, unbuttoned to show off hairless, bronzed pecs. A-list pretty boy or not, I had no interest in grinding his crotch. I flashed my usual "back off" face, a scrunched nose and cute smile while shaking my head.

He pouted. "But if you don't come closer, how am I going to put my hand under your skirt and get you off right here on the dance floor?"

When he grabbed my wrist, I didn't even think. I pivoted

at a hard angle to free from his grasp and slammed my fist down on his forearm. My ankle wobbled in the heels I wore as I stepped back, hands raised in a guarded stance before I realized the setting and dropped them.

"What the fuck?" Dude rubbed his arm. His face winced in pain.

Krav Maga, baby. Looks like that shit comes in handy after all. I'd taken the course over the winter with my friend Megan, never actually thinking it would be something I put to use. My reaction might have been a bit overdramatic, but hey. At least I knew it worked.

I tossed my hair and scowled. "Who said anything about you molesting me on the dance floor? Did I ask for that? Did I say you could put your hands on me?"

He'd rolled up his sleeve, I guess to check for bleeding. "Damn, girl, calm down. Molesting? Jesus, don't get dramatic or anything. Just have a little fun. Don't be that girl."

That girl. I refused to flinch.

What a term. That Girl who can't keep her mouth shut. That Girl you meet at a party, charm the hell out of, and then never call again. That Girl who your best friend dates for a few months before finding "the one." That Girl who has a new obsession every few months but never committed for long.

That Girl. Yeah, I knew the label well.

But no girl, woman, or *human* should ever be touched without permission. And one perk—and sometimes curse— of being That Girl was that I didn't dilute the truth. When an entitled douchebag needed to hear it, all the better.

I curled my lip. "Damn, boy, why don't *you* calm down? Maybe you're from L.A. or something, all big shot with your rock-star friends, but in Tennessee we have manners. And we don't take kindly to guys who don't ask permission before putting their hands on a lady. Now, go on, get!" I stomped my foot and pointed across the room. My southern twang had grown with every syllable until I sounded like a caricature. Keeping a straight face at such a performance was difficult. Luckily, he gave me one more sneer and slithered away like the snake he was.

I looked around for my friends, but all I could see were glitzy people grinding on each other and swallowing pills with champagne. Everyone wore clothes I could never afford. For a moment, I felt out of place among all these VIPs.

Stop that. Are you going to let that slimeball ruin your night? Or are you going to get a drink and resume dancing your ass off?

Much better plan. I weaved through the crowd to the bar, only to bump into a very cute fella en route. He had a lot of swagger about the fact that he was one of the hosts, but he also knew how to flirt without being a creep. I declined his invite to stay for the after-party, but he turned the night around.

Moving on always was the best way to get rid of bad vibes.

Two days after the party, I sat in my parents' dining room for Sunday dinner and wished we could gather in the breakfast nook instead. In there, I could eat with one foot on the comfy Parsons chairs I'd picked out when Mom remodeled. In here, the rickety wooden seats with needlepoint cushions forced my posture rigid. Mom called it "being fancy." I found the stiffness a little too fitting with the tone of the meal.

"Did everyone have a good week?" Mom passed the peas as she spoke. "Olivia, what have you been up to?"

Really, Mom? We even have to use the fancy version of names? Should I call you Claire in that case? I can't be Liv with a linen napkin in my lap?

But Mom was the sweetest, and so I swallowed a bite of a roll and played along. "I was at a party Friday. That was kind of cool. Did you hear that a local guy won on the show *American Pop*? His name is Jesse Storms." Only Mom nodded. "Well, it was his event. He's recording here."

"That's where you were?" Tom asked.

I nodded at my brother. "Yeah, Nick's doing his album."

Mom pounced. "And who is Nick?"

"Oh, uh, Nick's just a friend."

In a classic older brother move, Tom's light brown eyes glinted at me being busted. I'd inherited Dad's Italian genes with my dark hair and eyes, but Tom and Mom had fairer, softer features. Seated side by side and both assessing me, they made quite the picture of scrutiny.

A large gulp of water dismissed the heat that threatened to creep up my cheeks. Nick and I had let the term "friend" get too flexible lately. *Just a couple of silly make-out sessions. No big deal. Dating your ex's best friend, one of your dearest friends in the world, is not an option. Not like we're heading that way or anything.*

God, we've got to cool it.

Mom gave me the eye but spared more inquiry. "I'm glad you had fun. So, Will, how's work?"

Beside me, Tom's best friend set his fork down. He scratched the weekend stubble on his square jaw as if about to give the World's Most Interesting Reply. "Work is crazy since we expanded operations to Chicago. I've been up there more than I've been home in the past three months. It's going well, but busy."

Mom and Dad stopped eating and nodded like bobble-heads while their surrogate son droned on. His position as a big-shot marketing director at one of America's fastest growing cellular companies always got the 'rents drooling with admiration. Even Tom's stories from his nursing job were hardly competition to the glorious William Langer's tales. Only Tom's adorable daughter, Maddie, could compete in terms of entertainment, but that's a grandchild's privilege.

I picked at my peas and wished the afternoon would shuffle along.

Why hadn't I told them about the other part of my week-end? Why had I defaulted to parties and "just a friend" stories when I had, in fact, done something more purposeful that day? Okay, purposeful might be a stretch, but giving up my summer Friday to volunteer at Maddie's daycare had felt pretty good. They'd been short-staffed, and Rachel, Maddie's teacher, had asked if I was free to lend a hand as a "parent chaperon". I'd planned to hang with some friends that day, enjoying freedom from the drudgery of my corporate mailroom job. Instead, hours flew by as I monitored a coloring station, doled out snacks, and sang songs.

And loved every minute of it.

Maybe that's why I hadn't said anything. My parents were sweet to ask about my life, but we knew the score. Just like I had my place in my friend group, just like people who met me described me as cool, bold, or bitch depending on what they thought they knew, so too did my family look at me in a certain role.

With them, I was still the baby. Mom and Tom especially had always doted on me. Having a protective big brother who supported every whim I'd ever had probably had a lot to do with why I was so comfortable being myself and speaking my mind. No one thought twice if I blurted out more details than I should. Mentioning Nick was a great example of classic Liv over-sharing. My latest obsessions, from piano lessons to axe throwing, were all about "finding myself."

So volunteering at a daycare would've registered as deeply as dancing at a pop star's party. Silly as it was, helping Rachel had meant more to me than my family would understand. Those basic activities had somehow equated to a deep sense of fulfillment that I rarely got from a day of work.

By the time Mom brought out cake, I'd folded a napkin into an origami bird to keep myself entertained. Dad was asking Will about statistical data as if he knew anything about it. I caught Tom trying not to laugh and grinned at him, momentarily blocking out Will's voice. Maddie let out a wail from the bedroom as Mom cut the first slice, so I pushed my chair back and hustled to get her before anyone else could respond.

"Hey little girl," I cooed as I pushed the door open.

My niece was sitting up, blinking blearily amid a fort of pillows on my parents' bed. Her cries quieted when I crawled over and nuzzled my head against her belly.

"Livi," she murmured.

"You hungry, Mads?"

"Pink!" She grabbed a fistful of my hair and stared at the dip-dyed ends.

"Yep, still pink honey. Same as it was before your nap. Let's go find some food, okay?"

"Airplane?"

That big-eyed plea won every time. I rolled to my back

and hoisted her onto my shins, laughing when she shrieked with delight.

"Airplane! Airplane!" Her ecstatic squeals lasted until I lowered her down and lifted her off the bed.

"Ooh, you're getting so big." I grunted as her little arms circled my neck. "Aunt Livi's going to have start weightlifting to keep carrying you around."

"I want chicken."

"Very logical reply, my love. Chicken it shall be."

I bumped the cracked door open with my hip to find Will in the hallway, his hand on the bathroom doorknob.

Our eyes met, and he sneered. "*American Pop,* really?"

It took me a beat to realize that was a dig at my story earlier. *Dammit, always be prepared with a comeback when he's around.* "That shirt, really?"

Decent recovery.

He shook his head and shut the door behind him. Maddie laughed when I rolled my eyes and poked out my tongue. We traded a shrug—a gesture she'd learned recently—and continued to the kitchen. That kind of exchange was a typical conversation for Will and me. I'd gotten used to his snark years ago and had no problem giving it back or ignoring him completely.

Everyone drank iced tea on the back porch in the June warmth for another hour or so. When the glasses were empty and Mom couldn't stuff us with anymore treats, I buckled my niece into the back of Tom's SUV and jumped in the front seat. Since Tom and I lived together, carpooling to family dinner was usually a given.

"Liv, we need to talk," he said on the ride. I looked over, but he shook his head. "We'll have a beer when we get home."

I itched with curiosity by the time Maddie was settled in

with a coloring book and a cartoon. Tom and I went into the kitchen. He flipped the tops off two Jackalope IPAs and pushed one across the table to me. Straddling a chair backwards, he got right to the point. "You're not going to like this, but Will needs a place to live in July. They're renovating his building, and he's got to relocate until it's done. I said I'd talk to you about him staying here."

I coughed on my beer. "What? Him? Here? How long?"

Tom sighed. "Maybe until the end of August."

"You're kidding, right? This is a joke."

"Look, I know you two don't get along—"

"Understatement much?"

Tom scowled at my interruption. His voice had an edge when he continued. "Yeah, but he's been my closest friend through everything. He'd do anything for me—for the family—and you know it." He took a breath. "Besides that, he offered to pay me the cost of his rent for the two months. Liv, it would cover Maddie's daycare for almost *six* months."

My mouth hung open. "Shit."

"But your name is on this lease, too, and I won't say yes if you're not okay with it."

"Will knows you waited to ask me?"

Tom nodded.

"Did that piss him off?"

"No. He knew you wouldn't like it, but, again: your house, too."

I puckered my lips and listened to Maddie sing to herself while I thought this over.

Tom and I moved in together two years ago. Maddie was only a year old then, and Tom was a grieving widower. His wife Jenna had died from a blood clot, a complication post-pregnancy they said, but reasons didn't matter when someone's world crashed down. I was 24, on my last attempt at college, and had gotten the mailroom job. Moving in with the two of them was one of the greatest decisions I ever made. They gave me purpose and grounded me, and I adored the little family we had become.

But Will Langer.

Will and Tom had been friends since they shared a dorm freshmen year of college. Completely different majors didn't diminish their friendship, and they lived together for all four years. Will was Tom's best man at his wedding. To my parents, he was basically another son. He was from Texas if I remembered correctly, but he never mentioned his parents at all.

Facts aside, the man got under my skin like no one else. Any complimentary description I could offer—he was intelligent, confident, dedicated—was eclipsed by the arrogant attitude and brooding quiet that made his presence a heavy weight in the room as far as I was concerned.

That weight wasn't helped by the almost palpable dislike he had for me. I made sure the animosity was a two-way street, but whenever I opened my mouth, I could count on hearing a deep sigh. I'd have told him off years ago if it weren't for how much he'd done for my brother over the years, especially how supportive he was when Jenna died. And he was great with my parents. Since I loved my family so much, I kept our little fire at a low simmer rather than letting it boil over, but it wasn't easy.

Being That Girl sucked, but it was a better title than useless. And Will had made it clear for years that that's what he thought of me.

I avoided the jerk as much as possible.

That wasn't always true. I used to avoid him because I had a massive, top-secret crush on him. I also used to be a silly, dreamy kid with her head in the clouds.

But, money for Maddie's daycare. I couldn't say no to that. We never worried about making rent or eating or anything, but Tom and I weren't rich by a long shot. Raising a child alone was expensive, and to deny him such a cash source just because Will and I didn't get along would be colossally selfish.

I sighed again and drained the beer in a few pulls. "You know I'm going to say yes, you douche."

He chuckled. "You don't *have* to. Maddie can just, I don't know, start staying at home during the day. She's not too young, right?"

"Three years old? I'd say so. Hell, why haven't we gotten her a job yet?"

"Pack her Dora suitcase. We'll ship her to the salt mines tomorrow."

I grinned and shook my head. "I'd say you owe me, but you know I'm a softie when it comes to my big brother."

He clinked his beer against mine. "I will owe you for this one, but I'm hoping you guys can mostly avoid each other. He'll sleep on the futon in Maddie's room, and I'll put her in with me. Should be minimal impact on your life."

"Promise?"

"Well, sis, I guess that's really up to you."

I poked my tongue at him, and Tom flicked his bottle cap at me. Ahh, siblings.

2

WILL

She sat at Sunday dinner stirring her peas. Why stir peas? What an obvious cliché of ways to fidget.

When Claire asked about her weekend, my fork began to swirl the little green balls on my plate, too.

She stirred because she was bored. I stirred because I should've been.

My mind split in half. In the front of my brain, I reviewed my calendar for the upcoming week. In the back, I pictured Olivia Milani at a pop star's house party, swinging her dark hair and wearing a low-cut top and miniskirt, perfectly comfortable among models and celebrities.

I chose *not* to picture that Nick douchebag, whoever he was.

There were moments, not many but a few, when I wondered if my disinterest in Olivia was the wrong tactic. There were times—that one, for example—when paranoia gripped me, made me sure that I was pathetically obvious. If someone looked closely, would they see how mad she drove me? Would they know how I wanted to bust her balls for being so damn flighty? How badly I wanted her to take the potential she had and make it worth something instead of running away when life got hard?

How I wanted her long legs wrapped around my back while I got drunk on her flavor? How I'd have no problem letting her tie me up and punish me after I pulled on that dark mane a little too hard? How I wanted to tell her that through all her fads and crazy hairstyles, she stunned me silent with her effortless beauty?

Jesus, how did they all not see it?

I panicked as I described work, wondering if I'd just trailed off into a litany of filthy, explicit fantasies instead. Claire and Anthony, my surrogate parents, continued to nod and smile, so I wrapped up fast and shut my damn mouth. Claire cut cake, and Olivia disappeared at Maddie's cry.

I didn't intentionally run into her in the hallway. I certainly didn't catch the sound of Maddie's shrieking giggles, sidle like a creep to the Milanis' bedroom, and watch, fascinated, at the sight of Olivia on her back, her niece hoisted into the air.

Of course I didn't. That would be absurd.

I did want to get a rise out of her with my little jab about the pop star, though. I counted on the zinger she sent back. And, because there was clearly something wrong with me, I went into the bathroom with the stupidest fantasy in my head...

She set Maddie down and pointed to the kitchen. "Gramma has cake," she whispered, her dark eyes on the little girl until we heard Claire's exclamation.

Then, she flipped her hair while she spun on her heel and gazed at my smirk. Her voice was as cool as the rest of her. "American Pop, that's right. What's it to you, Will Langer?"

But her finger hooked the belt loop of my jeans as her other hand fisted my shirt.

My throat was tight, muscles clenched with restraint. "I'm just wondering why you'd waste your time like that."

"What do you suggest I do with my time instead?"

I stepped backward into the bathroom. Her arm lifted as I pulled away, but she didn't release me; she followed. The moment she was through the door, I pushed it closed and flipped the lock...

I acknowledged being a total sleaze for thoughts like those. Olivia and I had never been familial, but I couldn't justify my guilt any more than I could stop my thoughts about her. They'd been part of me for so long, a decade at least, that I wouldn't know myself without them. I'd forgotten what life was like before she was in it. Before I adored Tom's kid sister and hated myself for it—especially after he made it very damn clear that she was off limits. I couldn't remember what it felt like, my heart before her. My soul before her.

Every part of my logical being rolled his eyes at the way I felt for Olivia. All good sense said I was absurd, that I should've found a wife and settled down already. That I should let her live however she pleased. Everything told me I was wasting my time.

And yet, the years went by and nothing changed.

God only knew how I was going to survive the summer if she agreed to Tom's plan.

3

LIV

June cranked up its heat per usual, and life rolled on more or less normally for a few more weeks. The big difference in routines came on Fridays. Summer Fridays were historically for sleeping late, watching trash TV, and maybe going to Jack's pool or hanging out at Megan's hair salon that she ran out of her home. They were *not* for waking up earlier than usual to be at daycare by 7 am. They were definitely not for spending five and a half hours singing songs and distributing animal crackers and crayons.

But Rachel called midweek saying I had been a huge help. She told me she'd gotten permission to ask me to assist again. On top of that, the head of the daycare wanted to know if I would agree to the gig through the end of July.

I hadn't hesitated to say yes.

It was still nothing major. As a guardian for Maddie, I could act as a parent chaperon so long as I was never alone with the kids. Still, I felt like I had done something important with my day every time I walked out of that little classroom.

Rachel and I sat together in the only adult-sized chairs

in the room on my third week. The kids were napping on rows of padded blue mats, so we had to whisper.

"You're a natural with the kids, Olivia," Rachel said with a smile. "But you're not a parent, right?"

I waved the thought away. "Oh, god no. Not even thinking about it yet. I love Maddie to death, but being an aunt is enough for now."

"Well, you and your brother are raising her well. I can tell she gets a lot of practice with conversation at home. It's so important to talk to them like people. Baby talk doesn't facilitate growth."

"We try." I hadn't considered the truth of what she'd said, but it made sense.

"I'm getting my masters' in child development right now, so those kinds of things interest me a lot. Uh, I hope this isn't presumptive, but you've seemed so involved in the class and curious about my job. I brought you something."

She reached behind her chair and handed me a canvas tote bag. I pulled out a large, soft-cover textbook on early childhood development.

"What do I do with this?"

Shit. I bit my tongue. My question hadn't meant to sound rude, but too often I let the thought train leave the station before I considered how someone would take it.

Rachel just laughed. "Whatever you want, I guess. I ended up with two copies last semester and thought maybe you'd be interested. If nothing else, it'll tell you a little more about Maddie as she grows."

I looked at her, my brows drawn. "Wow, thanks. I mean, I never really thought about this kind of thing before but thank you."

She nodded. "I understand. You're great with Maddie,

and you're incredible with the class. Just think of it as a little light reading on the brain."

I grinned, half in agreement and half with goofy pride. I couldn't remember the last time someone described me as incredible at anything other than telling people off.

Rachel returned my smile, and then looked around the room and sighed. "God, I wish we got naptime, too," she whispered, and we had to shush each other's laughter to keep the kids asleep.

At home that afternoon, I lounged on my bed and flipped the book open, planning to pass a little time by skimming it.

"Hey Livi. I figured you'd be getting ready to go out."

I jolted out of the book when Tom stuck his head in my room. My phone clock told me I'd been reading for three freaking hours. "Oh, uh, just—yeah, I should probably get going."

"How was daycare today?"

I pushed the book under my pillow before standing up. "It was alright. Just a day."

"I hear that." He chuckled and turned away. "See you later, sis. Have a good one."

"Later, Tommy."

Of course Tom had caught on to my daycare gig. His twelve-hour shifts at the hospital put us on very different schedules. Taking care of Maddie and dropping her off were regular parts of my routine, but there was no way to hide getting up early just to take her to school. When he noticed the week before, I'd told him the partial truth: they were short staffed, and the money was a good little bonus. He hadn't asked for more details, and I hadn't wanted to share.

Why are you being such a geek about this thing? It's literally no big deal. The money was minimal as an aide—not that the money was great for the teachers, but at least it was a living —and the whole thing was temporary. Why, then, was I tight-lipped like it was a friggin' black ops mission?

"Whatever." I jammed the book in its bag and went to find an outfit.

Ooommm. My eyes opened to gaze at the pale orange ceiling. Sweat pooled in the hollow of my throat and slicked my hair, but I resisted the urge to towel off until I'd sat up. Beside me, Megan polished off a bottle of water. We silently rolled up our mats and went for the showers.

Hot yoga had become my obsession last fall and showed no signs of growing dull. Ninety minutes of cathartic sweating was pure bliss in my book. On top of that, the bonus of brunch and best friend time afterward made a perfect Saturday morning, especially on the Saturday Will moved in.

"Your new ink is gorgeous." I eyed the colorful tree on Megan's shoulder while we dressed.

"Checking me out, chick?" She ran a fingertip over the fresh tattoo. "It took about four hours. Which, let's remember, I spent alone, thanks to your 'super busy Friday'."

I flicked water droplets from my hair at her. "I *said* sorry, you ass. Maddie's daycare needs some extra help."

Megan stepped into her shorts and wrinkled her brows. "That's where you've been? Sounds... enthralling."

We walked out of the yoga studio and down the block to Sky Blue Café, our usual spot. I shrugged, hoping she didn't notice my held breath. "It's alright."

"If you say so. Latte or regular coffee today?" She slid into the booth already eyeing the menu.

"Latte. Saturdays are for indulging."

The drinks arrived. I searched for a good topic to chat about. Obviously, I wasn't going to start gushing about toddler cognitive theories.

Meg beat me to it. Her hazel eyes flared as she took her first sip. "I forgot to tell you. I have our next big thing."

"Oh? Do tell."

She thumbed her phone and grinned. A second later, mine buzzed with a link. "CrossFit, baby. We could be some badass bosses."

I skimmed the info page she'd sent and snorted. "Could be? Tuh, as if we aren't by nature. But I hear this is intense, and we just took that Krav Maga course in March. That stuff works, by the way."

Meg set her mug down with a bang. "Stop, hold on. Did you use the crane technique and not tell me? Liv Milani, did you sweep the leg?"

We laughed at the *Karate Kid* references for the millionth time since enrolling in the self-defense class. "Not even close, but I used the wrist grab defense on an asshole at the Jesse Storms party a few weeks ago."

She gave me a slow clap. "You're my hero. So, how is it a bad idea to add burpees and rope climbs to your repertoire?"

"Am I in training for X-Games or something?"

"Nah, just for life, yo."

We clinked mugs to that.

She gestured to her phone again. "Look, it's four classes for a hundred bucks. Let's see if we like it. If you wuss out, I bet you can get a refund."

"Name the last time I wussed on anything."

"Exactly. We can start Tuesday."

"Ugh, fine. Bought." I tapped the screen hard for dramatic flair.

Megan grinned. "Speaking of that party, how's Nick these days?"

I shrugged and stashed my phone. "Meh. Haven't heard from him in a while. I tried texting a couple times, but no response. Working on Jesse's album is making him kind of crazy."

"So I should cancel the order of monogrammed towels I bought you guys?" Megan laughed when I flipped her off. "Come on, 'fess up. How, um, *serious* did y'all get?"

"God, you are nosey."

Her eyes widened. "He was on top of you so bad at my place that one night, I thought *I* was getting action. Besides, he is pretty cute. Come on, give me the scoop."

I groaned so loud the people at the next table looked over. "Nick and I are friends. Maybe we, ahem, blurred a few lines a couple—three—times, but it was just fun. It's not like we were in the throes of a passionate affair. Now he's busy and so am I. Who cares?"

Megan drummed her fingers on the table. "I hear there are going to be some new faces at David and Aaron's party tonight. You coming?"

I arched a brow and picked up the check. "That could definitely be fun."

She winked at me as we slid out of the booth. "Fun indeed. I'll see you in a few hours."

"Pray for me. It's jerkface move-in day."

"Om, girl. Om."

We kissed cheeks goodbye. I headed for my car humming the Imperial Death March as I braced to "welcome" Will into my home.

His black Audi was parked in my spot in the driveway. A fancy-looking bicycle leaned against the side of the house. "Great start, buddy boy. Thanks for leaving me to park on the curb." I stomped inside, grumbling under my breath. The living room was quiet, but the floorboards upstairs creaked as muffled voiced drifted down. I followed the sounds.

Maddie squealed when I peeked into Tom's room. She sat in a heap of clothes with a crown on her head and a pink tutu over her clothes. "Hi, Livi! Toys!"

In the corner, Tom and Will wrestled with the toddler bed. There was a futon in her room that Will would use. I wondered how he felt about the idea of living for two months in the pastel beach décor I'd painted for her third birthday. *I hope Tom makes him use the SpongeBob sheets.*

I bit my cheek to keep from cackling and caught Tom's eye. "Do you need help?"

He shook his head. "Nah, we've got it. We're going play clean up in a bit, right Mads?"

She grinned at her father, oblivious.

"Okay. Guess I'll be in my room."

"Sounds good." Tom turned back to the bed, which I noticed Will had been studying the whole time.

"Hello, William." My voice was flat and louder than needed. *Got something to say about how I could lend a hand? Maybe you'd like to critique my outfit or—*

He glanced at me over his shoulder. "Olivia."

I sucked my teeth in reply and disappeared to my room. The textbook was on my vanity table, easily accessible on my way to the bed. I kicked my sandals off and flopped down with my highlighter and pen in hand.

Shrugging off Megan's question earlier was pretty impressive. I had basically lost all chill on the subject of child development. I'd taken to reading the textbook on my lunch hour during the week. My head was full of facts and questions that had no outlet except for the whisper sessions with Rachel on Fridays. Yesterday, I'd finally asked her how one became a daycare teacher. Nonchalance was my goal, but that crumbled when she'd grinned and promised to forward some information.

Okay, so this is your latest thing. Cool. But it's not a big deal, so of course it's not worth telling Megs about. Being a helper will be over in a couple weeks. Becoming a teacher or something would require a college degree, or at least a certification, which you don't have. Don't get carried away.

I frowned at the book. What was the point of all these notes, or even bothering to read on, if that were true?

It'll help you be an awesome aunt. You know you're good at that.

Reason enough. I opened the cover and dove back in.

4

LIV

Maddie was amped when I picked her up on Monday, so to wear her out we played one of our favorite games: "Concert." For this, we both dressed up in my flashiest clothes and put on lipstick. I sang and danced around the living room while she bopped to the music and squealed with laughter.

We did several oldies and a couple new hits before I called up my theme song and signature number, "Let 'Em Talk" by Kesha—the clean version, of course. This song always required a lot of jumping around and throwing my hair, leaving me sweaty by the time it was over, but damn it was a fun one to shout-scream.

At the first chorus, I noticed Maddie was also jumping around and shaking her head, clearly trying to copy me. When I waved a finger, she did it right back, puckering her little lips as a mirror to my pout. *Ooh, a new development!* My brain split between the performance and trying to recall what the textbook had said about mimicry.

Guess I was a little too absorbed because I failed to hear the back door open.

"*Oh-oh-oh*—oh, god, really?" I twirled around and found Will leaning against the wall, arms crossed, a sardonic curl on his lips. "How long have you been there?"

"Long enough. Don't let me stop you."

I glared at him, but then spun to Maddie and threw myself on my knees at her feet. She dropped to hers too, arms flung wide, and Jesse Storms could keep the arenas full of screaming fans. My niece's grin was enough for me.

"More, Livi! 'Call Me Maybe'!"

I cringed. Will snorted. "Let's go eat instead. How about a cookie?" I suggested, just short of pleading with a toddler.

Maddie wouldn't be moved.

Will also wouldn't move. I don't know how he didn't hear the curse-laden directions to go away that I mentally shouted at him, but he just cleared his throat and gave me another one of those smug smirks.

I'd made the mistake of doing this song one time, and it had automatically become Maddie's top request. Since the child was diabolically irresistible, I had little choice but to pretend her big brown eyes were the only ones watching while I made my hand into a phone and went for it. Watching *her* make a phone hand and try to mouth the words made everything a little easier. Still, the second the song was done, I shut off the stereo and hurried us to the kitchen. Maddie kept warbling as I settled her into the high-chair and began to make dinner.

"I don't think I ever heard that whole song before." Will strolled in and dropped into a chair at the table.

"Oh please, that's totally your ringtone."

He nodded. "It almost was, but since I couldn't find your version for download, I didn't see a point."

Did Will Langer just make a joke?

"You can sing," he said when I didn't reply.

"Not nearly as well as some of my friends."

"Well enough to handle that maddeningly catchy song."

"You loved it. You stayed for the whole thing."

"It was... mesmerizing."

"I usually am."

"Mm-hm." His dark eyes fixed on me in a way that made me fidget. I tugged at my cutoff shorts and scratched my hip to play it off, but Will didn't speak again. At last, he checked his phone, and I turned my attention to the stove.

Maddie began to babble at him about school. I listened and pretended I wasn't while he questioned her about coloring and playground. "And what about your teacher? Is she nice?" he rumbled, his deep voice gentle and strangely adorable as he spoke to her.

Maddie squealed that she loved Miss Rachel, but then added, "Livi's the best."

"Liv is your aunt, not your teacher."

"And teacher too!"

I hurried to set the plate in front of her and ruffled her hair. "Shh, eat up, sweetheart."

Will cocked his head. "What does she mean?"

I ignored him and poured a glass of iced tea, but then I sat down at the table and shrugged. "I've been working as an aide at her school. It's just a temp thing for extra money, no big deal."

"That's a lie," he said without hesitation. "There's no way that money is worth the time investment."

I bared my teeth. "Look, I'm sure you bill at a thousand bucks an hour—"

"No, I meant—"

"But some of us have to hustle for our paychecks. So, don't start about how poor I'd have to be to take a job, alright?"

Will slapped the table. Maddie startled, and we both glanced at her, our glares turning to sweet smiles. She grinned and went back to her grilled cheese without further ado.

Will's voice was tight as he returned his attention to me. "Calm down."

"Tell me to calm down again, and I'll put your ties in the paper shredder."

Dark eyes rolled. "You are so dramatic. Can you please listen for a minute?"

"Can you please try talking without sounding like a total d-bag?" With anyone else, I might've regretted sounding so harsh. Will pushed my buttons like no one else.

The muscle in his jaw flexed, but then Will blew out a soft breath. "An aide at a daycare is minimal money. If you wanted a second income, you could find any number of things to do that would pay far better and be *far* easier. Therefore, your claim that it's no big deal isn't true. You must be interested in the work. Tell me more."

How did he know that so easily?

"Did you always want to be in marketing?" The question was meant to redirect, but I knew it wouldn't. Will Langer wasn't the sort to be distracted if he was interested in something. And, for whatever reason, his analytical stare was trained on me at the moment.

"It wasn't my dream job. I wanted something that would require strategy and creativity but that would also be lucrative. Marketing was a good fit. Why? Are you thinking of becoming a teacher?" He leaned forward, elbows on the table, that stare intensifying.

Roll your eyes. Laugh. Shrug. Do something! Despite the directions my conscience shouted, I sat there mute, tea glass at my face. Finally, I set it down and licked my lips.

"I," I started, but then snapped my mouth shut.

"What would it require? What age group would you teach?" he asked like I had said yes.

"I don't know yet," I mumbled. "I just started."

"What made you think—"

"You know, it was easier when you were being a jerk about the money. Maybe you should just tell me it's silly, not grill me on details."

Will sat back. His eyes widened, but then he clenched his jaw. "Typical," he breathed. Louder, he said, "Then you chose the wrong person. If you want to hear it's silly, then ask a fool for his opinion. Don't waste my time."

I hid my face in the crook of my arm. "Ugh, for one second could you stop being weird and just, I don't know, pretend I'm not me? Give some encouragement that isn't so damn cryptic."

Silence followed. I peeked up and found him on his phone. He set it down and cleared his throat. "Shoot for the moon. Even if you miss, you'll land among the stars."

We stared at each other a long moment before I began to laugh. Will pressed his lips in a line, but his grin broke through. I wiped my eyes and held up my middle finger. "That's what I think of your words of encouragement, Langer."

He hummed. "Then next time, Milani, don't ask me to pretend that you're not you."

My brows lifted, but Will's expression didn't waver. Before I could think of a reply, Tom strolled in. Will eyed me again, then turned to greet him.

"How's it going, Livi?" Tom asked as he straddled a chair.

"Good." I jumped up and began to make another grilled cheese. "Want a sandwich?"

"Sure. Are you going out tonight?"

I nodded. "There's a show at Third and Lindsley."

"What about, uh, what's his name? Nick? Still hanging out with him?"

"Mm, not really. Haven't heard from him lately."

"Dick." Tom's voice had a big-brotherly edge to it as I set the plates in front of us.

"It's cool, Tommy. We may hang out again or maybe not. I'm good either way." Even as I spoke, it struck me how familiar a thing it was to hear myself say. I took a big bite to dismiss the thought.

"You shouldn't be. You shouldn't take that from a guy," he grumbled.

"Ugh, Tom. You are so not my dad."

"Ugh, Liv, sound a little more like a five-year-old, little sis," Tom groaned back with a chuckle.

My eyes locked with Will's again as I looked away from Tom. For a moment, I forgot to chew. His expression was blank, but instead of an eye-roll or sneer, he just arched a brow at me. I blinked, and his eyes got narrower—but his lips curled in the faintest of smiles.

"Gotta go." I jumped up and rushed out of the room before I could begin to think about what the hell that look meant, or why it felt so damn good to have finally talked to someone about my latest whim.

One night later, a super toned chick in a black tank top and biker shorts smiled brightly at the group of nervous-looking people I stood among. I glanced around the warehouse-style facility that was the CrossFit gym, then over at Megan. She grimaced.

"Okay, guys, let's get started," Ms. Biker Shorts said with wicked enthusiasm.

In the hour-long "beginner" course, I'm pretty sure I sweated off at least ten pounds. The muscles in my calves were jelly when I stumbled to the locker room.

"Dear god, why did I suggest this?" Megan groaned.

"Clearly you're a masochist." I dropped to a bench and tried to muster the strength to peel off my shirt and crawl to the shower.

She put her hands on her hips. "We need beer, stat."

"Oh, look! You found my second wind." I laughed and got moving.

At the closest pub, we downed what was possibly the most rewarding beer ever before letting the waiter talk us into ordering food. "Burgers for my ladies," he said as he delivered the plates. "What are you two up to that's got you so hungry?"

"We've been at CrossFit." Megan rested her chin on her hand and flashed a flirty smile.

He whistled. "Y'all must be pretty tough."

Her smile got wider. "Damn right, buddy."

"My name's Adam, and I'll be back to check on you in a few."

"What do we think?" Megan asked as he sauntered away.

I glanced at his retreating figure and shrugged. "He's cute. Not my type, but you should get his number."

"Oh, suddenly you're so generous. Trying to make up for ditching me at the party last Saturday?"

The weekend party had indeed featured some new faces. One of the guys, a friend of a friend, had been cute and fun. We'd wound up flirting all night over a wicked game of Cards Against Humanity, but there was no great spark to make it memorable. Besides, Megan had been having plenty of fun with our friends.

I harrumphed an objection as I ate. She poked her tongue at me, so I stuck my tongue out at her—with food on it.

Megan clapped a hand over her eyes and laughed. "God, you're disgusting. Please tell me that adorable move was how you snagged... what was his name?"

"Chad, maybe? Something like that."

"Seriously? You don't remember his name so you're calling him Chad?"

We giggled, and I shrugged. "It was a party, not a date. I didn't even give him my number."

"Why not? Was Chad not tall, dark, and handsome enough for you?"

"That's not my only type," I grumbled, and then grinned. "It's just my favorite."

Megan eyed Adam across the room. I followed her gaze. He was talking to another waiter, cheek creased in an easy smile as he pushed his sandy blond hair away from his face.

Megan hummed. "Well, here's to whatever your pleasure."

I laughed and lifted my beer. "Amen, sister."

"Are we going to Jack's for the Fourth tomorrow?" she asked once she'd unglued her attention from Adam.

"Yeah, but I may need a wheelchair after the workout tonight. My glutes are already killing me."

"Hydrotherapy, baby. The pool will soothe all your aches."

"Here's hoping."

Meg's hazel eyes narrowed in a way that made me pause. Her assessing gaze was uncanny and far too insightful. I braced myself.

Sure enough: "I've let you hide for too long. What in the hell is with this daycare business?"

I thought about the email I'd gotten from Rachel yesterday that outlined how to become a certified teacher. I thought about how liberating it had been to talk about my new thing, even if it was with freaking Will Langer.

And then, I nodded and spilled it all. "Well, since you asked…"

5

WILL

The Fourth of July was on Wednesday, thereby derailing the momentum of the week. There were barbeques I could've gone to. Clients and colleagues loved to host, but I wasn't in the mood to socialize and then go right back to the office the next day. Better to get a jump on a few things and enjoy some quiet.

Tom had a 12-hour shift, and Maddie was with her grandparents. Liv had bounced out of the house earlier in beachwear, shouting goodbye to her brother, not bothering with pleasantries for me. Just as well.

I started the day with a long bike ride, which was typical for a day off. Most of the afternoon was spent working at the kitchen table. By the evening, I'd made an impressive dent on my personal and professional to-do lists. Dinner sounded good, but I decided to wait a bit and zone out with some TV before making any decisions. My ass had barely hit the recliner cushion before the back door opened.

Olivia appeared. She stopped short when she spotted me. Her dark eyes rolled, which made mine do the same.

"Hello, Olivia."

The look on her face said she caught the way I mimicked her from Saturday when I moved in. Really, what did she want from me? I'd been working on fitting that damn bed into a tight corner, and it wasn't as if we were in the habit of hugging hello.

"William." She fiddled with the belt on the sexy getup she wore, shorts and a top all in one, whatever that was called. In it, her legs looked even longer, her tanned skin even more gold. *Get out of here, Liv. I have no idea what else to say to you.*

The frown she usually wore when she looked at me didn't waver, but she didn't leave, either. It was clear she'd been swimming given her clothes and hair, so I used that as a reason to mess with her.

"Is this a pit stop between parties? Time for a wardrobe change?"

God, you're such an asshole to her. I hated parties as a general rule because I found them exhausting. Still, there was a morbid fascination with what it would be like to be out with Liv, to see how she owned a room just by being in it. I couldn't tell her that. I also couldn't ask why she spent so many evenings out when she wanted to become a teacher. The next certification exam was in August, a fact I learned when I researched the subject after our conversation the other day. Shouldn't she be studying?

Shouldn't you mind your own damn business?

As ever, the queen of snark didn't disappoint in her reply. That I-hate-you look turned into a saucy sneer. Her jaw clenched, but her comeback didn't miss a beat.

"Nah, not really. I've been tripping balls since noon and am probably seconds from passing out in a pool of my own vomit. Thought I'd call it a day."

My brow wrinkled as two images, one childish and the other very much not, competed in my head as an interpretation of what she'd said. "You've been what?"

"Forget it."

Loser didn't need saying. The implication was clear. Liv's sneer deepened before she strolled past me into the kitchen.

"Fuck," I sighed under my breath as I snatched the remote, needing a distraction. Since it was July 4th, I knew just the thing:

Do-do-do-do do-do-do-do...

Liv skidded back into the room, a tall glass of iced tea in hand. Her brows arched. "What the hell are you doing? Did I just hear *The Twilight Zone* theme song?"

The TV answered for me. "Submitted tonight..."

I nodded, not bothering to explain that this was a tradition for me. "There's a marathon every Fourth."

A delighted smile creased her face, lighting her up like I usually didn't get to witness. Liv flopped down on the couch, her glass held high so as not to spill. "Hell yeah. I was going to go upstairs, but it looks like you're stuck with me now, Langer."

"Hooray." I muttered it. I wanted to laugh it. For just a second, I wondered how awkward this might be, but the show absorbed us both.

Many episodes later, I rose from the chair and headed to the bathroom, unable to hold out another half hour. Dusky shadows darkened the house as streetlamps flickered on outside. When I returned to the recliner, I realized the TV was the only thing illuminating the room. Hours had slipped away, and we'd been too engrossed to notice.

Salty, buttery aromas hit my nose. Liv appeared with a fresh drink and a bowl of popcorn in her arms. She sat on the center cushion of the sofa and began to munch. Dinner had been a thought ages ago. My saliva glands were working overtime.

"That smells delicious."

I glanced at her, waiting for the zinger about making my own or how much she was enjoying it. Instead, Liv thumped the cushion beside her without blinking from the screen.

"Then come have some."

When an opportunity presented itself, my instinct was to assess the situation from all available angles and look for the best outcome. This approach, much as I hated to admit it, was probably largely a result of the first time I met Olivia Milani. Nonetheless, it had served me well in business over and over again.

And so, in grand fashion, I overthought the offer until Liv cleared her throat, an obvious message of *what are you doing, Langer?*

Go for it. I went to sit beside her, and she passed me the bowl. "Thanks," I said. "I didn't know you liked this show."

"Well, you see, I have good taste. So that would be a big fat duh." She shook her head and licked her index finger.

Blood rushed to my dick as I watched her finger slide between her lips. Her cheeky tone just made it worse. I returned the popcorn to her, grabbing another handful as I did.

Before I could compose a good reply, Liv waved me off. "Ooh, hush, this is 'Time Enough At Last'. It's one of the first I ever saw, and I swear it fucked me up big time."

"Indeed." I chuckled, anticipating the sick plot twist at the end.

How I thought I could focus on the show with Liv Milani seated beside me, I have no clue.

She smelled like summertime. Chlorine and sunscreen

wrecked my concentration from the opening credits, and from there it only got worse. Every little sound or move she made vibrated my senses. When she shifted, our shoulders rested against each other. I swallowed a groan. Why did she have to be so warm, so fucking beautiful? *What does she usually smell like? How is she not bothered by us sitting like this?*

Because she doesn't care about you, ass.

But then Liv tensed. I watched in my periphery as her chin lowered, her gaze on my hand as I reached for more popcorn from the bowl in her lap. Her breath turned to shallow puffs, and I withdrew fast.

"I'm sorry, am I taking too much?"

She jumped. "Nope! It's cool. Have as much as you want."

I thought that's what I was doing. Unsure what had gone wrong but certain something had, my shoulders stiffened. "I'll go back to the chair."

Liv gripped my arm, her tone much more natural. "Don't make things weird, Langer. Just eat the damn popcorn."

Her hand constricted, and again I had to keep myself from groaning. *Harder, Olivia. Let's find out how much I can take.*

Don't make things weird indeed. We had two more months of living together. I crooked a smile and lowered my shoulders in a strange and silent truce. Liv nodded once and passed me the bowl.

Instead of going back to the TV, though, she pulled her hair into a high ponytail and tucked her legs on the far cushion, angling her shoulders toward me a bit. I didn't give a damn about the show anymore. I shifted to face her, too. She jutted her jaw, a silent invitation for me to start a conversation.

My brain raced through a dozen potential topics, but one was most on my mind. "I'm curious. What does it mean to trip balls?"

She laughed. "It just means you're high AF."

I stared.

"Oh, um, high as fuck. Usually like on acid or whatever."

"I see. So, what's that like?"

My brows pinched together because I knew too well that I sounded like a pathetic nerd. No one I knew used such slang, so how could I be expected to keep up? It wasn't my fault I'd gone from a "drugs are evil" upbringing to a workaholic adulthood.

But Liv didn't laugh at me. "I don't know."

"Oh?"

She shrugged and flashed a cheeky smile, putting on a strange, cartoonish accent. "Don't do drugs. Drugs are bad, m'kay?"

Bits of popcorn flew down my throat. Cough after cough exploded out of me as I wheezed through uncontrollable laughter. When I turned watery eyes to see her grinning, she thrust her tea at me. I drained most of the glass before I could breathe again.

"Holy shit, that was the most uncanny *South Park* impression I've ever heard."

Her giggle was a sound of pure happiness that hit me with age-old memories. She gave a little bow. "Why thank you, thank you."

"You always were too damn funny." I coughed again and pushed my hair away.

The delight on her face died. "You don't think I'm funny. You think I'm useless."

Useless? Jesus, how wrong could someone be? Liv was maddening, flighty, and smart-mouthed to a fault. She ran away too fast and hid behind her razor wit to keep from getting real about anything. As someone who'd spent his life burdened with responsibility, I envied and hated that about her.

Liv Milani was also bursting with talent, brilliant, warm, and the biggest-hearted person I'd ever known.

"Is that what you think I think of you?" She rolled her eyes at my question, but I shook my head and turned to her even more. "Liv, I—well, fuck what I think. But you're not useless at all."

"Why do you hate me so much?" she blurted, biting her lips in a line.

Oh, god, I don't. But I understand why you think I do. My eyes widened. "I don't hate you."

"Sorry, Will. It's dark in here. Maybe you're confused. It's me, Liv. Your nemesis, remember?"

The dim room didn't hinder my vision. I could see her perfectly. I could see the guarded pinch in her shoulders, the quick breaths she drew through parted lips.

I could see when her expression softened from careful to curious. I could see the way her gaze scanned my face and lingered on my mouth. I could "see" every beautiful detail of the woman I knew so well and yet not at all.

"Nemesis. Now there's a word," I said at last to break the tension. "Can you define that, please?"

"An enemy, right?"

"Let's find out." I lit up my phone and searched. *Oh, fucking hell. Too perfect.*

I couldn't help but smirk as I put the phone away and looked at her again. "Not exactly. A nemesis is 'the inescapable agent of someone's downfall.' What do you think about that?"

Another absurd fantasy flashed through my head.

Olivia grinned. "Hell yes, I'm the agent of your downfall. I will bring you to your fucking knees."

I laughed. "Come on, Liv. Don't you get that's exactly where I want to be?"

"What?" Liv's yelp was hoarse and high-pitched, almost guilty. It made me wonder if she'd been thinking something similar. Her chest heaved with ragged breaths, eyes round and fixed on me.

The TV went black in a station glitch before I could reply.

The silent room belied both of our heavy breathing. I couldn't tear myself away from the stare she had locked on me, but I knew better than to even think of leaning toward her. I tightened my shoulders and balled my hands into fists. "You heard me. Are you the agent of my downfall, Liv?"

She wet her lips. "I might be."

Fuck. My nails cut into my palms, but I nodded. "Yeah, you certainly might be."

"Are you thinking..." She cut herself off with a lemon face and quick shake of her head.

"What?"

Another headshake was my reply, so I rose and went back to the recliner. The show resumed. Very slowly, so did my pulse.

But I couldn't let it go, so at last I murmured, "Yes. Yes, I was."

I sensed her stare. "You were what?"

"Thinking."

A long beat passed before she snorted and found some of her usual snarky voice. "Don't hurt yourself, buddy boy. Wouldn't want you to strain anything."

I grinned, and damn did it feel good. As the show closed out, I glanced over to find her gazing at me. She crooked a hesitant smile, and my own widened. *Maybe this summer won't be the nightmare I'd feared.*

But then Liv's face shuttered. She tossed the bowl on the coffee table and rushed for the stairs without a word. As her bedroom door closed, I leaned back and sighed.

Or maybe it would be a whole new kind of nightmare.

6

LIV

The next morning when I passed Will in the hallway, he barely gave me a grunted, "Hey," in greeting.

Back to normal, thank god. If he'd been even a little bit different, I would have had no freaking clue what to make of it.

I leaned against the wall once he'd gone and replayed yesterday's whole weird session in my head. Why the hell had his hands been so damn interesting when he reached for that popcorn? They were just hands, for crying out loud. Why had it been so dark in the room? That had to be why all of a sudden Will Langer had looked far too appealing.

I closed my eyes, recalling the way he'd bit down on that full bottom lip of his as the silence got awkward between us. The way he'd pushed those long fingers through his dark hair was too damn sexy to ignore.

Nemesis. The agent of your downfall. Fuck yeah, I'll be the agent of your downfall, Will Langer. Why don't you fall on those knees and—

"Stop it," I mumbled, scrubbing my face with both

hands and slapping my cheeks lightly. "Back to normal. Nothing to see here. Move along."

I forgot about our journey into the Twilight Zone when Rachel called at lunch to say I'd be helping with the five-year-old class this week. By the time I walked into the classroom the next day, all my mind could process was how huge a difference two years can make.

The kids bombarded me with questions the moment I arrived: "I like cookies, do you?" "Why is your hair two colors?" "Are you our new helper?"

The teacher swooped in, introduced herself as Miss Mary, and the day began. I supervised several kindergarten-level activities, like counting to ten and playing with letters to spell words. At recess, I played cowgirls.

It was so much fun. I knew I couldn't tell anyone about it because I'd have sounded totally corny. The evening teachers relieved us at 2:30, and the goodbye hugs I received had me grinning like a total dork.

"Miss Olivia! Miss Olivia! Listen to me!" Amira, one of my students, tugged on the hem of my shirt, so I turned and knelt beside her. She danced around and began to sing the alphabet. I had to reach out twice to keep her from toppling over from a bit too much enthusiasm, but my grin got even bigger.

I applauded when she finished with a drawn-out Z. "Amira, that was wonderful. You even remembered the QRS part this time." She high-fived me and then ran back to the mat. I grabbed my purse and followed Mary outside.

Mary laughed once we clocked out. "I've been a kindergarten teacher for thirty years, and I know when someone has the knack. You, dearie, should be a teacher."

"Oh my god, really?"

"I wouldn't say it if I didn't mean it."

My heart leaped, but then I took a breath. *You're Liv, remember? That Girl has whims, but the mailroom job is the best you can do for a steady gig. Okay, so Rachel and Mary both said you have talent. So Megan encouraged you to go for "it"—whatever that means. She's your best friend. She's supposed to cheer you on. So... so Will Langer kind of, sort of, acted like you being a teacher was a legit thought.*

I gave Mary a close-lipped smile. "I'll think about it. Thank you so much."

"See you next Friday, dear." She hugged me quickly and went to her car, leaving me with plenty to think about.

My whole life, whenever I'd had the idea to try something new, I'd just gone for it. As kids, Tom and I would play in the park after his soccer practice. If I wanted to turn a flip on the monkey bars, he taught me how. If I wanted to do a bicycle kick even though I didn't play soccer, he taught me that, too. If I landed on my ass, I'd just laugh and get back up. Mom would look on, sometimes swooping in to monitor, but they never reprimanded me for trying.

The same was true of social situations. If I was having an argument, Tom coached me on how to speak my mind. It was a trait I needed little help developing, but his caring nature and status as best big brother ever also taught me to look out for those I loved.

No matter what, I knew I had a safety net. But this daycare gig was different. It was a path I'd have to walk alone. It would be hard. I would have to commit, to be the adult ensuring the safety of children with no way to escape should things get hard.

Did I really trust myself to commit to a life path that required responsibility and patience? Did I really want to smell like crayon wax and baby wipes on the daily?

Maybe so.

7

LIV

A week slid past while I muddled all this over. Tom and Will double-dated Sunday with some women Will apparently knew from work. Why any woman would agree to a date with him was beyond me. His grump was so ingrained, I almost felt sorry for the chick forced to sit across from him. At least the lady with my brother got a good dude.

Megan and I had our final intro CrossFit class Tuesday, and then I helped Mary again on Friday. Nashville was hot and sweaty as usual for July, so downtime was mostly spent indoors under powerful air conditioning.

Summertime or no, I was ready for my hot yoga session the following weekend to give CrossFit a rest. That night, my buddy Jack's band, Cellar Door, had a gig. Megan wasn't free, and Nick was nowhere to be seen, but the show brought a lot of my friends out. An impromptu party commenced when we commandeered a section in the back.

I sat across from my friends David and Kira, a local musical duo in their own right, and beside their manager, Aaron. We'd just clinked glasses when I looked up to see

Ben Addison pulling up two chairs at the opposite end of the table.

Ah, dear Ben. If it weren't for him, I wouldn't know the crew. Ben and I dated almost three years ago. He was my "type" for sure: quiet, intense, dark, and super sweet underneath. There was nothing romantic between us anymore, but our relationship had been a real one, not just casual dating. I was quitting college when we met, but he always took me seriously. I appreciated that. Things had fizzled between us, but we'd remained best buds.

Well, except for that one Valentine's Day a couple years ago when we were both a little lonely and...

Friends. Just friends. Great friends.

Besides, the second chair was for his girlfriend, Celeste. She flashed her gorgeous green eyes and smiled at the group while he draped his arm across the back of her seat. Ever since Celeste had come into the picture, I'd known that Ben was off the market for good. No hard feelings, seriously. I was so happy for him. Celeste was Ben's obvious soul mate. They weren't married, but—

But then Celeste lifted her IPA to her lips, and damn if she wasn't rocking a beautiful diamond.

I wasn't the only one who noticed. The table exploded with shouts of congratulations. Luckily, the show hadn't started, or we'd have derailed everything. The couple smiled bashfully and touched their foreheads together through our toasts. I'd like to say it was cheesy, but in all honesty, they were adorable.

"When the hell did this happen?" I asked with a grin.

Celeste's smile thinned at my question. We were civil, but not friends. "A week ago. We hadn't told anyone until we called Nick last night."

I didn't miss the way she looked at me when she mentioned her cousin, but I pretended not to notice.

"A toast!" Aaron declared, and we all raised glasses for the happy couple.

Cellar Door killed their first set as usual. When the house lights came up, I slipped off to the bar for a refil.

"Hey there," Ben said with a smile when he leaned his elbows beside me.

I smiled back and lifted my whiskey. "Congrats, my friend. I'm thrilled for you guys."

"Thanks. How's everything with you?"

"Can't complain." We sipped a moment, and then I heard myself say, "Guess I shouldn't expect to hear from Nick anytime soon, hmm?"

He slid his gaze away. "Uh, I wouldn't, no."

"Kind of shitty, to be honest. Your boy just stopped calling." With Ben, I knew I could be as blunt as I wanted, even about his best friend.

"Yeah."

"I knew the deal." It stung that a friend like Nick would ghost after flirting with me like he meant it, but there was no big surprise. Ben nodded, and I tossed my hair. "Whatever. I'd say tell him to text me if he wants, but why bother? I'd like to think I'm worth a little more than that."

"Much more," he said with conviction, and I threaded my arm through his as we moseyed back to the table.

The show was a blast, but I went home unusually thoughtful for a night out. None of our group had been serious enough about anybody to get engaged yet. Thrilled as I was for Ben, and doubtless about his and Celeste's love, it changed the game in a way I hadn't been ready for.

Add that to the knowledge that Nick had indeed dropped me like yesterday's underwear, plus a couple of bourbons and a beer, and that lonely feeling I chose to ignore most of the time rubbed a little raw.

Tom's car was missing from the driveway when the cab dropped me off. I slipped into the dark house, glugged water and an aspirin, and tiptoed upstairs. Dressed for bed, I peeked into his room to find Maddie asleep, then noticed light under her bedroom door.

"Yes?" Came the muffled call to my impulsive knock.

I stepped into the room. "Hey. Where's Tom?"

Will turned from where he stood at the dresser, and I immediately regretted barging in there in my pajamas. My pink cami and shorts left very little to the imagination.

Will's gaze swept over me twice before meeting my eyes. His throat bobbed with a swallow. "Out. Tom is… out."

The urge to slink away was strong, but Olivia Milani slunk for no one. I took a breath and blazed ahead. "The chick from last weekend?"

Will nodded and turned back to the dresser. Those moments of intense staring from the 4th seemed long gone. *That's right, boy, hide from me. One or two conversations doesn't mean we're pals. You probably don't even care, do you?*

"Cool. Well, good talk. Have fun with whatever you've got going on in that drawer. Must be fascinating."

Shit, wrong move.

Will lifted his head and faced me again. He nodded at me and twisted his lips, and again I wanted to flee. "I was trying for a little decorum, given that you walked into my room dressed like *that*."

"This is my house. I'll wear what I like and go where I want." I tossed my hair. If I had to do battle in nothing but underwear, I'd be damn sure he got all my attitude.

He nodded, still with that wry smile on.

I scowled. My defenses wavered to frustration and

fatigue. "Leave me alone. I don't need your shit, okay? Not tonight."

"What's wrong? Your night out didn't live up to your expectations?"

Well, kind of. I swept aside that knee-jerk thought. "Piss off, Will. My life isn't your business."

"Indeed."

Why is he pushing your buttons? He's hardly said anything. I couldn't let it go. "You would assume that partying is all I'm about. It figures you'd reduce me to that."

He stepped closer. His pouty drawl practically dared me to punch the smug off his face. "Aw, did I hurt your feelings, little Liv?"

An angry flush heated my cheeks. "You wish you could hurt me."

"You wish you weren't hurting."

His calm, blunt words threw me. I clenched my hands into fists and stuttered, "You don't know me."

"Really? I don't know you? Are you sure about that?"

I took half a step back at his intensity, but my only reply was a strong shake of my head.

Will opened his mouth, but instead of whatever he was going to say, he smiled. "You're so angry. Look at your hands."

My knuckles were white, nails dug deep into my palms. I sneered. "Ooh, I take it back. You can read me like a book. Angry, ha. What do my hands tell you now?" I held up both middle fingers. "There's mad for you, dick."

"Oh, how clever. Go to bed. I'm tired."

My eyes almost fell out of my head. It took all my restraint to keep from shouting that no one told me what to do. I remembered Maddie just in time and hissed instead. "Kiss my ass, Will."

"Bend over, Liv."

I narrowed my eyes to slits before I kissed my palms, spun around, and smacked my glutes as I stormed out of his room.

That bastard laughed as I shut the door.

This was the weirdest summer I could remember, and it wasn't even half over. One second everything was changing. In the next moment, routines reset back to normal, and I was left wondering if I was losing my mind. No one else seemed so upside-down. Tom and Megs were their normal awesome selves. Even Will acted like everything was the same.

Which, I guess, it was. God, maybe I *was* losing it.

Megan and I were nervous about keeping up at our first "all levels" CrossFit class the following week. Tuesdays were for novices, but this Wednesday was our 3rd time. It would be a true test of how dedicated we might be to this new adventure.

"I'm mentally in the pub already," Megs declared on our way into the gym.

"You're mentally already flirting with—you're kidding me." My dig about Adam died the same moment that my feet stopped moving. "Oh, god, please no."

Megan's blonde ponytail whipped her face when she spun to me. "What's wrong?"

"We have to leave. Come on, find the fire escape."

"We are not leaving! What's wrong with you?"

I nodded pointedly and spoke without moving my lips as if stealth would somehow help the situation. "See that guy in the blue shirt and black shorts?"

She pulled me forward but followed my gaze. I dragged ass, watching her brows lift when she spotted the target. "Might you mean that *hot* guy in the blue shirt?"

"Megan Riley! Shut up!"

"Woman, have you lost your sense? That man—"

Was striding our way. She squeezed my arm while I braced against the annoyed gaze locked on me.

"You've got to be kidding," Will said.

"Took the words out of my mouth. What are you doing here?"

"The same thing I've done every Wednesday for two years. Don't remember seeing you around before."

I rubbed my eyes. "This is our first all levels class. We got the intro package."

Will hummed. Megan still gripped my arm. I lowered my hand, and he sighed and turned toward the class. "Good luck keeping up," he said as he walked away.

I glanced at Meg, who finally released me. "Have I ever mentioned Tom's friend, Will?"

Her lips twitched. "Mr. Douchebag Know It All who's invaded your house for the summer?"

"That'd be him."

She laughed. "Well, slap me twice and call me Shirley. He was *not* what I'd pictured."

I pinched her, but she just laughed again and hurried us to the group.

We warmed up with jumping jacks and push-ups. *Don't care, don't care, don't care*, repeated rhythmically with every clap of my hands or bend of my elbows. Halfway through, I changed to *Screw him,* just to shake things up. So what if he was into my newest thing? I could kick ass and pretend he wasn't there.

But then the instructor announced that the workout was

a partner activity. I latched onto Megs, but died inside when we heard, "Newer people should be sure to buddy with a more seasoned friend."

"Let's see what you've got."

I turned, more than a little surprised Will had voluntarily approached me. The cocky smirk on his face didn't dismay me in the least. He crossed his arms, the contours of his thick biceps straining the deep blue fabric stretched across his broad chest.

Wait. No. His stupid arms were crossed over his stupid chest. End of story.

Megan laughed. "You two have fun." She blew me a kiss and vanished.

I squared to Will. All around us, friendly-looking people paired up and gave each other pep talks. In my icy corner, I shivered and stared my nemesis down. "You think I'm scared?"

He chuckled. "Never. But I'll make sure you can't move when you're done."

"You'd love to put me in traction, wouldn't you?" His brow lifted, and I huffed. "Whatever. Bring it, Langer."

"With pleasure."

Kettlebell swings, jumping jacks, pull-ups, and burpees sound like a reasonable workout, but a WOD, aka workout of the day, is killer. This was an "AMRAP," as many reps as possible for one minute each. We would do each exercise three times over with a minute rest in between. The point of partners was for support, both physically and emotionally, but I expected very little of either.

We took our place in the circuit to wait for the starting buzzer. I bent in half and touched my toes, my ponytail cascading over my head.

"You should tighten that elastic, so your hair doesn't distract you."

I righted my posture. Arguing was pointless because he was right, but no way could I let Will Langer tell me what to do. "Should I tuck my shirt into my pants, too? Or maybe just take it off?"

His eyes glinted. "Your words, not mine."

I ignored that and gestured at his shirt. Stepping closer, I pointed to the matching blue headband that kept his black hair off his forehead. "Whatever. Not all of us can afford a designer gym outfit."

Will swatted me away, but he seemed very far from his usual, annoyed self. "A, I don't call my clothes outfits. B, you should spring for one. It's hot as balls in here, and the shirt helps with wicking sweat. The shorts, well," he shrugged. "They're just really comfortable. Like wearing a hug. I mean, a hug for my ass, but still."

Giggles bubbled out of me without warning. I clapped a hand over my mouth and doubled over. Since when was Will funny?

His words replayed in my head, and I stopped and made my hands into a T. "Hold up. A week ago, you were asking me what tripping balls meant. Now it's 'hot as balls' in here?"

He blinked several times. "Er, well, I suppose it was a funny phrase. Must've stuck in my head more than I realized."

"My, my. What have we here? Looks like I might be rubbing off on you a little bit."

Despite his dark complexion, Will flushed. His eyes sparked with mischief, though. "Now there's a phrase."

"Oh shut up. You know what I meant." I laughed again,

glad to let it be an excuse for why my own cheeks were warm.

A grin was clearly trying to break free on his lips when I wiped my eyes and reached to tighten my ponytail. He managed to keep it in check. *Shame.* When he'd smiled on the 4th at my *South Park* joke, it really had been a pleasant sight.

The countdown clock to start the workout went to under a minute. Will glanced at it and nodded at me. "Game face, Milani. Let's do this."

The whistle blew. Side-by-side, we swung the kettlebells, threw them down, and went straight into jacks before running to the pull-up bar. Will did a bunch of reps while I fumbled with the assist strap. He looked over, and I scowled.

"Don't tease me. I need the support."

"It's okay. Wait." He stepped close and placed both hands on my waist so I could steady my feet in the strap. "Is that good?"

A little too good. I nodded, battling to stay focused on the task when I could still feel where his hands had been on me. Why were my sides so warm? *Did he squeeze me a little? Or did I imagine that?*

He stepped away while I finished my first pull. Will assessed my form with an approving nod before he finished his reps, but he helped me down when the whistle blew. *He definitely squeezed me that time... Or I'm delirious already. Probably that one.*

"Now, drop for burpees," he said.

Jesus, this was tough. By round three, my imagination had no time to play games. Even the jumping jacks were a struggle. I became convinced they were shortening the rest minute more and more every time. "Pick up your feet" and, "Hold your form" were the only encouragement I received, but Will's gruff directions did make me grit my teeth and push harder.

My hands could barely hold the bar when he steadied me for the last time, but Will seemed to be able to go forever. He curled up and called me out when I failed to get my chin over the bar.

I wailed. "I'm gonna vomit."

"Not until after the whistle. Final set, come on-*umph*," Will grunted when I basically fell into his arms as he helped me out of the strap.

"Sorry, sorry," I gasped. I clutched his shoulders and scrambled to get my footing.

We took a mutual step back. "Burpees," he muttered.

Jump back, pushup, jump up, high-five my partner. Again, again, again. My lungs burned, breath wheezed, and twenty seconds were still on the clock. "Can't..."

"Hell yes, you can. You will not quit." He smacked my hands with more force, and my hatred for him momentarily distracted me from the fact that I was dying.

The whistle blew for the last time. Everyone applauded, but I collapsed on the mat, gulping air. "Shit," I rasped. "*Shit*."

Will dropped beside me. "Well done."

My head lolled to the side to look at him. "Huh?"

"Not that I'm surprised. You've always been good at what you want to be good at. And when you want to be good at something, well," he shrugged, his gaze on the mat between his bent knees. "You're incredible."

"*Huh*?"

"You heard me."

I struggled to sit up. "Uh, thank you?"

Will got to his feet in a single motion and pulled me up. He looked me in the eye, nodded once, and walked away.

I was still reeling from his words as Megan and I hobbled to the showers. She tried to bring up my partner over beers and burgers, but I simply didn't have the energy for the frustrating confusion that was Will Langer.

Weirdest of all, neither of us mentioned our run-in to Tom.

WILL

I walked into the house deep in thought, barely saying hello to Tom and Maddie. Upstairs in that pastel-hued bedroom, I stretched out on the futon. I opened Google Photos and scrolled through old albums, way back to twelve years ago. Freshman year of college.

I got my first cell phone before I boarded the bus out of Dallas. It was one of those prepaid deals that cost almost nothing and had terrible service. But it had a camera, and so the start of life in Tennessee was the start of my recorded history. Everything before existed in memory.

Photography had quickly become a favorite hobby. I still enjoyed it, especially since now I could afford a top-of-the-line phone with the best camera available. The only problem was I worked too damn much to make good use of it anymore.

But back in those early days of independence and learning to make my way, I roamed around Knoxville on weekends taking photos. Buildings, nature, and tiny details I spotted that no one else seemed to notice filled these old albums. At first, I'd sorted them by topic. As time went on, I'd reclassified them into years.

My eyes skimmed over the shots as I scrolled, looking specifically for—

Yep. That one.

Tom's and my dorm room on move-in day. The photo was of the two of us, standing together in the center of a freshly unpacked room. Our tight smiles said that we barely knew each other, but Claire had wanted a photo of her son and his new roommate, and so this pic got snapped.

My grin faded as I lowered the phone. The photo was a moment, but that whole day had been on my mind while watching Liv crush tonight's workout. Move-in day was the first time I met Liv Milani. Good god, was I unprepared.

Poor social skills. Skinny body. Disproportionately strong arms and shoulders. I walked onto the University of Tennessee campus as an awkward, shy 18-year-old. All around me, station wagons were lined up. Fathers and mothers shuttled boxes into the dorms, smiling bittersweet smiles at their babies going off to college.

I had a duffle bag, backpack, and two $100-dollar-bills in my wallet. I'd gotten off the bus downtown and walked about four miles to campus. After 20 hours on a Greyhound, the exercise had been welcome.

According to the slip of paper tucked next to the Benjamins in my bifold, my dorm number was 514 of Morrill Hall. The elevator was packed, so I took the stairs and found myself in the common area for the floor. Kanye West and Tim McGraw vied for top billing from speakers in different rooms, but it all sounded like a cacophony to me. I didn't even know who Kanye or Tim were. Neither of them would've been allowed in the home I grew up in. It would take a while to find my interest and taste in music.

Mercifully, my wing of the cross-shaped floor was quieter. I hurried to the end of the hall and slid my key into 514. Half of the room was already claimed. Boxes were stacked, some still unopened, and posters hung on the wall. The bed was neatly made.

And occupied.

All I could see from the doorway were legs, crossed at the knees and bent so one foot rested on the bed. Even from my angle, there was no question that this was girl. Her Converse sneakers were sideways on the floor, her socks were lime green, and she was reading *Slaughterhouse-Five*— one of the life-changing books I'd gotten my hands on Sophomore year of high school. One of the books that pushed me to break out of the ranch-and-religion world of my upbringing.

I wasn't thinking about that, though. My stomach was too busy knotting up in dismay. "Um," was all I could manage.

She snapped the book shut and sat up. Yanking her earbuds out, she tossed the novel aside. She swung her legs into a cross-legged pose.

"Oh, hi," she said with a smile.

"Hi."

I didn't know what else to say. She seemed to be waiting for me to talk. This equated to us staring at each other for an eternally awkward moment before I forced myself to shuffle into the room. I skirted the perimeter to the empty bed, realizing as I did that I probably looked like a man in a lion's cage. The girl watched me curiously, but I didn't speak —or take my eyes from her—until I'd dropped my bags on the bare mattress.

"Um, I... I didn't..." I stumbled into silence, knots in my tongue. I hadn't spoken in over a day. Besides, I had no practice talking to unexpected strangers.

"Sorry, uh, I didn't realize this was a coed dorm," I managed at last.

Her eyes flickered back and forth quickly, but then she got to her feet and crossed her arms. "Well, obviously."

"Yeah, but I mean... it's just that..." I scratched my head and reached for the slip of paper in my wallet with my dorm info on it. My roommate's name was Tom Milani. As far as I knew—which wasn't very far, honestly—there was no female name that Tom was short for.

I looked at the girl again. She seemed young for a college freshman. She was tall, but her limbs were a little skinny for her hourglass figure. Besides that, she had braces. I frowned and looked at the paper again.

She cleared her throat. Her voice was lower, rougher. "Yeah, we got lucky on that, huh? Plenty of chicks right here in the building. I know security can be a bitch, but I bet they're not that strict, right?"

My jaw unhinged when she winked at me.

"Besides, I've got your back if you've got mine. We'll make a code and shit, right buddy?"

"Um." Words didn't even try to come to me.

"What's your name, pal?"

"William."

"Billy, good to meet you. I'm Tom."

I cringed at the nickname but slowly stuck out my hand. She took it, gripped me so hard I thought my fingers would break, and then began to laugh. Her grip relaxed, but she didn't release me. I stood there like a helpless dope—not like, I *was* a helpless dope—and she giggled like a schoolgirl.

Which was exactly what she was.

While we stood there holding hands, the door swung open. A guy stepped in. His head cocked in surprise at this absurd scene. A suspicious smile formed as he looked at my companion. "What are you doing?"

She dropped my hand and tried to stop her laughter. "Just joking with your roomie," she said sweetly. Behind Tom, a man and a woman appeared, loaded down with Target shopping bags.

And me? Still the helpless dope.

I shoved my hand into my pocket, only to take it out again when Tom crossed the room. "Hey, you're William, right? Tom Milani. Good to meet you, dude. These are my parents, and I guess you already met Livi."

The girl scowled and pushed his shoulder. She stuck out her hand again. "It's Olivia," she declared with a spark in her eye.

I hated her in that first moment.

No. That's a lie. I hated myself in that moment. Liv was, then and always, funny, brash, and bold. The total opposite of me. I hated myself for being so woefully unprepared for life on my own. I hated that I couldn't find my tongue or have the sense to realize this kid was joking with me. I hated that she made me want to laugh at myself when I didn't know how.

I hated it—and I admired the hell out of her for it.

As the years of college went by, I got to know the family. I moved past that hatred. I grew into myself. Then, anytime Liv popped up in my life became an event. I was never sure what she'd say, how she'd make me laugh with some absurd remark, but she never failed to deliver.

From that first day on, she was exactly what she wanted to be. And whatever that was in the moment—from a prank-pulling smartass to a sweet little sis to Tom—she was incredible at it.

Just like I'd told her.

8

LIV

Me on Friday: "That's right, Vanessa, my hair is *brown* and *pink*. Raise your hand if you have brown hair. Good! Now, what letter does pink start with? Good, Ryan! And what are some other things we can think of that are pink?"

Me on Sunday: "Do you think that I need your help? Get over yourself. I don't need your sympathy. You'll be history in no time."

This summer was wild.

The Sunday night fiasco was one of those moments where I knew I should've just walked away and didn't, but damn. Megan was hell-bent on seeing Celeste's ring and gushing over it while I was still getting my head around how this wedding would change the crew. Running into some redhead chick that was apparently Nick's flavor of the month had been a bit too much for this girl to take. To be fair, she handled my attitude with a lot of style. I felt a little remorse at being so harsh, but screw you, Nick Field. Ghosting was never okay, not even on randos you met at a bar. At least tell someone no thanks. A best friend *definitely* deserved more respect.

My cranky mood followed me into the next day. Tom's shift was noon to midnight, so he got Maddie ready to stay with Mom and Dad while I stomped around the kitchen that morning. He gave me a concerned frown when I appeared with my purse and keys.

"Everything okay, sis?"

I shrugged. "It's fine. I just hope it's a quiet Monday."

"Me too." He laughed, and I ruffled his hair and hurried off to work, already looking forward to an empty house later. With Tom and Mads out, I could run a bath, play music as loud as I wanted, walk around naked, and eat takeout in front of the TV.

The obvious foil to my plans didn't occur to me.

I'd gotten so used to the Audi in the drive that I barely saw it anymore. Plus, with Tom's car gone, my usual spot was available. The shadows were long when I lugged two arms full of groceries through the back door. I staggered through the living room and into the kitchen, only to find Will at the table, sipping a glass of whiskey.

"What the hell?" I gasped as my adrenaline spiked from the surprise. "Why are you sitting in the dark?"

"It's not dark yet."

His snarky reply was enough to turn adrenaline to ire with everything else weighing on me. No apology? No offer to help with the bags? Fine. No sweetness from Liv. "Bullshit."

"I take it our recent bouts of civility are over, huh?"

"Civility? You mean how we've been able to occupy the same space without tearing each other's hair out? Yeah, it's been a real love fest, hasn't it?" I rolled my eyes. "Creep."

"Brat," he whispered into his glass.

"What was that?" I slammed the coffee canister on the counter so hard the cupboard popped open. I banged it shut. Making noise seemed a good way to get my mood across, but Will didn't reply. I glared at his easy posture in that damn chair. *Leave him alone, Liv.*

Advice I didn't heed. As usual. "Don't you have anything to do tonight?"

He reached for the bottle. "Sorry. I don't have a club to hit, a 'just-a-friend' to party with, or—"

"God, what is your fucking problem?" I threw my hands in the air.

"You are." His chair scraped the linoleum as he jumped to his feet, all the casual disinterest gone. "You're so rude and self-centered it's absurd."

I had to step back when he loomed over me. At 5'10", not a lot of people towered over me like Will did. It was more than his 6'3" frame. The man knew how to make his presence felt.

My voice was strong, though, when I sucked a quick breath and said, "What are you talking about? I am not."

"Oh no? You started with me before you were even through the door. Didn't even bother to say hello or consider that I just got off work, too. You go through life on a whim, always looking for the easy road. You think you can shoot off any smart-ass remark without regard to how you sound, however inappropriate it is, and everyone will just shrug and say, 'That's Liv.' Stop acting like a child. Just look at you, a grown woman with pink hair. When are you going to wake up?"

A volcano erupted in my chest. "You better back off before I smack the shit out of you."

"See? Even that. All talk. If you want to smack me, don't talk about it. Do it. You have permission. If you're bold enough to go through with—"

Before I realized what I was doing, my palm cracked

across his left cheek so hard it stung *me*. Will's head snapped to the right, absorbing the blow, the outline of my fingers already visible.

I trembled with anger and more than a little remorse when his eyes locked back on me. But the train had most definitely left the station, so I squared my shoulders and refused to budge.

His lips curled into a snarl that turned into a laugh. "Fuck. I didn't think you had it in you."

"Fuck *you*."

"Did that make you feel better?"

"You're a douchebag."

"Not what I asked." He stepped even closer, but I couldn't think straight to back up. "I asked if you liked hitting me. If it made you feel better."

I lifted my chin. "Damn right I liked it. Been a long time coming."

"Then do it again. I dare you."

"Why?" I sneered. "Does it get you off?"

I blinked. In that instant, his face was an inch from mine. His breath warmed my cheek as he said slowly, "You're goddamn right it does."

I threw my left hand this time, giving him twin welts on each side of his face. The red marks stood out in stark contrast to the smoldering darkness of his eyes. I shook with rage, hating everything about him, but mostly hating how impotent he could make me feel.

Will took the blow and then looked me over, snarling that laugh again. "Well done."

I scuttled backward. He followed, step by step, until my shoulders met the wall. His hands rested on either side of my face, pinning me. The welts on his cheeks had barely subsided.

"What's the fair response to allowing you the pleasure of smacking the shit out of me? How do we make this even?"

"I guess you can hit me?"

He scowled. "As if I'd ever hit a woman. Jesus, Liv."

"I don't know then." I groaned and squeezed my eyes shut, stomping my foot in frustration at this mess.

"Can I touch you?"

The anger in his tone had ebbed enough to make the question a curious one. Enough to make me freeze. I opened my eyes and looked up at him. The restraint he radiated was so palpable that I imagined straps binding him in place.

Slowly, I nodded. He reached out. His index finger skimmed my jaw down to my throat. I tipped my chin up, eyelids fluttering against my will.

"That's not revenge for a slap, William."

"Oh no? Would you like me to be rougher?"

My pulse thundered as I gazed into his dark brown eyes. He stared right back into mine.

"Yes."

Will's hand opened around my throat. Those long fingers constricted in a light squeeze. I squealed in surprise and gripped his wrist, and he relaxed again.

"I can feel your heart racing. What's the matter? Did you think you were the only one who knew how to play rough?"

"Who's playing? You've had that coming forever."

Will grunted. "Be careful, Olivia."

Why did those words send a jolt through my body? *Why* was there an impossible ache between my legs? *Oh, hell no. Don't you dare, girl.* I swallowed around his grip and looked into his eyes—

His eyes, which regarded me with the same intensity, but absolutely no hatred. Panic fluttered up my throat. It was more a sensation of scrambling for solid ground than worry for my safety. I knew that Will had no intention of hurting me. That he would never hurt me. The moment the thought came to me, I realized I'd known it for over ten years. *That squeeze felt kind of good, though.*

"Will, please," I whispered.

"Please what?"

I just shook my head. He tapped his fingers against my neck in a silent request for an answer. And, dammit, as he did, I itched to touch him.

"Please," I repeated, the longing in my voice embarrassingly obvious.

"Please *what*, Liv? Let you go? Squeeze again? Don't hurt you? What are you begging me for?"

"Don't hurt me." I refused to beg for anything else.

God bless. I could barely see straight, much less think. This whole exchange had kindled a wildfire of fury, frustration, and want inside me that I couldn't get under control. The want was the worst part, the lighter fluid I hadn't expected, the element that made me angry at myself, too.

Since when do you want...

That dark hair. Those inky, black-brown eyes. His large, warm hand on my throat.

I drank him in, every inch I could see or feel, and my desire flamed brighter. *What is wrong with you? Will Langer detests you, and you have nothing but contempt for him... Right?*

His voice registered through my hazy thoughts. "...can do as you please, but never make it worth anything. I can't stand to watch someone so completely waste her time. Are you listening?"

"No," I spat. "You're boring the shit out of me."

His fingers clamped down enough to make me gasp. "Am I?"

"Damn right."

He relaxed his hand and drew in a long, shaky breath. "You drive me crazy."

"Back at you."

The silence stretched. I needed a knockout blow of a burn. Something that would make him walk away. But that achy fire inside me was messing with everything. Instead of the clever jab I'd intended, what fell out of my mouth was:

"I bet your dick is so hard right now."

"What do you wager?" Will bared his teeth with a hiss, but the flush on his cheeks suddenly had nothing to do with my attack. He blushed a dark red, his pupils dilated in a look of pure guilt.

I wet my lips. "Are you?"

Guilt turned to anguish. "So much it hurts."

The room spun. Heat broke like a dam between my legs, but I shook my head. "What the hell are we doing? Why? You can't possibly think that we're going to—"

His hand disappeared as he took a giant step backward. "We're not 'going to' anything, Olivia. Don't worry, you haven't driven me that insane. Tom would kill me, and I'd hate myself if I—"

I guess it was my expression that stopped his words. I couldn't be sure and didn't care. My spine went straight, but everything else inside of me collapsed in queasy humiliation. Ben was engaged, Nick was douche of the year, and now this?

"Really, Will? You'd hate yourself?" My voice was too soft, too hurt, but I couldn't fix that.

He narrowed his eyes and stepped toward me again, but I recoiled. "Not like that," he said gruffly. "I meant—"

Two tears spilled down my cheeks. "Good job, asshole. You won. I'm out."

Those dark eyes softened in regret when I pushed past

him and hit the stairs running. He called to me, first from the kitchen and then again much closer, but I sprinted for my bedroom and swung the door behind me.

It jumped open with a sharp slap. "Wait."

I wheeled to him. "Go away. You won, you hurt me, now leave me alone. I don't—"

"God, stop for a second. I didn't mean—"

"I heard you, but you did mean it. You meant it, and you're probably right, and fuck you get out." My voice broke, and I scowled. "Go jerk off to the fact that you made me cry. I'm sure that plus a little hand lotion will be enough to—"

"I said *stop it*." He was so close that I paused, my gaze on the carpet in the dim light of the setting sun. I wiped angrily at my face while he said, "As usual, you don't understand because you don't care to. You heard what you wanted and—"

"What I *what*?" My head snapped up. "You think I want to hear that I'm a basic slut?"

I blinked at the baritone rumble in his chest, easily one of the angriest sounds I've ever heard in my life. Both hands cuffed my neck, thumbs pressed into my chin lift my gaze, but his hold was soft and weirdly reassuring. "Never, ever say that again. I would kill the bastard who thought that of you. Understand?"

"You're too close," I whispered against his face.

"You're shaking like a leaf," he replied in a similar whisper.

"You're a little intense." My lips twitched. "As usual."

With a wry twist of his mouth, Will lifted one hand to wipe my tears. The pad of his thumb brushed across my cheek once, then again. "What I meant to say, Olivia, is that I'd hate myself if, after all these years, I... snapped and... I mean, if I couldn't resist the chance to..." His words tripped, but his gaze didn't waver from my mouth.

I swallowed hard, mostly to keep from doing something crazy like moaning or worse, and Will's arms shook with restraint. His hold slid from my throat to the back of my head.

"Fuck," he sighed. "Fuck it all."

His whiskey-flavored tongue slid across my lower lip, and I whimpered in a sort of horrified relief. My tongue flicked out to meet his, but the force of our kiss when our lips sealed together was so powerful that I cried out and stumbled back.

"Shit, wait."

"As long as you need." He nodded, stepping away with his palms up.

I sucked in one breath. Then, I reached for the crisp fabric of his dress shirt and pulled.

Will crushed me against his body. His size and strength dwarfed me totally, and I fell into his arms under a wave of irrational desire. Our lips and tongues clashed, unrelenting and hotter than anything I'd ever known. I clung to him so fiercely that my nails cut into my palms, even with his shirt between them. Will held me so tight, there was no way he was going anywhere.

We stumbled backward, bouncing off the wall and the dresser before we fell to the bed, clumsy and blind to everything but each other. I hit the mattress on my side, but Will had me on my back in a blink.

"This is so fucking wrong." His voice was a deep, dark rumble as he kissed down my neck.

"Uh-huh." I whimpered, squeezing his hips with my knees.

"But, god, I just—" His lips found mine again. I raked my

nails over his hair, then pulled so sharply that he hissed and lifted up. His eyes narrowed in a lusty glare. "What are you doing to me, Olivia?"

My pulse pounded against my ribcage. "Just messing with you, William."

"Oh, yeah?" One hand planted by my head to hold him up. Will caressed my face, my shoulder, down to my hip. My shallow breath was audible in the silence, and he smiled faintly. "Just messing with me, huh? You really, *really* love messing with me. Don't you, Liv?"

His fingers slid across my hipbone, then up the center line of my body. I tensed when he skimmed between my breasts and flattened his palm on my heart.

"Uh-huh. That's all this is," I panted. "Not like I want you or anything."

Will closed his eyes a long moment. "Then I should get up."

"No way." I clawed at his neck and brought him down for another kiss. His tongue stroked mine, hips flexing against my core. Stars exploded behind my eyes. I moaned as my head lolled back.

Will began to kiss down my collarbone between my shirt lapels, his breath warm against my burning skin. "You drive me crazy," he whispered. "I want you to know how that feels."

"What are you going to do to me?" Dear god, I was literally quivering.

That wicked mischief was back in his expression when he hovered over me again. "I'm going to make you scream till you're hoarse."

I hummed. "You wish you could make me scream."

"No, Olivia. I *know* I can."

I yielded to his warm, open mouth as soon as it met

mine. While we kissed, Will shifted so that one knee was outside my hips. He palmed my breast and swished his thumb over my bra until I grunted and shuddered. Then, he laughed and reached for my buttons. With each one he popped, long fingers tickled over a little more of my bare skin.

He got four open before his phone rang.

The ringtone was shrill in the heady silence, and we both jolted hard. My eyes flew open. Will was already up on his knees, phone in hand.

"Langer. I've already left the office today. Fine. I'll be there in twenty. Fine."

He climbed off the bed and turned away. "I have to go."

"Good," I croaked.

"Indeed." He smoothed his shirt and opened the door. "I... well."

But that was all. He was gone.

I collapsed back on the bed while the burden of his presence slowly faded. "Holy fucking shit," I said aloud, hand on my heart.

9

LIV

Reasons why I hate Will Langer:

    -He's an arrogant jerkwad.
    -He thinks I'm a useless brat who does nothing but party.
    -He parks in my spot and drinks my whiskey.
    -He's a terrible kisser.

I sighed and scribbled out that last one, then kept scribbling until the page looked like a tumbleweed of silver ink. The pen bounced across my journal and to the floor. I left it there and picked up "Rebel," my favorite shade of MAC lipstick. The deep violet was a perfect match with my getup: an aqua and black tank top with a lace back, shredded jeans, and ankle boots. My hair was flat-ironed so that the dark, shiny crown contrasted with the bright pink bottom. After this week, a little edge seemed apropos.

The list in my journal had been built over the last several days while I skulked around and avoided him at all costs. Megs had been down to take a break from CrossFit, and I'd taken the plunge and registered for the online training to become a certified daycare instructor. That kept me preoccupied. For his part, Will was pretty scarce around the house.

Tom asked me to keep Maddie tonight, but I'd had tickets to Ruston Kelly at The Cannery Ballroom for ages. Luckily, Mom and Dad were happy to give up their Friday, so my guilt at telling him no wasn't too severe. Not that he ever minded, but I never wanted to let my brother down.

I rolled my lips with an audible pop and jumped up, ready to weekend.

Tom was in the kitchen when I went to make a sandwich. He grinned at me and lifted his tea in salute.

"Wow, bro. Looking sexy," I said with a smile. Tom always rocked a shabby-cute vibe. Tonight, he was sharp in a patterned short-sleeved button-down and chinos, hair combed back from his freshly shaved face. This was a serious upgrade from the scrubs and tees he usually sported.

Tom straightened his collar and made a face. "I still clean up okay, huh?"

"This is the third date in a couple of weeks. Spill some details." I picked up half the sandwich and leaned against the counter.

His smile deepened as he studied his glass. "Her name is Erin. She's a paralegal. An acquaintance of Will. She's twenty-eight, lives on her own, and," he shrugged, "I like her."

I jumped up and down and squealed. "You're *smitten*. Look at how smiley you are!"

He flipped me off.

"Tom, are you—oh."

We both looked up when Will appeared in the doorway. He eyed me briefly before addressing Tom. "Sorry I had to take that call."

"No problem, man. Want a drink?"

Will exhaled and nodded. He crossed his ankles and leaned one shoulder against the doorjamb. "Whiskey, if you're pouring."

"Tough week?" Tom handed him a glass.

Will downed the shot. "Total shit."

Neither Tom nor I spoke. Will looked around and seemed to finally realize we were waiting for him to continue. "Sorry, I'm not used to talking about my day. Yes, work was a disaster. The newest ad campaign is a week off track thanks to a lack of planning. We could've avoided it if I'd been informed about last-minute revisions. I've spent the week doing damage control and still got handed my ass from the VP."

Tom winced. "Sorry, man. Sucks."

Will shrugged it off and crossed the room to put the glass in the sink, right beside where I stood. "Hello," he muttered.

"Sorry you fucked up at work."

"Liv," Tom said sharply, but my attention was on Will.

His sigh was loud and annoyed. The twitch of his lips was anything but. With his back still to Tom, Will caught my gaze. That elusive smile flickered again, but he used his usual tone to me to say, "Thanks so much, Olivia, but I didn't fuck up. My employees did, so I had to deal with it."

"I bet it's fun working for you."

"People don't usually complain."

"I bet they said the same thing about Mussolini."

"*Liv*," Tom snapped.

Will's head dropped with another sigh, but he didn't try to control his grin this time. I bit the inside of my cheek and widened my eyes. This was at least the second time in a month that I'd made Will Langer laugh. It was pretty damn satisfying. Almost as satisfying as pissing him off.

Not quite as satisfying as when his lips—*Stop it!*

Will scrubbed his face and turned around with a neutral expression. He traded a look with Tom, who rose from his seat and smiled.

"I'm sure Stacy can take your mind off work for a while," my brother said. "Let's get going."

"You guys are double dating?" I clamped my lips shut too late. Why the hell should I care? Why the *hell* was my stomach at my knees?

"Yeah, Erin works with Stacy. Uh, she's Will's... friend." Tom's phone chimed as he spoke. He grinned at the screen, seeming to have forgotten the conversation. "Have fun tonight, sis."

"I intend to. See you tomorrow, Tommy." He chuckled when I winked and blew him a kiss, grabbed my purse, and disappeared.

On the ride to the show, I decided I'd belt a few shots to warm up, then get lost in the music and let the night go where it would. When I ordered a Four Roses on the rocks, though, the scent of whiskey called up every thought I wanted to avoid. Namely, how it tasted on a certain jerk's lips.

Megan knitted her brows when I pushed the glass away. "What's wrong? That's your fave."

I smiled. "Pacing myself."

"Why the hell would you do that?"

She grinned and nudged the drink toward me, so I cheersed her and faked a sip.

"Ooh, look who's here," she said, her attention diverted to the entrance.

I turned to see "Chad," the guy from the party a few weeks ago, strolling our way. He wasn't what I remembered, but I'd been in an anything-goes kind of mood after Nick. I vaguely recalled him mentioning that he worked with David or Aaron, but he wasn't part of our group. The anonymity had been ideal then. He'd struck me as sweet and considerate with a tennis-player build. A good choice for an evening of flirting and games.

Tonight, though, his smirk was more than a little cocky. The slightly-too-big polo he wore changed his look from slender to lanky. Still, he'd been nice, so I nodded hello. Megan hopped off her stool to make her way to a cluster of our friends while the guy took her seat.

"I hoped I'd run into you again," he greeted me. "Buy you a drink? Another one of those?"

"Maybe a club soda for now," I said when the bartender appeared.

His name wasn't Chad, it was Cam, but he didn't mind my error. I didn't mind his arm on the back of my chair as the show began, but that was mostly because I was too engrossed in the music. Anytime he inched closer, I shifted away. I could tell he was a little dismayed, but That Girl got to say who touched her and when.

When the show ended and the house lights came up, Cam and I traded a smile. He motioned for another club soda for me and a beer for him.

"What do you do, Liv?"

"I'm a teacher." The lie came out of my mouth so easily.

He laughed into my ear. "You must be the hottest teacher in the state. I pity your male students."

I batted my lashes even as I leaned away. "I teach kindergarten."

"Really? I saw you as a high school art teacher. Kids, huh? That's cool. You like it?" I nodded, and he leaned in again. "Teach *me* something."

I laughed and nearly inched off the stool in an attempt to get some distance. "I'm pretty sure you know how to count, Cam."

"I could practice on your toes if you wanted to get out of here."

He hadn't finished the suggestion before my brain punted it away. He was nice enough, albeit a little pushier than the first time we met. And, yeah, we'd kissed at that party weeks ago. But this was headed nowhere. I flashed a tight smile and wrinkled my nose.

"That looks like a no," Cam said.

"Not tonight, thank you. Actually, I've got a little headache. Think I'll go home."

"Aw, come on. Don't tease me like that." He pouted playfully, but I heard the edge in his tone.

"I'm sorry if you misread my intentions. See you around."

I hopped off the stool but whirled when he clasped my arm. His grip wasn't tight, but I jackknifed my elbow free without thinking. *Damn, those self-defense lessons were clutch.*

"Excuse me." I glared at his hand where it still hovered midair.

Cam blinked and lowered his hand, a frown creasing his face. "Excuse you. We've spent the whole night together. Are you really going to lead me on?"

My brows went up. "I didn't lead you on. Nobody made any promises."

We glared at each other a beat longer, but he shrugged and turned to the bar. I scowled at his back, then whipped out my phone and hurried for the exit. Uber would be on site in five minutes, so I sent a text while I waited.

Me: I'm taking off. Prolly skipping yoga 2moro btw.

Megs: kk, g'night! Xoxo

I'd planned to let the night go where it would. Didn't expect that to be an early bedtime, but oh well.

10

LIV

I walked in the house sober as a priest and went straight for the kitchen. The smell of bourbon had made my stomach dip all night. Now, I wanted the taste in my mouth like no other. Lights were unnecessary. The streetlamp shone straight into the kitchen window, and I knew the house blindfolded anyway. I poured a shot, tipped it into my mouth, and held it there until it coated my taste buds and burned my sinuses.

That burn ran down my throat and lit up my chest when I swallowed. It chased away the meaningless little ghosts that haunted my thoughts. I poured another and left it on the counter to get a glass of water.

Maddie's tippy cup wobbled and fell when I pulled the fridge door open. "That's why God made lids," I whispered to myself as I bent to retrieve it.

Once I poured my drink, I shut the door—and turned around to find Will in the doorway.

Chilly water splashed on my feet and jeans as the cup slipped from my hand. "Jesus," I gasped.

"Indeed. And you give *me* shit for not turning on lights?"

The irony, I had to admit, was strong.

"I didn't know you were home," Will said as he stepped into the room.

"Sorry I forgot to text, *Dad*. Swear I wasn't a minute past curfew."

"Don't sass me, little Liv."

His darkly playful words made me blush. More bourbon called my name, so I sat on the counter and picked up the highball glass. Will flipped on the light.

God. Bless.

His work suit had gone from crisp to casual. Dark chocolate trousers and a tan vest were complemented by a sky-blue shirt with two buttons open. The sleeves were rolled up, showing off his forearms. He'd ditched his tie. His hair was mussed.

He was the perfect kind of rumpled. It would've been sexy as hell—if he didn't look like he'd just fallen out of someone's bed.

I looked away. "Where's Tom?"

"He went to have coffee at Erin's."

"Is that what the kids are calling it these days?"

Will chuckled softly but didn't reply.

"So, what? Did you get yours to go? Single shot on the fly, maybe a dollop of foam, huh Langer?"

He rubbed his jaw and prowled toward me. "Actually," he murmured as he stopped just in front of my knees. "I wasn't in the mood for coffee tonight. Bourbon sounded much more appealing."

I held out the glass. Will stepped even closer. His fingers brushed mine as he accepted it. Barely a swallow was left, and he tossed it back.

"Help yourself."

"Don't tempt me," he rasped, banging the glass on the

counter by my hip.

Good god, how was I supposed to remember why I hated this man when he sounded like that?

Will took a step back. "What happened to your plans tonight?"

I cocked my head at his question.

"You said you weren't home until tomorrow. It's not even eleven pm."

My pulse karate kicked my ribs. His casual tone was so obviously fake. When he combed his fingers through his hair, that rumpled look went from *I just got laid* to something more like *I wish my brain would shut up*.

Precisely what I'd been thinking all week.

Get real, Liv. Whatever was brewing between us had to be a mistake. Just more of the weird voodoo this summer had stirred up. I knew it, and I had no doubt that he knew it, too. One part of the see-saw could easily be set back to its usual indifferent equilibrium. All I had to do was shrug off his question, indicate how absolutely none of his business my plans were, and end this. He'd probably be relieved.

Instead, I jumped down from the counter and said the most recklessly awesome, brilliantly foolish thing of my life.

"First of all, I said I'd see Tom tomorrow. As in, *he* should be out all night. Second of all, the concert was a blast. It was so good," I stepped forward and crossed my arms, lips curled. Alarms blared in my head that I totally ignored. "It was so good, I... screamed myself hoarse."

Will's eyes were midnight. "Don't bullshit me. Don't fucking dare."

"Whatever do you mean, William?"

He took two steps forward, which meant I took one back. My ass hit the counter. His hands slapped the laminate to pin me in place while I fought hard to keep from flinching.

Why the hell did you do this? Why the hell indeed. Will Langer had always sparked a hypnotic fascination in me. Teasing him was dangerously addictive.

Kissing him was even more so.

Will's shoulders were at his ears. His arms caged me, but he left plenty of space between our bodies. "What do you want from me, Olivia?"

Something in his tone stripped me of my bravado and struck a nerve. *You have no business messing with him. Silly little Liv. Stick to what you know. Just because being in his arms gave you all the feels doesn't mean it was anything to him.*

I looked down. "Nothing. What the hell would I want from you?"

"Look at me." He repeated it twice before I huffed and met his gaze. "*What* do you *want*, Liv?"

I huffed again and rolled my eyes. "What do *you* want, William?"

A tiny smile ghosted his lips and eyes before he blinked hard and scowled. "I want you to stop deflecting. Nothing more than that. Punch me, tell me to fuck off, push me away and get the hell out of here. End this now. Tell me what a bastard I am."

He bent his elbows to bring us closer, dropped his voice, and said, "But whatever you do, Liv, be damn sure it is exactly what you want to do."

Exactly what I want?

I sucked my lip between my teeth and shook with chilly potential. Then, I exhaled and gripped his collar. A little tug brought us nose-to-nose. I inhaled his clean, spicy scent. Lavender and black pepper. The bourbon became a dizzying top note.

I know exactly what I want. Dammit.

Will didn't move, so I tugged again and opened my lips.

Our mouths grazed each other and sent bolt after bolt of electricity down to my toes. His breath was shallow, lips dry and soft as they dusted mine.

"I hate you," I breathed.

"I know."

"Kiss me, Will Langer."

Will froze, then grinned, all in the split second before he drowned me in a kiss.

As soon as it started, my hands were on his face, his on my hips. I swayed, weak-kneed at the blinding intensity. That brought his arms tight around me. Again, I was crushed against his body. Again, I capsized under this wave of desire. His tongue coaxed mine, urging me to open wider and take more of his kiss until the moment he broke away.

"Fuck this."

His rumble stopped my heart. But then he grabbed my wrist and pulled me to the living room.

Will dropped onto the couch. I was straddling his lap before his ass hit the cushion. He gripped my shirt, fingers dug into my back while we kissed. I quit petting his face and opened his vest and the rest of his shirt buttons. Will growled when I grabbed his lapels and tugged him impossibly closer.

I pushed the shirt off his shoulders and peeled up his undershirt. We might've gotten the thing off without actually breaking our kiss, but I might've been a bit delirious, too. My palms slid down the hard, smooth contours of his arms and chest, and he slipped his fingers under my bra straps and flicked them down.

"Take this off," he breathed. I realized then he'd already unclasped the back, so I yanked the bra through my shirt.

His hands took a rough, greedy journey down my arms to my hips, then back up. Will teased and played with me until he learned exactly what made me squirm and sigh the most. When I began to whine, Will cupped my breasts in his palms and dropped his head.

"*Fuck*," I hissed when he sucked on my nipples through my thin cotton shirt. The added caress of his thumbs along my lower curves made me dig my nails into his shoulders.

My shirt stuck to my skin from the moisture of his mouth. Slowly, he withdrew and ran his fingers where his lips had been. I shuddered and gripped my hair. "Oh, god."

You are in Will Langer's lap, sighing like a porn star. What. The. Fuck?

He lifted my hands from my hair and laced his fingers through mine. His palms on my knuckles, Will began to move our fingertips down my face.

"Shh," he whispered when I tensed.

I exhaled and kissed him again, this time with a new, lazy tempo. Never before had touching myself been so interesting. We skimmed my jaw, my throat, over my pounding heart and lower. He guided us over my breasts with slow movements that made me stall out on the kiss.

"Does this turn you on?" he murmured, pinching my nipples between my thumbs and his fingers.

I nodded, eyes closed.

"Say it."

I opened one eye. "Yes, it turns me on. As if you don't know."

He laughed and pinched again. My hips bucked, my spine arched, and Will leaned forward for another warm, wet suck.

"Will, what are we *doing*?"

"Good damn question." He sucked again while we held me to his mouth.

His hips flexed. I bucked a second time, and the friction

became the conductor for the first pulls of a climax. I moaned, the tingly pleasure beginning to simmer in my bloodstream. Will answered with his mouth and his lips.

I tumbled off his lap to the cushion, one foot on the floor. "Come on. You did this to me, so help me out."

Dark eyes blinked open. "I did what to you?"

My face got hot. "Shut up and finish what you started."

He smiled. Not a smirk like I expected. A smile. "Is that a two-way street?"

I smirked. "You'll have to wait and see."

He popped the button on my jeans. While I scrambled to peel them off, Will jumped up and pulled me to my feet, his arms wrapped around me from behind. "I can't watch this," he breathed in my ear. "If I watch you come, I'll lose my fucking mind."

"I think you already did." God, talking was hard

"Indeed." His lips clamped down on my neck, teeth scraping my skin into his mouth in a vicious bite.

I yowled, and Will breathed a laugh and bit harder.

"Fucker." I gasped and pulled his hair—but I also dropped my head to give him better access.

"Get back here." His voice was so low and gravelly it was almost comedic.

I wasn't laughing, though, as he held my jaw and swiveled me back to his lips. I forgot I was standing up. Between how tightly Will held me and the unreal tease of his caress, the fact that my feet were on the ground became completely irrelevant.

He coasted his hand down to my hip. I lifted to him, head bobbing in a lazy nod. Will hesitated, then skimmed his fingers between my legs.

"Christ," he groaned and stroked again. "How can you hate me so much and be this wet for me?"

I'm not sure if you can blush when your face is already flaming hot, but if you can, I did. "That'll happen when someone sucks on your tits, dummy."

"Liv?"

I waited.

He growled into my ear. "Scream for me."

Before I could say, "No way in hell," Will took a deep, uneven breath, hooked the elastic of my underwear, and shoved two fingers inside me. Fiery pleasure ripped up my spine, and I clamped on my tongue to hold in the *mmm* that vibrated my throat. I thought vaguely of the popcorn bowl a few weeks ago, how I'd noticed how long and lovely his fingers were.

God, they *really* were.

Will's forehead hit my neck. Breathy profanities fell from his lips now and then that only thrilled me more. His arm across my ribs twisted so he could tease my breasts, and that started my detonation.

Don't scream, don't do it, don't you dare...

"Oh, fuck, yes, please yes, more..."

Maybe I kind of shouted. Definitely not a scream, though.

When my body stopped convulsing, I went limp in his arms, so wrung-out and blissed that I couldn't begin to think. He held me up so firmly that I didn't worry about my buckled knees. My head lolled, and he nuzzled my neck.

And then he said, "You can scream better than that."

My lips curled. "Damn right I can."

I grinned deeper when he chuckled, then opened my eyes and gazed at him through my fallen hair.

Will's smile faded into an intent stare. He tilted his head. One broad palm pushed my hair off my face, coasted to my neck, and brought me back for a kiss.

But that kiss was the shot of whiskey to sharpen my senses. I went from hazy and satisfied to a woman on a mission. I whirled in his arms and whipped off his belt to shove his pants and boxer briefs to the floor.

Good lord.

William Langer was blessed. I raked my gaze from his dark hair down the lines and angles of his strong body, but my eyes settled on the perfection in my grip. He was long, hard, and absolutely beautiful. How unfair for such a perfect body to belong to such an arrogant jerk.

Such a jerk. I bit my lip when my heart throbbed with affection.

Slowly, I met his gaze. "Your turn to scream, Langer."

Will bent to my grip, hands braced on my shoulders, my hair in his fists. "I'm going to fuck a blister on your hand. And possibly rip this pink out of your hair."

"I won't let you last long enough for any of that bullshit."

Touching him was so hot that I started to get achy all over again, but as promised, he didn't last long. Impossible, with my bicep flexed in a vise-grip and all the moisture from his crown against my palm. I twisted my wrist and stroked harder when he tensed.

"Come on, boy. Make a mess for me." My voice was a dark, lusty dare.

Will buried his face in my neck as his hips jerked. My poor shirt. The thing had just dried up top when it was warm and soaked all over my stomach.

Slowly, I let go. Will lifted his face. He stepped back, hitched his pants up his hips, and—laughed.

"Shit," he rasped, reaching out to touch my neck.

I fingered the tender skin and pursed my lips. "Turtle-necks in July? Really?"

We both smirked, but my rush faded fast, replaced by a question I could see mirrored in his eyes.

What have we done?

Will reached for me, but I backed away and nearly fell on my ass to step into my jeans. "Don't. Just don't."

He didn't. Speak, touch me, move—whatever finished my command, he obeyed. Why this sudden obedience hurt so damn much, I'm not sure. What I did know was that I had to do the one thing I wanted to least.

I looked into his eyes.

Those inky pools gave me nothing. No hint of emotion. It was an expression I knew well.

Jaw cocked, lips twisted, I opened my mouth, but *mistake, fuck you,* and *never again* all jammed up my throat so bad, I couldn't swallow. With one more look at that unyielding face, I spun around and got the hell out of there.

11

LIV

When I finally rolled out of bed the next morning, the thought of facing him in my house nearly made me crawl right back into the sheets.

I fled to my parents' house instead.

I knew it was a cop-out even as I texted Tom from the safety of my room to let him know I'd pick up Maddie today, then sidled like a ninja to the back door. There was no point in calling it anything but cowardice, but I needed a few hours of sanity before I could see Will Langer again.

The pool was a perfect excuse. With the sweltering July humidity, Mom didn't bat an eye when I showed up in a cover-up and flip-flops to spend the day swimming and pushing Maddie around in her float.

Mom appeared from the house when I'd tucked Mads in for a nap in her inflatable boat in the shade. I stroked lazily to the side of the pool for the glass of tea she proffered.

"Unsweet with mint and lemon, just like you like it," she said with a smile.

"You're the best."

She settled into a chaise and pushed her sunglasses up her nose. "How are you, sweetheart?"

"Good."

"You always say good, you know."

I shrugged.

She gestured to the trees. "It's just us right now. I'll ask again. How *are* you, Livi?"

I put my elbows on the concrete. "I'm... weird, Mom. It's a weird summer. Feels like a lot of things that were always true aren't anymore."

Mom nodded. "Funny how change happens in spurts, isn't it?"

"It doesn't feel very funny. But yeah."

"Is there anything you'd like to talk about? You can pretend like you're thirteen again and tell Mom all your secrets if you want."

"You always knew how to keep it in the vault." I grinned at the nostalgia. There was no way in hell last night was up for discussion with a single soul, but I set the tea down and opened up.

"I've been thinking about changing jobs," I said, then outlined the basics.

Mom beamed. "I always thought you were amazing with children. You were so good with your younger cousins, even when you were a teen. Now, obviously, you're a champion with your niece."

"Aw, Mom, thanks." My grin turned goofy.

She laughed. "Anything else?"

"Ben is getting married."

"Give him our congratulations—right?" Her smile turned to a grimace fast. "Or—oh, were you two—"

I crossed my arms into an X. "I'll give him your best. I'm totally happy for him, and of course we're still friends. I don't know why I mentioned it. I guess it's kind of a big change, and not just for him. It's... I don't know."

"Realization that you're at that phase of life?"

I nodded and chewed my lip. "Kind of, exactly."

"Time catches up, doesn't it?"

"That's for sure. Thanks for listening, Mom."

"Is that all?"

"Eh, you know, those are the big ones. Other little things are different, too, so I guess they add up. Um, oh. I started doing CrossFit."

"Is that safe? That self-defense class was one thing, but I've heard CrossFit is something different." She sat forward with a frown.

"Nah, it's just a tough workout is all. It's hard, but it's fine. The instructors are really good. Megan and I joined. We ran into Will there, actually."

Drown me now. My stomach knotted just to say his name. Why in the hell had I brought him up? My goal for the day was to clear my head. It was as if I couldn't resist.

Mom hummed agreeably. "And then there's Will at your house. That's sure to cause a fluctuation in routines."

"Yeah, pretty much," I mumbled. "We try to avoid each other."

Or drink each other's souls. Depends on the moment.

"You used to get so excited when he and Tom would come visit from college. It was the only time I could get you to help with housework voluntarily." She chuckled.

"College guys to hang out with? Is it really a surprise that a high school kid would geek about that?" My smile was like a crack on a sheet of ice.

"Well, you always did worship your big brother. He was so protective of you. After your surgery—"

"My what?" Thoughts of Will scattered.

Mom blinked. "Surely we've told you about this? You were about three, and you hadn't started to talk beyond basic sounds. Turned out you had fluid in your ears that made you nearly deaf. A surgery cleared it all up, but Tom was so worried about you. He was so helpful as you recovered. That might've been why he became a nurse, now that I think of it. Anyway, you know he always looked out for you. Sometimes I worried that we babied you too much, indulged too many of your whims. But I'd say you turned out, my bold, beautiful daughter."

I'd been listening intently to a story I had no knowledge of, but her compliment made me grin. "Thank you, Mommy. Although I do enjoy a good whim."

"I know you do. And we all know you caught up on your verbal skills with no problem." We laughed together, and then she said, "But the point was how you'd get excited when the boys came home from college. I know it was largely because of your brother, but you and Will got along fine back then."

My stomach dipped. "Well, we don't now."

"Wonder why?"

I bit the inside of my cheek as long-buried memories came to life. There had been a time when Will and I were pals. Not friends exactly, but he used to smile at my silly teenage nonsense. That flat expression didn't start until—

With a hard exhale, I dismissed those thoughts and shrugged off Mom's question. "I guess we just don't. Too different, maybe."

She smirked. My mother *smirked* at me. "Or too same. Stubborn and proud."

I dunked under the water and stayed there until my lungs burned. When I resurfaced, it was to the sound of her laughter. "Precisely, young lady," she called.

We spent a couple more lazy hours in the sun before Mads and I headed home, detouring to the grocery for dinner supplies. Tom met us in the driveway with the look of a man who'd gotten laid after a long drought. Maddie zoomed to him for a hug, so I went inside to start making burgers and mashed potatoes.

The gods gifted me with an empty kitchen to cook in. By the time I shouted that dinner was ready, I was summer Saturday chill.

That, of course, ended quick.

Will and I caught eyes as we all sat down to eat. I looked away first. "So, Tommy," I said, "you look pretty refreshed for someone who was out so late. What time did you get home, anyway?"

His light brown eyes rolled, but there was plenty of swagger in the way he reached for the ketchup. "Uh, about eleven."

"A.M.?"

"Something like that," he chuckled, reluctantly returning my high-five.

"The best kind of Friday nights last until Saturday morning, huh brother?" My words were teasing but the look he flashed told me Tom knew how happy I was for him.

We slapped hands again. When I reached for my fork, Tom did a double take. His grin turned wicked. "How was *your* night, Livi?"

I tore my burger in half. "It was alright."

"Just alright? Nothing at all interesting? You're glowing a little bit."

"Uh, hello? I spent all day at the pool." Now my burger was in quarters, but only one bite was missing I started peeling the bun.

"Yeah, right. Shame on you, little sis." Tom pressed a fingertip against my neck and cackled. "Busted."

Shit, that damn bite mark. Being at the pool all day, I'd somehow managed to forget the blue and purple oval that had made me cringe at the mirror this morning. I slapped my hand over the spot. "Shut up, Thomas."

He laughed harder. "How did Mom not notice? God, you always did get away with everything."

I glanced at Will. He had one elbow on the table, fist at his mouth, and *laughter* in his eyes. I wasn't sure if I wanted to deck him—or let him give me another mark.

"Don't tease me, Tom. It was just—I mean, I didn't mean for... ugh, shut up okay?" I hid my face.

To my absolute horror, both men laughed. Tom continued. "As your big brother, it's my god-given right to tease you about everything, but *especially* about letting some guy suck on your neck. That's reckless, that is."

"Messy even." Will's murmur dropped my heart to my knees.

Tom loved it. Even with my eyes still hidden, I heard him clap Will's shoulder as he said, "While we're on the subject, how'd your night end up with Stacy?"

Suddenly, I was very interested. I propped my chin on my hand and batted my eyes. "Yeah, Will. How was your date?"

"Fine."

"Aw, come on. Poor Stace was only fine?" *What the hell is wrong with you? Shut up!*

That got me a long, withering stare. "My night ended exactly as I wanted it to, Olivia. Any more questions?"

I nodded at Maddie. "Sure, but nothing appropriate for the dinner table."

Exactly like you wanted? As in, you wanted *this to happen? As in, you'd thought about it? As in... you didn't want more?*

"Liv?"

I shook my head and looked over at Tom. "Yeah?"

"The brewer's festival is next weekend. Should we go again?"

I brightened. "Heck yeah! You should bring your lady. It's high time I met her."

Tom nodded. "I'll see if she's free. Are you bringing anyone?"

"I might see if anyone else is going and meet up there. Are *you* coming, too?" I jutted my chin at Will, and Tom startled.

"I know nothing about this," he said.

"Beer, fun, music—obviously your idea of torture. Figured since you live here, you're on automatic invite."

"I'd hate to cramp your style."

"Tuh!" I tossed my hair. "Honey, you'll never cramp this style."

Tom chuckled. "Come on, dude, it'll be fun. You can bring Stacy if I'm bringing Erin."

"I'll come."

I stood up and grabbed all the plates. "Bet you can make *it* exactly what you want, too," I said. The perfect parting shot.

Or possibly a Freudian invitation. *Shit.*

Megs: Ready to sweat tonight? Bring it, baby!

The message lit up my screen at lunch on Wednesday. I sighed.

Me: I guess. You sure you're up for it?

Megs: lol I'm sure jerkface won't bully you too badly. Woman up & be there!

"Exactly what I expected, from you, Megs," I muttered to the phone.

In the hopes of manifesting my goal, I'd deliberately not packed gym clothes that morning. Ultimately, all that resulted in was me flying home and running straight back out the door to make it to class on time. At least all the rushing meant no time spent hiding from Will. Luckily, it wasn't a partner's night.

Workouts crushed and showers completed, Megan and I were on our way out the door when Kelly, the trainer, smiled and motioned us to the front desk.

"This is y'alls last session. Have you thought about a membership?"

We leaned on the counter and looked at the menu of prices. "I don't know," Megs murmured.

"Aren't you hooked? You could—oh, wait. Hey, guys? Can I get a little testimonial over here? These guys will talk you into it."

Of. Course.

Of course Will and two other guys were now heading our way. Of course both of the other men wore open, friendly expressions while my nemesis locked eyes with me and refused to blink.

One of the other dudes started talking up the community vibe, the physical challenge, etc. All of it made me want to say, *thanks, buddy, got it* after fifteen seconds. All I wanted was to escape the strange cocktail of anxiety and tingly pleasure simmering in my abdomen as I gazed into those dark eyes. What the hell was going on in his brain? Was he mad? Regretful? Absolutely indifferent?

Megan nodded along. She seemed unruffled, even

though I was sure she recognized Will. "Yeah, I get you. And we do like it, but we have yoga, and—"

"What don't you know? You should absolutely do it." Will spoke to me as if the other three weren't there.

"It's so intense," I almost whined.

His look turned condescending. "Can't handle it?'

God, he knew my triggers. "Please. I can handle anything."

"Then get the membership." He looked over my shoulder. "She's in, Kelly."

"Did you just dare to speak for me?"

Will hesitated, his brows pinching together.

"Damn right you didn't." I glared at him—and slapped my credit card on the counter.

"Well, okay then. Guess we're in." Megan produced her card, too.

Poor Kelly. Her friendly testimonials had turned into a battle of wills, but she nodded as we pushed our cards toward her. Behind me, I heard Will's hard exhale before the door chimed open, indicating the men had left. Megs and I signed our receipts and headed for the parking lot.

"That was weird," she said once we strolled out into the evening heat. "He is a bit of a dick, huh?"

"Understatement of the year, my friend." *In all the meanings of the term.*

We slid into a booth at our pub, enjoying the air conditioner after such a sweaty hour. Adam approached and tossed napkins on the table. "Hello, lovely ladies."

"Well, hello Adam." Megan's smile went full watt. We placed an order after they flirted for a few minutes. Once he strolled away, I raised an eyebrow.

"What?" She blinked, trying to look innocent.

I wiggled my brows and made a kissy face. "You two need to do it already."

Megan laughed. "Oh, please. Do not make that face, you hypocrite."

"What are you talking about?"

"That bite on your neck? Hello, genius?"

"Oh god bless it." I banged my forehead on the table. I'd worn collared shirts all week, but in my rush to the gym it had slipped my mind.

"That Chad is an animal, huh?"

My head snapped up. "What? Who? Oh. His name was Cam."

Megan's laugh died. She tilted her head, eyes narrowing. "You might as well have just said, 'his name was Mud.'"

I shrugged and picked my nails.

"He gave you a bite so deep that it's still there after half a week, and that's all you've got?"

"It's...he wasn't..."

Megan's brow shot up. "Ooh, it wasn't Cam?"

I gave a shrug/headshake. "Look, let's change—"

No such luck. Megan spoke over me. "Who the hell was it, then? You two were at the show—"

"I didn't like him, okay? He was kind of pushy, so I bounced."

"And then?"

Adam saved me with our food and more smiles for my friend. That gave me time to scramble for a story and mentally kick my own ass for not just nodding to the Cam thing. As he strolled away, I knew I had nothing that would redirect her curiosity. Sure enough, her gaze returned to me while she sipped her beer.

I puffed out a breath. "It was just a random hook-up.

Nothing to tell. Just a one-time thing, a crazy mistake, and it's over."

"Say how you really feel," she teased. "Disappointed much?"

"No. It's fine."

"How did you meet?"

I shrugged—and then realized my shoulders were tired of doing that. *Please, please just let it go, Megs.*

She was quiet a moment, eyes flickering in thought. I'd just reached for my beer when she coughed and slammed her glass on the table.

"Will. It was Will."

My jaw unhinged. I just barely kept the drink upright as it slipped from my hand.

Meg's grin split her face. "Oh holy shit, I am so right."

"It... wasn't?" I stuttered, blazing with embarrassment.

She began to laugh. "Nice try, kiddo. God, so obvious! You could've sliced the tension between you and served it for dinner. How did I not get that sooner?"

"How did you get that at all? Megs, you *can't* tell."

She shrugged. "Who am I going to tell? And why would I? But wow, that's a mess, yeah?"

"No, it's not a mess. It's not a *thing.*"

"Not a thing my ass. That man devoured you with those gorgeous eyes. I mean, damn Liv, he's *hot.*"

My head hit the table again. "How about we shut up a little bit? Please?"

"I take it he was good."

I grunted. "But he's such a smug bastard. You heard him tonight. He's so condescending to me all the time."

She laughed again. "Yeah, and you ate it up and gave it right back. That was classic flirtation."

"No, that was real. It's been real for *years.*"

"Everything okay here?" Adam asked.

I peeked up and smiled sweetly. "All good, thanks. Boy stuff."

"Ah-ha."

"Adam, did you ever fight with a girl you liked? Just to flirt?"

He frowned at Megan's question. "Not that I remember. I'm a little more straightforward in my tactics... like switching sections with my buddy so I can wait on a girl. That's more my style."

Her lips curved. "Oh really?"

Adam smiled back and leaned on the table. "What do you say, Megan? Can I get your number?"

We traded glances. Slowly, she turned back to him. "Give me your phone." He laid it on the table, and she typed in her number. "Sorry it's not a napkin for me to put a lipstick stain on. Modern age, you know."

"I'll be okay. I prefer lipstick stains on my face anyway." Adam pocketed his phone and strolled away.

We looked at each other and dissolved into girly giggles. "Oh my god, that was the cutest thing," she hissed.

"Smooth AF."

As we ate, she said, "Anyway, about Will. So what if you want him? Nobody has to know—oh, shit, but Tom..."

"Who said I wanted him?" I nearly screeched.

"You *don't*?"

I swallowed. "Can we not talk about this please?"

She chuckled. "It must've been good to get you that tongue-tied."

"Megan," I warned.

"Okay. But it was, right?"

I rolled my eyes. "Yeah. You could say that."

She winked at me. "That's my girl."

12

WILL

"What do you think, Will?"

Matt and Carlos stared at me, but I had no response. I didn't even know what the hell we were talking about. Politics, probably, but local, state, or national? Environmental? Financial?

Who the fuck cared? Who had time for political theory when Liv Fucking Milani had rocked my world and then turned into a ghost for the past four days? Why weren't we all discussing this point instead?

Right. Because you're a 30-year-old professional, not a middle schooler at a slumber party.

"Sorry, long day at work. Say again?" The classic code for I wasn't listening, but at least it got my head back in the conversation. I picked up the topic—urban development—and threw out some insights from the latest *Washington Post* editorial as we ate.

"So how about those new girls at CrossFit? What do you think their story is?" Matt said as we waited on the check.

Carlos shrugged. "I figured they were a couple."

"They're not."

Matt chuckled at my declaration. "Either way, the Italian one seemed to be giving you a run for your money, Langer. I've never seen someone dared into a gym membership before. Guess y'all know each other?"

We rose from the table, and I crooked a tight smile I didn't feel. "You could say that. I have to run. See you next week."

Alone in my car, I gripped the steering wheel and exhaled hard. *Know each other, yeah sure. A decade of forced indifference boiled over into the hottest Saturday night I've ever known, and I've gone and pissed her off again. You could say we're acquainted.*

I walked into the house just as Tom was carrying Maddie upstairs for bed. The recliner seemed as good a place as any to continue replaying those moments at the gym when we couldn't take our eyes off each other—all up until I defaulted to pissing her off, just to get her to commit.

What is she thinking about all this? Is she thinking about it? I envisioned the flush that had started tinging her cheeks anytime we interacted. *She's thinking about it.*

Logic said that she could be feeling one of many things, from embarrassed to guilty to angry. Angry was a worst-case situation because it could mean she felt used. That would be a nightmare.

Although logic said all those were options, instinct told me that another possibility was that she felt just as I did: conflicted as hell and desperate for more.

While I assessed the situation, the back door opened. The woman of my dreams and nightmares walked in. She glared when she saw me, but again she wore that beautiful flush that gave me hope. Her dark hair was loose around her bare shoulders, legs miles long in black jeans. How did she take my breath every damn time I looked at her?

Enough. We need answers. My pulse kicked up as I swallowed hard and muttered, "Please don't walk away."

She huffed, but she didn't leave. Arms crossed, she glanced around. "Where's Tom?"

"Upstairs putting Maddie to bed."

"What do you want, then?"

"I'm sorry I spoke for you."

Her fidgeting ceased, eyes blinking rapidly as she focused more on me.

At last, a chance to clarify myself without her threatening to castrate me first. "You never need someone to speak for you. I didn't intend to, and I'm sorry if I did."

"Damn right... thank you."

"You're welcome." I wanted to laugh at her change of tone, but the sincerity was obvious.

"So, um, that's all?" Her fidgeting resumed. It made me want to pin her to the wall and kiss her until she redirected all that energy into dragging her nails down my back.

The recliner snapped closed, and in a second I stood inches from her. This was my opportunity to say everything that had been on my mind for half a week. "That's hardly all, but I can't get two seconds alone with you before you run away."

Panic flared in her brown eyes. She shook her head and stepped back. "Don't."

"You already said that. And I didn't. I'm waiting for you to."

"What do you want me to say?" she hissed, both of us too aware that Tom was upstairs. "You want me to say it was a mistake? That I was drunk? That we... I don't know what?"

"If that's the truth." Her words punched my sternum, but anything was better than guessing how she felt.

"Fuck you, Will."

Amusement tugged at my lips despite the tension. "Is that a curse or a request?"

A laugh slipped out of her, clearly unbidden, and I smiled a little deeper. Relief wanted to flood my system, but we hadn't reached anything definite yet. The heart of the matter had to be said.

The next words out of my mouth were so dark, so dirty and wrong and *hot,* that adrenaline surged my system just to say them. "Do you want *me* to say it was a mistake? That I feel guilty? That Tom's little sister off limits?"

She sucked on her lip, that flush turning darker red. "If that's the truth."

I shook my head. "Oh, Olivia. I am not *nearly* that good of a person."

Terrible person, asshole friend, absolute prick. Whatever title I deserved, at least I knew the truth. I didn't feel the least bit guilty about obliging her wish to kiss her. I'd do it again and again if I had the chance.

Liv trembled and sucked in a deep breath. She moved so we were nose to nose, and suddenly that chance was potently real.

"Are you telling me that you *don't* think it was a mistake?"

I leaned even closer. "Fuck *you,* Liv."

Goddam, she tasted good. So good, I moaned as our lips fit together and our tongues stroked, soft this time. She wrapped her arms around me, and I held her perfect body tight to mine. No panic or anger. This kiss felt practiced, like we'd done it enough already to know how to meet the other's desire.

I nibbled on her lip, then licked it slick once more before I had to pull away and crash us back to reality. Liv wobbled as I released her, so I put my hands on her shoulders as her eyes slowly blinked open.

God bless.

Those eyes sparkled under an absolutely perfect glow on her cheeks. Her lips were blushed, even fuller than usual. The tiny, dazzled smile that played there softened everything about her. For just a moment, this sassy, brilliant woman was blissed.

Because she kissed me.

Holy fuck.

"You look fucking beautiful after I kiss you. Electric." My voice was raspy, and I couldn't care less.

"I feel nuclear."

I kissed her again for that.

"Will," she croaked when I pulled away. "What are we *doing*?"

After days of analysis and years of strategic maneuvering, the answer was suddenly clear:

"Foreplay."

13

LIV

Over the next few days, I studied and got deep into my teaching coursework. I went to work. I talked, texted friends, ate meals, did all the regular stuff I was supposed to.

But that word, that one word, became the filter on all my waking moments—and maybe my non-waking ones, too. Hazier than any starlight effect could ever be, *foreplay* blurred the lines of logic and fantasy.

It was the thought when I stared into space after looking at the textbook too long. The whisper in my head while I went through the motions at work. And definitely the word behind my eyes when I went to sleep at night. It vacillated between conjuring a queasy, yellow dread, like we were headed toward a total train wreck, and tinting my world with a rosy hope that I would die before I admitted to a single soul.

Every time the word rattled too loudly, I'd snap back to reality, tell myself that this was foolish—that Will Langer and I didn't even like each other, had *never* liked each other —and try to move on with life.

Will, unfortunately, made that hard to remember. He

was a little too good at this whole foreplay bit. Every interaction we had spun my head all over again.

Case in point: I was curled on the couch with Maddie Thursday afternoon watching *My Little Pony* when Will got home.

"This sh is weird," he grumbled, careful to edit his language for my niece.

"There are men your age who obsess over this show. Which is your favorite?"

He snorted.

I stood and turned up the volume, so Maddie's attention stayed focused on the show. Certain she was rapt, I faced him with my hands in my back pockets and flashed a daring grin. "I want to do my hair like the shy one."

Will groaned. "Tell me you're joking."

"What's your problem with colorful hair? A lot of people have it."

He twisted a lock of mine around his finger and tugged gently. "Like you need anything extra for everyone to see how beautiful you are."

A smirk curled my lips. "I wear it like this because *I* find it pretty and fun, thank you. Has nothing to do with others' opinions."

He arched his brows. "Fair point."

"I do have them once in a while, despite what you think."

He stepped closer and put his lips to my ear. "I think you're the cleverest woman I've ever met. I also can't help but think about how hard I'd have to pull this hair until you begged me to stop."

I wound his tie around my hand. "You're the one who'll beg."

"I'd beg you right now if I thought it would help."

"Hungry, Livi!"

I jumped out of my skin, chirping loudly, "Me too, Mads! Let's go to the kitchen."

Will laughed as Maddie went running ahead of me. I kept one eye on her, pulled on that tie, and stole a kiss before hurrying to make dinner.

Sexy as that was, Will *really* shook me Friday afternoon. Maddie had dozed off snuggled beside me on the couch again. I lay on my back, staring at the ceiling. The door clicked open, and he appeared, upside-down in my line of vision.

"Hi," I murmured.

His brows furrowed. "You want a drink? Looks like you've got a lot on your mind."

I carefully moved Maddie to the mat inside her gated play area. Sure she was settled, I followed him to the kitchen to sit on the counter while he poured. We clinked and sipped in a weird silence. Acknowledging each other and sharing a drink were alien for Will and me. By the tension in his shoulders, I guessed he was quite aware of it, too.

"What are you thinking about?" he asked, elbows on the counter, gaze at the wall.

"Since when do you care?"

Will snorted. "I care."

"No, seriously. Since *when?*"

Dark eyes cut to me. "What are you asking?"

I sucked on my lip. "I was thinking... about... a long time ago."

Shut up, shut up. I sipped and imagined the burn torched my words. Words I'd scribbled in my journal this morning. Words that I hadn't thought of in eight years.

But Will's attention was captured. He turned, drank, and

waited. I shook my head and rolled the glass between my palms. "Say it," he said.

"Do you remember—"

"Yes."

I twisted my lips. "You don't know what I was going to—"

"That night we talked till dawn."

I squeezed my eyes shut. Watery memories of a night that I'd almost convinced myself was a dream—no, that I *had* convinced myself was a dream—floated up. "We were drunk."

"And you were a baby."

I twitched my lips again. "I was eighteen. It was a graduation party for all three of us."

"No. We'd been to a party off-campus. Then we went back to the apartment and—"

"Tom passed out—"

"And you and I... talked. About everything." Will paused. I heard him drink since my eyes were still squeezed tight.

"You're pale," he said.

"I hadn't thought of that in a long time. I don't remember much about it. Just that we talked. That we... I thought you..."

I thought that, at last, at last, *the secret fascination I'd had with you as I grew up had a purpose. A reason. I thought you liked me.*

"I did."

My eyes flew open to find Will staring into his glass. A line cut between his brows, but I was certain I hadn't spoken. He sighed. His head bent a little lower. "Oh, god, I did."

Is it weirder that I didn't finish the thought or that he didn't need me to?

Those fingers—*mm, those fingers*—sliced through his
dark hair, and my palm itched jealously. I reached and
pushed my own fingers from his temple to his neck. Will
wore his thick, wavy hair with just enough length to keep it
stylish, not frizzy or moppy. Sliding my hand through it gave
me the best kind of chills.

I didn't want to think about the past anymore. "Your hair
is very touchable. That's what I'm thinking now."

He pushed off his elbows and stood between my
knees. My hands played, making his curls stick up
everywhere.

"You can touch it whenever you want," he sighed with a
blissed expression. "You can touch *me* whenever you want,
Olivia."

My pulse jumped. "Is that an invitation?"

"Mm-hmm. A standing one."

"Since when?"

Will palmed my waist and pulled me closer. My knees
spread to let him lean until we were nose-to-nose. "Since
you wanted to," he said before our mouths connected.

"Will," I said between kisses. He grunted a reply, so I
pulled back just enough to say, "This is such a mistake."

It was the first time I'd said the m-word aloud, and the
taste in my mouth was bitter with doubt. But it *was*, wasn't
it? There was no way something that felt this right with
someone this wrong could be a good thing.

Right?

Will's eyes opened and fixed on me. "Should we stop?"

"We have to." Even as I said it, I leaned for his lips again.

He recoiled.

"Fine, Olivia. If that's what you want."

And with that, he turned and disappeared. By the time I
hopped off the counter, he was already upstairs.

That encounter wasn't exactly foreplay. Why, then, did I spend the night staring at a single page of my textbook and wake up the next morning with him still on my mind? Passing him in the hall didn't help given the tight black shirt and shorts he wore, a bicycle helmet dangling from his fingers.

After that vision, even yoga couldn't clear my head, and that's saying a hell of a lot.

At home, I threw on cutoffs, a graphic tee, a purple plaid button-down, and black ankle boots for the beer festival. With an application of MAC's "Pink Nouveau" for a daytime look, it was time to go. I scuttled downstairs.

"Bout time, sis." Tom smiled when I appeared in the kitchen.

I blew him a kiss and pushed my aviators on, following them to Tom's car.

"You two in the back," Tom instructed. We were going to pick up Erin. Tom was our driver since he wouldn't drink before an overnight shift.

"I feel that if I ride shotgun, it sends an important message about my role in this family," I teased. Tom rolled his eyes, and I grinned. "On the other hand, I'd hate to stick her next to Will, so I guess I'll sacrifice."

"What a hero," Will said.

"Now kids," Tom drawled as he started the engine. "Seriously though, Liv. Can you take it easy on her? I like this girl. Can you try not to intimidate the hell out of her?"

"Intimidate? Moi?" I laid a hand on my heart, and both men laughed. "I'll be nice, Tommy. Just for you."

At Erin's, Tom parked and went to the door, which left Will and me alone in silence. He gazed out the window. Try as I might to focus on my phone, I couldn't resist sneaking looks at him. He wore a fitted gray Henley and dark jeans. Even seated, his clothes accentuated his body in a way that made it impossible to forget that I knew what was underneath.

"Erin is really sweet. Try not to bowl her over."

I startled at the break in silence, then scowled. "Oh, so we're back to smartass remarks about what a 'brat' I am, are we?"

He didn't look at me. "I thought that was what you wanted."

An old hurt twisted my heart in a way I didn't see coming. I bit down on my cheek to will it away. "It was never what I wanted. You don't have to be so goddamn cold to me."

That finally turned his head. I braced for that impassive expression. I didn't expect to see anguish instead.

"Yes, I do. I don't know how else to stay away from you, Liv. And you said just the other day that we had to stop what had started. So, here we are."

"Did you want to stop?"

He didn't reply.

I punched the seat. "Dammit, Will, answer me. Did you?"

The muscle in his jaw bulged. "Dammit, Liv, you still aren't hearing me. I want you to know what *you* want."

The hurt throbbed in my chest, and suddenly, the car was too small. Torn between bursting into tears and ripping his clothes off, I yanked open the door and stepped out. Nashville's summertime humidity was never so refreshing as when I sucked in a breath of air that wasn't saturated with the tension between us. Not a moment too soon, the front door opened, and Tom and Erin walked out.

14

LIV

Several hours and quite a few beer tastings later, Erin and I were shout-singing "Wrecking Ball" on the ride home, laughing as we drowned out Miley Cyrus on the stereo.

She reached into the backseat to high-five me as the song ended. "Oh my gosh, this has been amazing. I'm so glad we finally met, Liv."

I gave her another high-five. "Definitely. Nothing like beer and shenanigans on a Saturday afternoon to become instant friends."

Erin had been quiet at first. After a few samples of beer, we'd started to laugh and chat. She was indeed sweet, and we got along great. Mostly I was happy for Tom. His gaze followed her while I coaxed her from one adventure to the other all afternoon.

Tom parked in the driveway and turned to the group. "I've got about two hours before work. Erin, do you want to grab some food before I take you home?" She agreed. "Great. I'll get changed and we'll take off. Liv, you have plans tonight?"

"I'm sure I can find some trouble to get into. You two

have fun." The beer and sun were catching up with me already. Inside, I flopped on the couch, and Tom made his way upstairs to change. Erin and Will chatted softly while I dozed, completely content.

"I'm out, sis." My eyes opened again when Tom put his hand on my head. I sat up with a yawn. Erin waved at me from the door. Will sat in the recliner.

"Okay. See you tomorrow. Erin, hope to see you soon."

The door closed. Neither Will nor I moved.

All alone. So, what next? Are you going to be responsible and go upstairs? Or are you going to sit here and fantasize about your nemesis on his knees in front of you?

I tilted my head back and closed my eyes. Every passing moment wound me up more. No amount of good judgment could stop me from wondering if he was thinking anything close to the recklessly hot thoughts I was.

Okay, hoping he was thinking them.

The angel on my shoulder threw up her hands. *Fine, sit here and fantasize. Since when did you know how to be responsible anyway?*

That thought made me frown. I *was* responsible. I was responsible enough to care for Maddie, to help out at the daycare, and to hold a steady job and pursue any number of hobbies I liked. I had no problem dressing myself or eating right. And dammit, I was one of the most loyal friends someone could have. Why didn't That Girl deserve a little more credit?

Was it really *irresponsible* to admit how drawn I was to him suddenly? And not just the physical part. Will had been dropping lines all summer that boosted my confidence. What was wrong with wanting more of that energy in my life *and* to be hit with lightning bolts of passion every time he touched me?

"Are you asleep?" Will's question softly sliced the silence.

I shook my head and stared up at the ceiling. When he didn't say more, it occurred to me that he wasn't struggling like I was. He said he wanted me to know what I wanted. Did that mean he was cool either way? That this was just a fun fling that he could take or leave?

Confirmation was necessary, even if I didn't want it. I kept my tone sleepy and disinterested as I asked, "Did you have fun today?"

"I did," he replied in a similar voice. "A lot of fun."

"Erin is great. Good match you made. Tom couldn't keep his eyes off her."

"Mm-hm."

"So, what exactly was fun for you? I mean, you don't really do *fun*."

"I don't do fun? What does that even mean?" His tone was still soft, but the challenge was there.

"You're Mr. Serious. You sneer at fun."

"Forgive me for acting my age."

"Eighty, right?" I tried to keep my smile at bay. *This* was fun.

He sighed loudly, and I dared to glance at him. He gazed back at me, brows drawn but a hint of a smile on his lips. "You think you know so much, don't you?"

I nodded, and his eyes rolled.

"Eighty. I guess that'd make you about eighteen, right?"

"Are you suggesting I'm barely legal?"

His eyes widened. "Dammit, you win," he grumbled.

"It's all I do, baby."

Will recovered fast with a mischievous glare. 'So, how long have octogenarians been a fetish for you?"

"You ass." I chuckled, pleased when he laughed. too.

Before I could tell him how absurdly much I liked making him smile, Will's next words dissolved all my mirth. "I'm not always serious, you know. Just like you're not always temperamental."

I, and all my defenses, leapt up. "This is exactly why I don't like being around you. We're just chatting, and out of nowhere, you insult me. You make me feel so foolish." I bit my lip and wished I'd kept that last part to myself.

Will sat forward, elbows on knees, eyes narrowed. "How did I do that?"

"You just called me an airhead."

"I did not."

"Temperamental. Flighty. Airhead."

"No, Liv. Temperamental. Changing before something gets tough or too real."

My brows knitted together while I considered his interpretation.

"But, like I said, not always."

The sexy rumble in his voice made my heart skip two beats. I cocked my head. "What do you mean?"

His lips parted, then snagged in a half-smile. "Hula-hooping. You learned how to do that, right?"

Hula-hooping was one of the many activities I'd dragged Erin to that day. "Uh, yeah. I mean, I learned when I was a kid. So what?"

"Right. And now you're good at it." Will's voice was low and daring when he continued. "Watching you move today was very, very fun."

Sweet relief and white-hot desire gipped me. I hid my fists inside the sleeves of my button-down to keep from throwing myself at him. "What was fun about that?"

He might as well have been holding candy out to a baby.

Will kicked back the recliner and shut his eyes with a shrug. "Since when do you care?"

"You bastard," I whispered.

"You coward."

"*What*?"

Will didn't flinch at my screech. "Did I say coward? I meant rational, clear-thinking person. You're the one who said it was a mistake. That we should stop. What difference does it make why watching you hula-hoop made me fantasize about how you'd move over my lap?"

The room spun. I took a slow breath before speaking. "I said we should stop. But I didn't say I wanted to, did I?"

That opened his eyes.

Will put his feet back on the floor and crooked his finger. "Then come over here and let me show you just what I thought about. Unless, of course, you're still trying to be good."

I lifted my chin. "Oh, honey, I'll be good. I'll be fucking *great*."

He grinned. "No doubt."

But it was a long walk, those five steps from the couch to the chair. Every second built the anticipation, the desire, and the dark thrill of knowing that this was a point of no return. That Will Langer and I were about to—

I shivered when he rested his hands on my waist and lifted his gaze. One of my knees settled on the chair's arm. Will sat back and stroked my inner thigh. His breath was short and tight, eyes lust-drunk.

"Wait." His hand covered my knee and eased me back to stand so he could tug my shorts to the ground and push my plaid off. Will kissed my leg just below the hem of my tee and exhaled hard. "These legs. Goddamn. Come here, Liv."

He tugged at my t-shirt, but I needed no help to straddle his lap, cup his jaw, and seal our mouths.

Will's fingers clamped on my hips, but his kiss was gentle and restrained. Without words, his lips and tongue soothed the jittery adrenaline in my blood and turned it into a fire instead. Soon I was rocking my hips over the ridge in his jeans, lost in the kiss I craved like an addict by then.

Will pushed my shirt to my chin. I whipped it off as he cupped my breasts, dropped his head, and sank his mouth onto the swell of my cleavage. He pulled my skin between his teeth, then lapped his tongue across both breasts while one hand unclasped and flung the bra away. I didn't even try to keep silent when his lips closed around my nipple. He gave a hard suck and then a sweet tickle while his fingers teased the other one.

He worked slowly, switching between sharp sensations and gentle licks. I watched, fascinated by the reverence he radiated. Dark hair spilling over his forehead, eyes closed, mouth worshipping my body—holy hell, it was beautiful. My skin was splotchy, red and white and even purple in a couple of places. His scratchy stubble gave a delicious contrast to the wet glide of his mouth.

My ache for him grew heavy and hot. I rhythmically rolled my hips against him and clawed at his shoulders, cursing the fact that he was so clothed.

Will grunted an acknowledgement to my ramblings, but he didn't so much as pause. Fingers pulled at me, tongue circled the pink peaks of my nipples, and the edges of my vision began to darken. He blew a gentle stream of air across my hot skin, then kissed me again, thumbed me again, blissed me over and over again. I panted and spread my knees as far as the chair would allow to grind against his cock.

"Oh god, oh, fuck, oh Will, Will, *yes*." I screamed, shocked when an orgasm ripped through me. Will pinched hard, his face buried against my skin. I moaned again before I fell forward against his shoulder.

That was a first.

I sighed and sat up once I'd caught my breath. "Wow."

Will hooked my chin, but his jaw was set hard, expression dark. My smile faltered as I moved to cover myself, but he batted my hands away and stroked my collarbone.

"You're glaring at me," I muttered.

His eyes narrowed further. "I'm so fucking hard, my teeth hurt. That smile you're giving me isn't helping."

I swallowed a laugh and curled my lips into a sweet smile. "Will? I'm thirsty."

His eyes were midnight, voice a matching rumble. "Thirsty? How thirsty?"

"Parched." I trailed my nails down his chest and lowered my lashes. Sitting on his lap in nothing but panties should've felt weird. Sitting on his lap tingling from an orgasm should've felt like lunacy. None of it did.

He growled again. "You should probably take care of that."

"You're right." I hopped off his lap and grinned at his stunned expression. Tossing my button-down on, I spun for the kitchen.

He groaned when I sauntered back in, a glass of ice water at my lips. "Really, Liv? Does that quench your *thirst*?"

"Mm-hm. Want some?"

"Olivia, maybe you didn't pick up on the sarcasm. I give zero fucks about beverages at this moment."

"Come on. You give a fuck. Just one at least."

He groaned again, and I giggled.

"Look at you all frustrated. It *sucks*, doesn't it?" I chomped the ice.

"Don't give me your smart mouth, dammit. Get over here."

Oh, boy, this was more fun than I'd hoped. He stood when I approached, so I wrapped one arm around his neck.

I licked my lips and winked at his scowl. "Aw, come on Will. Admit that you like my smart mouth."

"No."

"Yes, you do. And you're about to like it a lot more. Take off your clothes."

What a show. I stepped back and watched as he reached behind his head to tug off his shirt. Dark hair shadowed his chest and trailed down those sculpted abs. His biceps flexed as he undid his jeans and dropped them to the floor. *God bless burpees.*

My gaze landed on his cock. It was even more beautiful in the light of day. Suddenly, I was very glad I'd gotten that glass of water. With another sip, I pushed him back down to the chair. My heart pumped hard while I kissed the curve of his neck and shoulder, then ducked my head and traveled down. On my knees, I licked him from hipbone to hipbone, tongue following the deep V-cuts on each side. Will cursed when I drew back for my water, but I shushed him and tipped the last ice cubes into my mouth.

"Chewing ice is horrid for your teeth," he whispered.

"Hush and learn." I palmed his hot, smooth skin and spoke around the frozen crystals. My lips closed around the tip and slid to his base quickly for the best effect.

"Oh, fuck. I *love* the ice."

"Mmm-hmm." My mouth was frigid compared to his heat. I began to tease him with my tongue pressed flat to his shaft, delighted when he hissed and groaned.

Playing was fun, but when the hot/cool contrast faded, he wrapped a hand around my ponytail and pulled the elastic out, fingers on my scalp. I took the cue and found a rhythm that made him mutter steadily in broken thoughts and slurred words. His hands in my hair and the thickness of his voice were perfect. Even better was the way his whole body responded to me.

And, wow, he tasted good.

Will's spine arched just before he exploded deep into my throat. "*Liv.*"

I sat back on my heels, and he slumped forward on his elbows to catch his breath. In the silence, I hugged my shirt around my body.

"Do not run away. I just need a minute."

"I don't want to run away," I whispered.

Will lifted his head just enough to meet my eyes. His were lit with a warm fire as he slowly dropped to sit on his knees in front of me. "What *do* you want, Olivia?"

"Did you really watch me today? Did you... think about me?" I pursed my lips and rolled my eyes to let him know that, despite the soft, hopeful, tone of my voice, the question was purely to mess with him.

He didn't buy it, dammit. He inched forward on his knees and kissed my neck. "What do you smell like?'

"Sunflowers."

He inhaled deeply. "Bullshit. Sunflowers don't smell."

He licked me, then laughed when I shivered. "I watched you all day, Liv. And I think about you all the time. You probably don't believe that."

I'd have believed anything with his lips on me.

I wrapped my arms around his neck and shifted to lie back, pulling him over me. "What do you think about?"

"This. More than this. Everything." He snuck into my shirt, his warm touch making me squirm.

"That's what I want. Everything. Fuck foreplay." My words were rough, thick with desire. Will was right with me. He lowered himself down, and I wrapped my legs around his back.

"I *definitely* think about that," he groaned when my ankles locked and my hips lifted.

Will's kisses left me helpless and moaning. We teased against each other, wet and slick with need, but he suddenly pushed away and stood up. "Liv, wait. Condoms. I'll be right back."

"No, don't go," I cried, irrationally panicked. "Don't. You'll think too hard. We'll say…"

"Shh, it'll be less than thirty seconds." He disappeared.

Less than thirty seconds later, he jumped off the last stair, threw himself over me, and kissed me deep. Less than a minute after that, my legs were around his back again.

But time was completely irrelevant when he pressed inside of me.

It was just a tease at first, maddening fractions of inches that made me whine and squirm. Will stared down at me intently, then wet his lips and thrust to the hilt until I groaned.

No. I screamed, dammit.

Everything about Will Langer was a challenge. Taking his cock was no different. He wasn't just blessed. He was perfect. Perfect fit, perfect angle, perfect everything. He knew what I needed, how to keep me on a razor's edge of unreal pleasure, how to make me love and hate that edge all at once.

"Thought you couldn't watch," I stuttered over the rhythm of our bodies.

"I can't watch you come," he huffed without blinking.

"But I'm going to come. Oh, god, Will."

His pelvis ground exactly where I needed it. Will ducked his head and licked my nipples when I clawed desperately at his back, but I knew his gaze was on my face when my eyes fell shut and my back went rigid in ecstasy.

Will waited until I went limp, then took me so hard that I had to grip his shoulders to keep from sliding up the carpet. He kissed my neck and murmured, "The agent of my downfall," in the breath before he pulsed deep and collapsed.

We lay together in silence a long time. I stroked his hair and smiled at the ceiling with a deep, to-the-bones sense of satisfaction. *My nemesis. You brought me down, too.* I wanted to tell him, but the quiet was too big to try to fill with words. Instead, I held him close and hoped he knew.

After forever, he stirred and sat up. "Are you hungry?"

"Starving."

"Do you want to go eat?"

My eyes widened. I caught my lip in my teeth and blinked as I put on my best valley girl voice. "You, like, want to take me *out?* On a *date?*"

"Forget it. Forget I said anything." He stepped into his boxers and collapsed in the chair.

I laughed. "I'll be down in thirty."

15

WILL

Liv. Liv and I. We just—

My phone vibrated and shattered my stupor. Tom's name appeared on the screen, and I went cold all over. He was the last person I wanted to think about in that moment. *I don't believe in fate, but fuck's sake. Is this some kind of penalty fee?*

I took a deep breath and steadied my voice. "What's up?"

"Hey, man, good news. Just got called off my shift for the night! Wondered if you and Liv were up to anything. Thought maybe either or both of y'all might want to hang out with us. Liv probably knows the perfect spot."

"Oh, yeah. Sounds good."

"I tried calling her, but she didn't answer. Can you pass the message?"

"Sure thing."

"Call me back, okay?"

"Got it."

Her footsteps on the stairs made me turn as I disconnected the call. As usual, her beauty stunned me silent. What was unusual was that this time, I didn't try to hide it.

She wore a long summer dress and sandals. Her hair was pulled back in a knot. Her lips were painted dark red, but that didn't matter nearly as much as the shy smile she wore as she gazed back at me.

"You look stunning."

"This old thing?" She tried to toss her hair but seemed to forget it was tied back. A self-deprecating cringe wrinkled her nose and made my heart jump.

"Um, were you on the phone?"

I'd nearly forgotten. My smile grew thin as I nodded. "Tom was called off his shift. Asked if you and/or I wanted to go out with them. He said you'd know a place."

Her expression fell before she could hide it, so I twisted my lips in agreement. Taking her out on a date held a certain reckless thrill, but alas.

"Sounds great. I'll just go change in that case. Tell Tom The Five Spot in forty-five minutes."

As she turned to go back upstairs, I grasped her wrist and spun her straight into my arms. The way she melted into my body made me lightheaded, but I kept it together to say, "What are the odds I can get a raincheck after CrossFit Wednesday?"

"Fair to good," she said. Her kiss said something a lot more certain.

I released her, and she disappeared again. Twenty minutes later, she was back.

"Good lord," was all I could say. Now she wore a short green dress with a black leather jacket and little boots. Her hair was pulled up high and curly—it definitely wasn't curly before. The red lipstick was refreshed.

"Good lord that was fast, or good lord this is a better outfit than the first?"

"Not better, just different. And yes fast. How did you do that?"

She laughed at me and led the way to my car.

I tucked her into the passenger seat, but by the time my door shut she was sitting rigidly, fingers knotted in her lap.

My stomach lurched. All the worries I ever held about such a moment were too close to reality. *Don't regret it Liv. No regrets.* "You okay?"

She blinked and crooked her lips. "Yeah, I'm not about to tuck and roll out, swear. Just... it's a lot."

"I know."

She unknotted her fingers, so I started the car and navigated to East Nashville and the bar. Tom and Erin were waiting for us when we arrived. I killed the engine and put my hand on the door.

"Wait."

I paused. We both stared through the window as she said, "Let's just go have some more fun. I don't regret anything, and I don't want to spend the night all awkward and weird. So, let's not, okay?"

All the air left my lungs. I couldn't try to be subtle. "Agreed on all counts."

That easy. Liv made a potentially painful night of tension disappear with a few words. I didn't have to analyze or theorize on how to act or what she was feeling. God, that woman was magical.

Magical and honest. We staked a table and ordered a round and some food, and it was simply a continuation of the afternoon. Liv chatted with Erin. Tom and I bullshitted and listened to the band. That easy. That *fun*.

When we'd finished our tacos and fries—delicious bar food after a day of drinking—Liv grabbed Erin's hand and escorted her to the dance floor. Tom and I watched, our conversation trailing off as the ladies danced together. Erin had been pink-faced and giggly most of the day, but I didn't expect her to be so comfortable dancing with another woman. She rested her arms on Liv's shoulders and swayed to the music.

"Wow. They're having fun."

I smirked at Tom's attempt at decorum. "You're the only person in this place of any gender who isn't allowed to admit that they're *hot*. I respect and pity you all at once."

He punched my shoulder, and I laughed.

"You are also the lucky bastard who has the right to cut in. Don't forget that."

Tom's eyes gleamed. "Excellent observation, asshole. Excuse me."

My attention lasered in on Liv while Tom wound his way through the crowd. When he got to them, Liv twirled Erin into his arms and stepped back. She swayed to the beat as she cut through the dancers, headed back to the table.

God, how does she move like that? I'd had the thought as she rode my lap earlier, but this was quite different. Olivia Milani moved through a throng of people with such confidence and energy that it was as if everyone stepped aside to make room. I got the sense she didn't realize her own power, and that made me envy and admire her all the more. I had no problem leading a meeting or being in a crowd, but to do it right required analysis and strategy, collection of data points at all times as I tried to gauge the mood. I was good at all those things because I'd trained myself to be. Liv's talents were innate. *Maybe she really is magical.*

Whatever she was, she was headed my way. And, when she caught my gaze, there was no mistaking the way her expression lit up. After so many years of watching her acknowledge me with apathy or irritation, there were no words to describe what that happiness did to me.

She ducked her head as she perched in the chair. *Are you shy around me now, Liv? How interesting.* I understood it, though. Given all that the week had held, if I let myself, I could turn into a stuttering geek in front of her just like our first meeting.

"Why didn't you come dance?"

I cocked my head at the question. "I never dance. While it is rather fun to imagine letting you show me how, I'm not sure that could be easily explained."

She flashed a smile as I emphasized the word fun, but her reply wasn't a tease. "I'd love to show you how."

The idea of dancing with Liv winked through my mind, even though I really didn't know how to dance at all. Blood rushed to my groin. *Now there's a fantasy I'd never envisioned before.* "Oh yeah? And what else would you like, Liv?"

Her wide eyes and short breath told me the answer.

The want in her look shut down a part of my brain. Erin and Tom were deep in the crowd, oblivious to everything but each other. I pushed my chair back and turned to the exit. "Follow me."

She hurried to catch up. I caught her wrist and power-walked us outside and around the corner.

"What are we—"

But her question died as I pinned her against the building and claimed her with a kiss. The bass from inside set the rhythm of my pulse as she hooked her leg around mine and melted into me, groaning when I held her tighter.

I could feel her body against mine, her lips, her hands. I couldn't, however, be sure I was standing on firm ground. Nothing about this moment seemed real. Nothing about it fit into the scope of my life at all.

"I don't dance." I pressed my hips against hers and sucked a kiss on her neck. "I also don't kiss in public, Olivia."

She groaned and laughed all at once. "Then what's this?"

I flexed again when she sucked on my earlobe. "Insanity."

She slid her fingers into my hair and caught my gaze. "Insanity indeed."

When we finally slowed down, I focused on her in the light of the streetlamp.

She flashed a sly smile and touched my lips. "You're pretty good at kissing in public for a novice. Lipstick all over your face gives you some cred, too. That's dirty hot."

I licked my lips, suddenly self-conscious. "It's noticeable?"

"Yup."

"It's hot?"

"Oh yeah."

"I don't think you understand. This is *not* me, Liv."

Her brow furrowed. "What does that mean?"

I caressed her cheek. "I'm not sure. But I'm very interested in finding out."

When I lowered my hand, she caught it and squeezed hard. "I'm interested in that, too."

She barely finished the sentence before I had her in my arms again.

Too soon, she groaned and twisted away. "Mm, come on boy. We've got to get back."

I growled, but I let her pull me back to the entrance.

As soon as we walked inside, I spotted Tom and Erin at the table. Liv's hand disappeared from my grip. She all but shoved me toward the bathroom. "Go wash your face," she instructed, but I needed no coaching.

I wiped the streaks of Liv from my mouth, sorry that I had to. Once I'd straightened my shirt and returned to the table, she was already there with a bourbon in hand.

"There you guys are. What have you been up to, Livi? Your lipstick's all gone."

She scowled at her brother through a sip. "So? I've had dinner and drinks. Gah, Thomas. what are you suggesting?"

He held up both hands and chuckled. "Nothing, sis. Just teasing you is all!"

Stop blushing, Liv. It gives you away. I tried not to smile as she poked her tongue at him. Tom shook his head at me, so I smirked at their exchange and said nothing.

"On that note, I think Erin and I will take off. Will, you don't mind taking Liv home, do you?" Tom looked back and forth between us.

His simple question emphasized the implication of him being gone all night. I shrugged. "Not at all."

"Don't bother. I'll probably hang out and dance awhile more." Liv's disinterest was spot-on.

Tom nodded. "Okay, whatever y'all decide. Have a good one, guys."

Erin kissed Liv's cheek, and they were gone. As soon as we saw the door close behind them, she grabbed my hand. "Come, boy."

My stomach clenched as she led me to the dance floor. "I don't—"

She turned around and put her hands on my arms. "You do right now. Just move with me."

When Liv decided she was going to do something, there was usually no talking her out of it. The band played some lighthearted indie pop song that I vaguely recognized. Its beat was simple enough. I shuffled my feet, mostly shifting my weight from one to the other as she swayed against me.

Although I'd hardly call my moves dancing, Liv beamed at me and put my hands on her waist.

"See? Easy."

Easy was holding her. Easy was the buzz her joy gave me. Being on a dance floor in a crowd of people was worth the cost for all that.

As soon as the song ended, I pulled her closer and murmured into her ear. "Let's go."

We rode home in silence, so of course my brain started to analyze the situation. *The agent of my downfall. Is this a mistake? Should we talk?*

But then her ecstatic scream from this afternoon echoed in my head. No matter where we were going, we were way past pretending this was an accident.

Liv reached over at that moment and squeezed my thigh. "Thanks for having fun with me today."

I swung the car into the drive and turned to her. "Thanks for letting me."

Her throat bobbed with a hard swallow. "My room's a mess."

"Somehow I don't think we're going to make it past the couch." I laughed as we walked toward the front door. Liv tugged my sleeve. When I turned, she threw herself into my arms, soft lips open and demanding.

My prediction was absolutely correct.

16

LIV

In the middle of that long night, I limped upstairs with stiff hips and stubble burn from my cheek to my ribs. Will's smile at my wrecked state was so smug it bordered evil. We kissed once more, and then he was gone.

I tumbled into my sheets and hid under the covers, listening to my breath. My mind opened doors that had been shut for a long, long time.

Will Langer needed a shave the first time I met him. As a 14-year-old, that alone was interesting and novel to me. I'd been giddy to help Tom move into his dorm. All morning, I'd been busy catching eyes with any college guy who looked my way. Tom finally wrapped his arm around my shoulder and said into my ear, "I'm going to pin you down and draw a Sharpie mustache on you if you don't quit."

Not that I was trying to catch a boyfriend. I hadn't even had my first kiss yet. College boys were as much a fantasy as Ashton Kutcher in *Seventeen*. Besides, I was still a gangly high school freshman with braces. Those boys only smiled at me because I geeked at them.

Tom and our parents went to Target for supplies, but I

wasn't in the mood. I promised to make his bed if I stayed behind. Tom glared at me and swore he was locking the door. I stuck my tongue at him, but honestly, I just wanted to read in peace. As soon as his bed was done, I flopped on it, headphones in, and got deep into *Slaughterhouse-Five.*

Between tracks, a subtle cough made me jump.

Will, I would find out, had just come from the bus station. He'd ridden all day and night on a Greyhound from Dallas. All he owned was stuffed into a backpack and duffle bag. Where his parents were, why he had so little possessions, and what that bus ride had been like, he wouldn't say. It didn't matter to my parents, though. Mom and Dad always just folded people into our family. Whoever Tom or I brought home and introduced as a friend were promptly fed and nurtured. They took him to buy supplies, then dragged him along to family dinner.

All I could do was stare.

He was so dark and quiet. His arms were so cut in his t-shirt that he looked like Popeye. More than that, he radiated this heavy energy, this seriousness. He was so much more of a man than any boy I'd ever known.

I wouldn't call my fascination with him a crush not then and not later. I had boys I crushed on, and I learned to touch myself to the idea of Romeo Montague from the 1996 film. Thoughts of Will Langer were forbidden, even alone in the dark.

Once, just once, I let myself think of him like *that.* My stomach dipped like the drop of a roller coaster, like Mom had just walked in, and I shuddered and buried my face in the pillow until my lungs burned. He was, quite simply, too much.

But, like Mom had said the other day, I did look forward to his and Tom's visits. Even though there was nothing special between us. Back then, he'd speak to me or let me tease him if I was in a particularly goofy mood. Tom was always the buffer that made it okay. He kept it from being awkward.

It wasn't until after high school, after that night when we talked until dawn, that he started looking at me with that blank expression and total indifference. Before that night, he'd put up with me pretty good-naturedly. On that night, we talked like two people who cared about each other's lives. But then, poof. I became nothing to him. Useless. Worthy only of a blunt remark or a teasing line at best. For eight years, that had been our MO.

And suddenly we were all over each other. *What the fuck?*

I threw back the covers and got out of bed.

Tossing my silk robe on, I padded across the hall, slipped into Maddie's room, and yanked his sheets away.

"What?" Will startled, jolted awake.

"You *hate* me, Langer." I knew it was too late, too long a day, too much booze and music and sex to think sanely about this. I couldn't stop myself. "Screw you, your superior attitude, and your *foreplay* game. You. Hate. Me. I hate you. We hate each other."

"Keep going," he rumbled.

Hands on hips, I stamped my foot. "Is my point not clear? I don't keep company with people who don't like me."

"You just let me use your body for two straight hours. We both seemed to like it a lot."

"Shut up. Exactly. What the *hell*, Will?"

His hand closed around my wrist and pulled. I tumbled down onto his chest with a yelp. Will flipped me to my side, his breath mingled with my own as he stroked my cheek. "Say it again."

"What?" My voice had gone from razor to butter knife.

"That we hate each other." His tongue skimmed my lips.

I buried my face in his neck and shook my head. "Don't we?"

I expected derision or a taunting reply. But Will stroked my hair and nuzzled me right back. "No, Olivia. We don't."

"But... but there's always been this wall between us." I lifted my head to try and see him in the dark.

Will's shoulders stiffened. "Uh-huh."

"What changed?"

I heard his smile. "I guess we found a door."

"Oh."

He petted my hair gently until I snuggled into his chest again. Falling asleep in his arms was the last thing I was going to let happen, even if my eyes got heavy while I pictured a door in a wall.

Will gently released me. "Go to bed."

I groaned and kicked my foot into the mattress. "Kiss my ass."

He palmed my backside and slapped hard. I emitted a weird hybrid of a laugh and a moan as I flexed my hips into his thigh.

"If you bend over, Liv, I will do anything you like to your ass," he breathed in my ear.

His offer had me aching despite our long night. There was no question of how he felt with those boxer shorts as the only barrier between us. With one breathless kiss, I managed to get out of bed before clothes came off.

"Maybe next time," were my parting words.

That bastard laughed at me all over again as I shut the door.

～

Will excused himself from Sunday dinner the next day. That let me spend the afternoon with my family without any weird tension. He made himself scarce when we got home that evening, too, and for that, I almost texted him a thank-you.

Work on Monday was the usual routine. For the first time, I felt like I'd outgrown such a mindless gig. Not only did I itch for something more meaningful, the ability to space out and daydream suddenly became too much time to ponder all these weird changes.

I replayed the weekend as I made the rounds delivering the first mail of the day. How had Will gone from being a non-factor in my world to taking center stage in every hot fantasy my brain could dream up? Why had that "door in the wall" materialized out of nowhere in this upside-down summer? For that matter, when would the spin cycle settle down? Nick and I weren't speaking. The daycare thing was its own bag of uncertainty. And now Will was in the mix. When would life go back to normal?

And how would I feel when it did?

I didn't want to look at those last two questions. Didn't want to admit to myself that I knew exactly how I'd feel. Instead of brooding, I put my mind on my teacher training for the rest of the day. At home, I set up Maddie's gated play space so she could toddle relatively unmonitored while I caught up on coursework.

Will came home to find me on the couch—the couch we'd severely abused just two days ago—with my laptop between my legs. I glanced up, but then refocused on my quiz. He knelt by Maddie and spoke to her. Neither of them registered very deeply because I had two questions left and I was pretty sure...

"A-plus! Woo! I am a legend." I flung my arms in the air when my results posted.

They both stared at me, so I slapped the laptop shut and rolled my eyes. "Sorry, guys."

Will lifted Maddie over the plastic gate. "Maddie, your Aunt Livi did a good job. Can you give her a high-five?"

She ran to me. I slapped both her little palms and hugged her tight before she went back to her play yard.

Will stood and shrugged out of his suit coat. He jerked his head toward the kitchen. I went to Maddie and pointed to where he had disappeared. "Livi and Will are right there, okay Mads? What do you do if you need me?"

"Just shout." She didn't even look up from her dolls as she parroted the instruction I'd taught her.

I kissed her head and went to find Will leaning on the counter, arms crossed, grin wide.

"You decided to be a teacher."

I hovered by the table and shook my head. "No, I'm just, um, doing a little... well, I'm getting certified, but that doesn't mean..." I bit my lip. "Maybe."

"Fantastic, Olivia. Really."

The admiration in his voice made me swell with pride. I drifted from the table to stand in front of him. "I got a perfect score on my quiz just now."

God, he really is beautiful when he smiles like that. Will uncrossed his arms and held up both palms, just as Maddie had done. I laughed and slapped his hands, but he splayed his fingers and caught mine. In a breath's time, he spun me around, the counter against my back.

"You deserve a gold star," he whispered.

"I'd take a kiss."

"I was hoping you'd say that."

Our lips met with a crack of energy. He slid one hand to

the back of my neck. With my shoulders supported, he encouraged me to lean until my spine arched and my head touched the counter. I pulled his shirt out of his slacks to skim his abs. He licked and nipped my exposed throat and then opened my buttons, baring more of me for his mouth.

"Your breath all ragged like that. Those little gasps that tell me what this does to you... Do you have any idea how hot you make me? How your sounds stay in my ears after we're done?"

"Oh, god, I know," I panted when he sucked hard. I reached for his shoulders and lifted up to press my mouth and body against him in one wild motion.

"Shh, wait." Abruptly, Will stepped back and cocked his ear toward the window.

At the same time, the baby monitor came to life with Maddie's excited shout. "Daddy's home!"

Will took another step away and raked his hair. "Go upstairs and fix yourself. I've got Maddie."

He'd already shoved his shirt into his pants and straightened his collar. I ran for the stairs and took them two at a time to the bathroom. Hair brushed, clothes righted, I floated downstairs, trying hard to replicate what Liv looked like when she wasn't giddy with pheromones.

The guys were in the kitchen. I must've looked fairly normal because Tom greeted me with a grin. *He has no idea. What would he say if he knew?* I glanced at Will, but he only met my gaze briefly.

Tom pulled me away from my thoughts. "Hey, sis. Glad you're here so I can remind you both that Friday night is Mom's birthday thing."

I nodded and settled in a chair. "I remember. She wants to go to some Asian fusion place across town. I made a reservation."

"Awesome, thanks."

Tom and I chatted about what to get Mom for her birthday. Will sat quietly across from me until Tom turned to ask about his day.

While the guys talked, I debated with myself. *Maybe we should tell Tom... Tell him what, exactly? He'd probably like knowing... What? That you're fucking his best friend? It's more than that... You think so, huh? How many times have you told yourself that, only to be on your own a few days later?*

"You okay, Livi?"

I blinked at Tom's question.

"That was a big sigh," he said, brows drawn.

I twisted my lips into a smile and shoved all those too-deep thoughts into a corner. *Just go with it. Let it be whatever it is. Don't make drama.*

"Great as always, Tommy."

17

LIV

"Don't hate me, okay?"

I looked up with one leg in my workout pants.

Megan tied her ponytail and wrinkled her nose. "I'm ditching you tonight. Adam switched schedules last minute. He called and asked if I wanted to go out."

"You're dumping me for sexy waiter boy?" I laid a hand on my heart, secretly relieved since I was about to blow her off for Will.

"Yeah, well, hate to break it to you, but you're lacking a little in the penis department. I feel extra bad since you clearly dressed up for me." She nodded to the outfit in my locker.

"Just trying to keep you interested," I said as we strolled to the gym.

"You don't really mind, do you?"

"Not at all. Actually, I—"

Megan sucked in a breath as our gazes landed halfway across the room. "Christ, Liv."

"What?"

"You know exactly what. That man has stripped you and

laid you out on this mat with his eyes. Damn, girl. I thought that wasn't a thing, hmm?"

My face warmed as I tore my attention from Will and looked over at Megan. "Well," I muttered, which was all it took to get her grinning like the Cheshire cat.

"What did I say? Megan Riley knows all, sees all. Her powers of insight astound. Cheers, love. You've made mama proud."

"Shut up. Let's go work out." I gave her a shove, and we headed to the group.

Five rounds of running, kettlebell swings, and pull-ups equaled shredded Liv. I dropped out of my last pull-up and tumbled to the mat, clapping clumsily when the rest of the class finished at their stations. Will dropped beside me and draped his arms on bent knees, winded from the last sprint. The sound of his breath was unnervingly hot. Before my fantasies could get too carried away, Megan stood over me, hands on hips.

"Come on, chick. It's time for a nice, cold shower."

"I'll meet you out front," Will said, helping me to my feet.

"What was that?" Megs hissed when we were out of hearing range. I nearly toppled over when she shoved me into the locker room.

"Um, he's taking me to dinner."

Her eyes went wide. "You're dating?"

I shook my head and stepped into the shower. "No, it's just whatever. You know."

With my eyes closed under the spray, I wondered if even I believed that.

We chatted about the workout while we primped. She dressed in a crimson sundress that went perfectly with her loose, dark blonde hair and showed just the right amount of skin to be fiery hot. I suddenly wished I'd brought a dress. Packing one in my gym bag had felt silly. Like I was trying too hard. I snapped an elastic around my hair and looked at my denim skirt and high-collared black tank with a frown.

Megs bumped my hip with hers. "You're perfect. Go get him, tiger."

Even with the distracting little smile that ghosted Will's lips when I appeared, I noticed the thorough assessment Megan gave him. Clearly, my best friend was reevaluating her initial impression. Part of me wanted to drag her to the side and tell her to stop. Promise her it wasn't like that. The other part of me knew she wouldn't buy it.

Mercifully, Megan didn't break stride on her way out the door. Will and I faced each other. That awkward, we-don't-do-this vibe sparked again. "I thought we could go to Sambuca. Sound good?" he asked.

"I've never been there, but sure. I'll follow you."

We drove a short distance to the Gulch and found side-street parking just off the main road. While I checked my lipstick, Will got out of his car and opened my door for me.

"Are we on a date, William?" The question was saucy but not sarcastic. I stepped out and cocked my head.

"Maybe."

The fact that we'd already slept together didn't stop the warm thrill that tickled through me. Still, I kept up the tease. "Keep your friends close and your nemesis closer, right?"

His eyes sparked as he pinned me against the car. "Like that, maybe?"

"Maybe."

But Will stepped back without a kiss. "Take my hand since we're on a date."

I slipped my fingers between his, and we strolled down the sidewalk. "Sambuca is swanky, isn't it?"

Will chuckled. "It's a good date spot. I'll say that."

"Your go-to for a first date, huh?"

"I go pretty regularly for client meetings. Sometimes just to sit and have a drink." He nodded across the street as we slowed in front of the restaurant. "That's home."

I turned to gaze at a massive building made of brick and glass. It sprawled out on both sides with a tower of units climbing into the sky in the center. My eyes bugged out. "Holy shit, you live there?"

He chuckled. "Usually."

It had never occurred to me to wonder where Will lived. But as I let him turn me away from that impressive building and into the dark, elegant lounge of Sambuca, my clothes suddenly felt shabby. I glanced over at his charcoal trousers and white linen button-down, cuffed at the sleeves and open at the neck. Trendy-as-hell shoes completed the stylish but casual look and made him hotter than ever. I dropped his hand and crossed my arms over my chest.

Will paused at the hostess stand. "What's wrong?"

"I didn't know it was going to be this fancy. I should've dressed up better."

He rolled his dark eyes and bent to put his lips to my ear. "What did I tell you? You don't need anything to enhance how beautiful you are. You could be in those jean shorts from Saturday. You'd still be the only woman I wanted to walk in here with. Now, stop being self-conscious. It's not a good look for you, Milani."

My face heated. So did all my sexy parts. *Don't get too giddy, girl. Be cool. Go with it.* "Damn, Langer. Watch it with those smooth lines."

Will pressed a kiss on my ear and reclaimed my hand.

He gave his name to the hostess, who smiled and asked that we wait a moment. I was reaching for a menu to peruse when—

"Liv?"

Will startled as adrenaline clenched my gut. I turned to find Ben Addison grinning at me.

"Well, hey, Ben. What are you doing here? Where's Celeste?"

"At work. I'm meeting James for a drink up on the roof to discuss the app."

"Are y'all still talking about that?" I had to laugh.

He did, too. "Yeah, yeah, I know. It's years in the making, but I think we're finally getting something going. Who knows what will happen?"

"Hopefully all good things."

"Thanks." Ben flashed a curious smile as he glanced at my hand laced with Will's.

We are so not ready for this on a first date.

"Oh, uh, I finished a workout and... dinner. Um, meet Will. Will, this is my friend, Ben."

"Sorry to interrupt." Ben used that tone guys have when they're deciding whether they're going to be dicks to each other and haven't quite made up their mind. His gray eyes remained steady, assessing and a little protective, like he always was with me.

"No problem." Will's voice was smooth but not warm.

God, I so have a type. Both men were both so self-possessed that it seemed like nothing could shake their poker faces.

Ben's eyes narrowed. "Do we know each other?"

"Couldn't say," Will replied at the moment I realized they might've met when Ben and I dated. I bit my tongue hard to fight the panic at this weird situation.

Ben considered a moment longer, then shrugged. "Maybe we met through work. Anyway, nice to meet you. Liv, great to see you. Sorry to interrupt."

"You're never a bother. Tell James hello. I'll see you both soon."

I hugged him. He nodded to Will and headed to the stairs just as the hostess appeared to guide us to a table.

Will slid into the cozy booth opposite me. His guarded look was in place. "I remember him. Not from work."

"He was my boyfriend almost two years ago. We're still friends."

The server approached for a drink order, so he shook his head and said, "Do you have a favorite wine?"

"Not especially. Something refreshing would be nice." *That sounds like I know what I'm talking about, right?*

"A bottle of Sancerre, please. And we'll start with the beignets."

As soon as the water was poured, he lasered in on me again. "Do you really think you can be friends with someone you used to sleep with?"

"Jealous?" I lifted a brow and toed his foot.

Will glared, although he returned the footsie gently. "Answer the question."

Well, well. He is jealous. I wanted to gloat, but I didn't push. "Possible and done. Ben's a good guy."

"Hmph."

The beignets arrived with a bottle of the most crisp, delicious white wine I'd ever

tasted. I stabbed one of the fritters and dipped it in the glaze. *A girl could get used to this.*

Will wasn't done with the conversation, though. "Why did you break up if he's such a swell guy?"

"We just fizzled out."

I paused mid-chew, thinking. That had always been my answer about Ben, but suddenly I could see the truth.

"I wasn't right for him. I'd just given up on college and didn't know what I wanted to do. He was already into his career. We were good together, but I think in the end we were just at really different places in our lives." I winced and looked warily at Will.

"That's an impressively honest assessment. Did you love him?"

I bit my lip and shrugged.

"Do you miss him?"

"I mean, he was probably the most real relationship I've had. Sometimes I miss that, but I have no regrets. He's engaged, and we really are friends. So, no, I don't miss him. Especially not with you and I—I mean, especially not since you've been annoying me so much lately."

Warmth blossomed in my chest. The line of concentration between his brows lifted into a sardonic smile.

"Is that what the kids are calling it these days?" he murmured, and I had to laugh at the use of my own phrase. He smiled back at me and reached for a beignet.

We chatted about music and CrossFit as we took our time with the appetizer, then ordered entrees. When we were done, Will poured the last of the wine into our glasses, and we sat back in the plush booth, perfectly sated.

"This is some, date, Langer. Delicious food, stimulating conversation, you all jealous over my ex—"

"Ridiculous. I wasn't jealous."

I took a quick breath but kept my smile. "Sure, whatever you need to tell yourself. But maybe it's time for you to give me a straight answer to a question I've asked about a hundred times. What are we *doing*, Will? Running into Ben was awkward, and we had a close call on Monday. I don't want to end up in some kind of rom-com situation where I'm hiding you in my closet or trunk or some bullshit like that."

I wanted my tone to be light, almost silly. As usual, it didn't work. He set his glass down and put elbows on the table. "What kind of answer are you looking for, Liv?"

"A straight one, Mr. Cryptic. Every time I ask, you redirect or just say we've lost our minds. I'm inclined to agree. Even so, it'd be nice to know the parameters of our psychosis."

His brows lifted. "Do you want to make this an official relationship?"

"No. God, no." I balled my hands into fists.

"It sounds like you might."

"Well, that sounds silly."

"Do you want me to commit to you?"

God, yes. I looked away. "Shut up. I just wondered."

Will paused so we could both take a breath. "What did you wonder?"

"Um. What is this for you?"

He motioned for the waiter and took his time with the wine before speaking again. "It's *good*, Liv. This is fun. You like to give me hell about being too serious. Maybe I am. When I'm with you, fun is a lot easier. Is that an acceptable, unofficial, response?"

The bill arrived. Will flipped open his wallet and dropped his card on the tray, all casual and easy. I forgot to offer to pay half because my gut clenched like I'd been punched. I grew very still, breath shallow, insides cold.

Fun. Easy. Story of my fucking life.

"Liv?" Will reached across the table for my hand.

"Don't touch me," I hissed, surprising myself with my intensity.

He recoiled, eyes wide.

I stood up and shoved my hands through my hair. "Uh, I'm so glad that I've been a good time for you. But screw that, Will. No."

"What's wrong?"

"I'm going home." I bolted for the door.

The heat of the evening engulfed me. I ran up the sidewalk and had just reached my car when he caught up. Will laid his hand on my shoulder. "Olivia—"

"I said not to touch me."

He dropped his hand, both palms up.

I took a shaky breath. "I'm not your fun, William. Find that somewhere else. I won't be that for you. I can't. I've been somebody's good time too much. You and I have too much history, too many complicated connections. Beyond that, you know what? For me, this was more, *official* or not. So, yeah. I'd rather leave it at that, thanks."

"Liv, wait a second. I know your default is to take everything I say as an insult, but good god. Having fun with you is incredible. It wasn't meant as a brush-off."

"Whatever. Let's just forget it."

Will's shoulders squared. "No fucking way. Just tell me what you want."

I reached back and opened the door, but Will's hand shot out and slammed it shut with such force that the car rocked. Being stuck between my car and his imposing figure had me mad as hell. I wanted to escape, to walk away, to forget this nonsense and say merci beaucoup to the universe for making me That Girl yet again.

"Let me go. It's easier this way," I said between clenched teeth.

"Not a chance. Talk to me."

"I told you. I don't want to be your fun." My gaze dropped to the pavement. Just saying it tightened my chest.

Will stepped back. His jaw tensed in a frown. "I got that part. So, what do you want?"

Wait, what? "Um, what do I want?"

"Yes, Olivia. What do you want us to be?"

"I... don't know," I admitted finally.

What did I want? I'd barely processed that he was refusing to let this—us—go. Most guys would've bolted, either from my anger or a conversation like this or both. Most guys would've been relieved to let me storm away, *maybe* would've texted me later to follow up. But no amount of venom seemed to faze Will Langer. Now, he was asking me to verbalize an ocean of confusing ideas standing here on a sidewalk. Hell no, I didn't know.

Will bent his head with a long sigh when I didn't say more. "You obviously want to define us, but you won't say it. Then you say you don't want just a good time, but when I ask you what you want, you don't know? Get real, Liv. Know what you need. You'll never be taken seriously if you don't."

I scowled. "And here we have it, the arrogant douchebag I know you to be. Expecting an answer after you just put me on the spot." I wished my voice was harder and stronger, but he was too good at summing up all my weaknesses.

Will sneered when I called him a douchebag. My icy glare seemed to have zero effect as usual. "You can call me names if it helps you protect yourself, but you know I'm right. A woman should know what she wants, on the spot or not."

"A little time to think would be appreciated," I muttered.

He softened a bit at that. "Fair enough. Let's do this, then. My car needs a tune-up. I'll drop it off Friday morning.

You can pick me up from work for your mom's birthday. We'll talk at my office. That gives you two days to think."

"Okay, but... what if you say no? To, um, what I want?"

Restraint radiated from his posture. "Then we'll figure something out. But until then, don't flirt with me. Don't look at me sideways. Don't touch me. Don't do anything to make me think about stripping you naked and hearing you say my name. Understand?"

"Fine. Same goes for you."

"Fine. Until Friday."

I stood there for a long time. The longer I stood, the more I wanted to escape my rapidly morphing reality, so I texted some people and went out. An hour later, my collection of friends had swelled, and we danced ourselves sweaty to 80s tunes at a bar downtown.

This Liv—whiskey-drinking, singing, dancing, and saying whatever came to mind—this I knew how to do. Careers and CrossFit and complicated men be damned. I could always be That Girl.

It was pretty cool, I guess.

But I did give my notice at work the next day.

18

LIV

Me: I need a friend. Want to be one? Drinks after work?

Meg: Ugh, I guess. But just this once, because secretly I don't like you.

Me: xoxo

"How was your date?" I slid into the booth across from Megan the next evening, glad she was available.

"Great. He took me to a comedy show. We had a lot of fun."

Fun. I flinched at the word. "And after?"

Megan took a slow sip of her martini. "I didn't sleep with him."

"I didn't mean that you did."

A pleased grin flickered on her. "He did kiss me, though."

"You look a little smitten."

She shrugged. Megan wasn't one to get hung up over a boy. "Let's just say I've got a feeling this could take me places."

"Awesome, Megs. Cheers!" I held up the vodka cranberry

that the server had just set beside me, and we clinked glasses.

"So, what's up? And how was *your* date?" She checked her phone. "I can't stay long. Promised my aunt I'd come to dinner tonight."

"I'll keep it brief." I took another sip of my cocktail and told the story. It was the super condensed version, but I took her from the way we'd started to last night's debacle, ending with, "Help me. He wants to know what I want. He says I need to tell him what I want us to be."

"Neck-sucking, dinner dates, and that hot body aren't enough, huh?"

"It's plenty. And it is fun, even though it's intense and a little aggressive and a lot overwhelming."

She wiggled her brows at *aggressive,* but I ignored it.

"I just can't be fun again right now. Especially not with him."

My best friend knew what I meant without any elaboration. "Then you shouldn't have lied about needing to define it. You want a commitment. What's wrong with that?"

I toyed with my glass. "What if he says no?"

"Dude, you have a funny type. That guy is a handful with the dark stares and the arrogance and everything. But the way he looks at you? More than that, the fact that he's waiting to hear from you? I mean, come on. You don't do that with someone who's a random good time. One thing though. You'd better be able to say out loud exactly what you need. From everything you've told me, he's no bullshit."

"That *is* what I need. Someone who doesn't bullshit—or let me, either."

"Ooh, I like that. Go with that." She nodded enthusiastically and drained her drink. "Sorry, but I have to split. Let me know how it goes. Oh, and one more thing. Never forget: if he says no, then you're still you're badass, beautiful self. Nothing changes that."

She blew me a kiss and slid out.

I sat back in the booth and toyed with my phone while I finished the drink. Instagram said Jesse Storms had just wrapped his album, but I didn't give much of a damn about that. I'd only started following him on impulse after that party so long ago. More important was the email I'd gotten this morning from Mrs. Harris, the owner of the daycare.

My brain was full on the way home. The feeling had become too familiar these days.

Tom and Will were eating dinner when I got in, so I grabbed a bowlful of pasta salad and sat down, smiling at my brother.

"Good news, sis. I've got a long weekend off next week. Want to come to Gatlinburg with us? Mom and Dad want to get a cabin. We can get a place with a pool, which Mads will love." He made a face at her, and she clapped.

Normally I'd be in for a trip to the tourist town in the Smoky Mountains, but, "Um, sounds great, but I don't think I can." I cleared my throat. "Actually, I have some news. I put in my notice at work today and, uh, emailed the director of Maddie's daycare. I've been working to get certified as a teacher, and the exam is next Thursday. Mrs. Harris said she'd hire me as soon as I can start."

"Really?"

Tom and I both looked at Will when he spoke. He busied himself with his dinner.

My throat tightened, weirdly defensive and nervous. "Yes, really. Have something to say about it?"

"About time you made the decision."

Tom groaned. "Sheesh, I thought you guys had been getting along okay. Did something happen?"

I coughed into my water. "Not at all."

"Sorry, man," Will said with a sigh. "I'm just tired. Long day. Apologies, Olivia. I meant to say congratulations, of course."

I didn't want to flip him off and roll my eyes, but I knew Tom was waiting for it. "Right, I'm sure that's exactly what you meant. Thanks ever so, dear William."

My voice was heavy with sarcasm, but there was no way I could meet his gaze. There was also nothing sarcastic about it. His support meant more than I cared to admit.

"You two are adorable. It's like having teenagers. Maddie, please never get older," Tom said, wiping her little mouth with a napkin. "Anyway, that's awesome, Livi. I'm so proud of you."

He grinned and reached for a high-five. I found a smile and slapped his palm, but I couldn't help but think of Will's high-five just days ago.

Tom cleared the dishes. "At least you'll have the house to yourself for a few days while we're gone. Will's apartment is ready this weekend."

"Good," I muttered, still unable to look at the man across the table. "When are you leaving?"

"Sunday according to the Gregorian calendar. I believe on your personal one, the exact time is 'not soon enough.'"

Tom groaned again, but his back was to us, his attention to the sink.

I glared at Will and bit hard on my twitching lips. "Clever."

Shit. That mischief was in his gaze. He glared right back.

"I hate you," I mouthed.

"No, you don't," he mimed.

Tom returned to the table, and we both snapped our gaze elsewhere. "*I want you, Will Langer. I want you to want me.*" *I'll say it, and he'll say yes...*

Right?

19

WILL

I'm so fucking proud of you for having the balls to do this. That was what my comment was meant to tell her.

For the first time, I think she got the message.

But there was a guarded tension to her shoulders that had been there ever since our date had gone horribly wrong. And there was a loop in my brain that wouldn't quit trying to figure out how in the ever-loving hell telling Liv that she made me happy had resulted in such a meltdown.

Why couldn't she just say what she wanted? What scared her about tossing that hair and stating the truth of the matter? Did she think that somehow that would result in her being hurt? What could she ask for that would be so ludicrous as to have someone reject it?

What are you scared of, Liv?

Twenty-four more hours of analysis until I could find out.

20

LIV

Dinner reservations were at seven. My story was that I had to have my fingerprints done for the daycare. I would go downtown in the afternoon to do it, thereby making it impossible for me to look after Maddie. Tom had back-to-back overnight shifts. Mom was happy to pick Mads up from daycare so Tom could sleep as late as possible, especially since she'd stay with them that night. It was a perfect setup, with plenty of time in the afternoon for me to get ready.

I'd actually gotten my fingerprints done on lunch Thursday. So by 4 pm, I was showered and standing in my closet, searching for the perfect outfit. Tonight's look had to kick a lot of ass. I had to walk into a fancy office, face Will, and be a charming daughter all at once. Yikes.

A journey to the depths of my wardrobe found just what I needed: black straight-leg capris and a royal blue wrap top that showed some cleavage but stayed firmly within the bounds of classy. I curled my hair into sexy waves. Bronze eye shadow and black mascara offset "Pink Pearl Pop" for my makeup. Nerves made me move fast, and in no time, I stepped into black heeled sandals and went to the mirror. The look was uncharacteristically elegant, but it worked. I glanced at the clock. I'd be a little early, but you can't be too careful with Nashville traffic on a Friday afternoon.

I parked in a garage under Will's office building and rode up twenty floors with my fingers in knots.

The receptionist looked up when I crossed the lobby to her desk. "Good afternoon, Miss. How may I help you?"

I almost turned to see who she was speaking to. People never addressed me so officially. *The outfit must've worked.* "Uh, hi. I have an appointment?"

"With whom?"

"William Langer?" *Why did his name come out as a question? Why do I sound like I learned to talk five minutes ago?*

"Your name?"

"Olivia Milani."

She glanced at her computer. "Yes, I see you're scheduled at five. He's on a call right now. Have a seat. I'm sure he'll wrap up soon. Can I get you anything while you wait?"

I declined and perched on a black leather chair by the wall. Afternoon sunlight poured in behind me. The whole lobby gleamed white and chrome. People buzzed back and forth down hallways behind the receptionist while I sat, watching the activity and trying not to look as wound-up as I felt.

The sound of his voice brought me to my feet before I even saw him. Will appeared from the hall on the left, in conversation with three other men.

"Will?" The receptionist called. "Olivia Milani is here."

His attention shifted from his companions to the receptionist, and then to me. Luckily, my legs knew to take a step forward. My brain sure as hell didn't do anything useful once I caught sight of the charcoal gray suit he wore. The lavender shirt and gray tie underneath made him hotter than ever.

He swept his gaze over me, mouth closed, jaw clenched. I felt the other men's eyes too but paid them no mind.

"I didn't know you were here already. Sorry to keep you waiting." His pitch was slightly different than I was accustomed to, but his business voice worked on my body as well as his usual growl.

I think I nodded. I might've just stared.

He turned to the others. "I'm going to miss the meeting since my five o'clock is here. Give me the minutes on Monday, okay?"

"You got it, Langer," one of the men said, his eyes still on me. Will nodded, and they continued on.

He stared at me a moment longer and cleared his throat. "Come with me. Ellen, I'll be in my office. No more calls today. Put it all to voicemail, please. I'm off soon."

The receptionist smiled, and he took my elbow and guided us back down the hall from which he'd appeared. Inside his corner office, my heels sank into the carpet while my gaze went to the view of the city. A huge mahogany desk faced me. A brown leather couch sat in the corner beside a door which, I had to assume, was his private bathroom.

"Not too shabby," I said when I'd gotten my jaw off the floor.

"Make yourself comfortable." Will shut the door and flipped the lock. He gestured, so I checked out his diplomas and the framed ads on the walls. I wandered to the window to look down at the river before scanning the desk. Precisely piled stacks of papers, a computer, and office supplies were the only decorations. Not a single photo or trinket in sight. *Typical Will.*

I looked up when he crossed the room to a cupboard by the couch and poured two bourbons. "Drink?"

"Yes, please."

"Have a seat." He handed me a glass and went to lean back in the executive chair on the opposite side of the desk.

I arched a brow, glanced down my nose at the functional chairs beside me, and strolled around to where he sat. "Love to, thanks."

Perched on the edge of his desk, legs crossed—then re-crossed, just to emphasize my complete comfort—I flashed a saccharine smile.

"Your ass is sitting on a three-thousand-dollar desk."

"It seems sturdy enough."

He sighed and stood to bring one of the chairs around to face his own. "Will that do?"

I took my time sliding off and settling into the seat. My palms were damp with nervousness, but messing with him was irresistible. Will leaned forward in his chair and set his glass on the mat on the desk, clearly ready to get down to business.

I took a sip of whiskey and tried to remember all the things I'd planned to say. "How should we do this?"

"Simple. We should talk honestly. Do you want me to start?" I nodded, so he said, "Well, then, the purpose of this meeting is to establish—"

I snorted into my glass. "Ugh, so formal. This isn't really a business meeting."

He threw both hands up. "Fine, then, why don't *you* start? Say what you came to say."

"I lied when I said I didn't want to define us."

His nod screamed *duh*.

"Okay. Okay. So." The bourbon burned my throat while I tried to unknot my tongue.

"Liv. Why are you so tense?" he asked gently.

I stared at him. "Hello? Because I'm here with you, telling *you* that I want us to *be official.* Us. Liv and Will. Two people who have spent their adulthoods rolling their eyes at each other. Now, I suddenly want—"

I stopped and stared at my lap. My volume cut in half as I said, "I'm nervous over all that. And I'm afraid you'll think this is silly."

My chair glided forward abruptly. Will pulled until our knees touched. "I *know*, Liv. I know it's crazy how we went from, well, us to this. Believe me, it's blown my mind since the first moment. But you know I don't think this is silly, or else you wouldn't be here. Just tell me what you need."

That simple statement hit a bullseye in my chest. When I chewed on my lip, his eyes darkened, so I leaned forward.

Will sat back with a shake of his head. "Talk first. Then I'll think about letting you kiss me again."

"Oh, please. You've thought about it the whole time."

He smiled. "I've thought about it since the last time I kissed you, actually. But I can hold out a little longer."

"So disciplined." I sighed, then gathered my thoughts. "Here we go. Yes, I'd like to define us. To start, I need you to be honest with me."

Our knees still touched, but Will slumped back in his chair in a perfectly casual pose. He rested his temple on his fist and nodded. "About what?"

"No, I mean... A lot seems to be changing in my life. I need someone to be honest with me about that. I, ha, like how you don't let me bullshit. And I like how you push me to know what I want. So, more of that honesty."

Will's lips curved into a small smile. "We can't happen any other way."

I nodded with another deep breath. "I figured, but I

wanted it said. Next thing. You don't have to make a lot of promises, but please don't vanish, okay? I don't want to text you one day and find you're not answering."

"I have meetings."

"No, I mean at all."

Will's brow creased, but he didn't speak.

"Tell me when it's over," I clarified.

He still didn't speak, so I rolled the glass between my palms and barreled on. "Last thing is that I'd like to know you weren't sleeping with anyone else."

Dark eyes went wide. "I am absolutely *not*."

Just say it all. "But if you do meet someone you'd rather be with, please don't disappear. Tell me first, although I guess that takes us back to item two. So, uh, I think that's it."

"All I've heard is that you'd like me to not be a complete asshole to you. How is that a request?"

I bit my cheek so hard I winced. "Like I tried to say the other day, we're complicated to begin with. I don't want to be your good time, Will. I'm aware that I'm nothing like other women you know. That doesn't mean it's okay for me to just be amusement until someone better comes along."

"Is that what you think this is for me? Just amusement until someone *better*?" Will looked out the window, then back at me. From his expression, I knew for sure that it never had been.

"That's what I'm not okay with it being for either of us. I need to trust that this is more because it sure feels like more. I don't want to be a fool this time around."

I looked at the remaining liquid in my glass and willed away a sting of tears. "I'd rather it be nothing than to have it... be nothing."

Will tapped his fingers on the arm of the chair. "You're still unhappy."

I drained the drink. "Kind of feel like I just bared some dark stuff, Langer. Not an easy thing to do when your nemesis is the definition of self-confident."

His short laugh made me jump. "Self-confident? Good god, Milani, how do you not see it?"

My brows tightened. "See what?"

Will just shook his head. "You want to trust me. I'd do anything to make that happen, but I'm not sure what it is."

"You've always been honest. Even when you're a total dick." We traded a smirk. "I do trust you, Will."

He drained his glass and slammed it on the desk, then held out his palm and guided me to my feet. "Liv, everything you want is a given."

"It's not a given for me, Will," I whispered. "Not at all."

Will shrugged out of his jacket and draped it on the chair behind him. I stepped closer, my hands on the cool material of his dress shirt, and looked up at him. Even in heels, he had a few inches on me.

He stroked my cheek. "You are so much more than idle amusement or a good time. I'm insulted that you'd suggest that was ever the case. I won't let you down. I swear I won't vanish or dick around. In turn, I really do want to have fun with you. All I ask is that you don't run from this. Have a little patience. Trust that we're worth the effort. Deal, Milani?" He quirked the corner of his mouth up.

My face split into a goofy grin. He'd made this so easy. I'd cycled through so many "relationships" that told me not to invest too deeply. Simply by being himself, Will Langer had upped my bar. I could've collapsed with relief. I laughed instead. "Deal. Yeah, deal, Langer."

This is happening. Will and me. This is a thing. Holy shit.

I wound my arms around his neck. "You just committed to me. Can you believe that?"

He backed me against the desk. "Liv, I committed to you when four little words came out of your gorgeous mouth."

"'Drugs are bad, m'kay?'"

He laughed. "Try, 'Kiss me, Will Langer.'"

Will groaned when our lips met, a desperate *mmmph* punctuated by his tightening embrace. It was the sexiest sound I've ever heard. There was no filter or editing. He needed this. He needed *us*.

Thank god it wasn't just me.

Liquid heat tingled through me as my pulse surged. I fell back on his desk and pulled him over me, our kisses so hard and deep that I forgot to breathe.

"Wait, Liv," he gasped, scraping his teeth along my chin. "We have to leave. You can't kiss me like this now—"

"I'll kiss you like I damn well please. And I do not care if we're late. See? I'm telling you what I want, just like you said I should. Proud of me?"

He chuckled between kisses. "Very proud. And in a lot of trouble for it."

I wouldn't have been opposed to letting him have me on the desk, but we managed to disentangle ourselves with clothes still intact. Will collapsed in his chair, his lips wet in the evening sunlight.

"Restroom's there." He gestured to the door but blinked twice as I sat up. "God, so electric."

He was right. I redid my hair and makeup, but the flush on my cheeks enhanced the whole effect. When I emerged, Will had donned his jacket again and leaned on the desk, waiting for me. We eyed each other across the room.

"The things I would do to you if we didn't have to go."

I walked to him and pulled on his collar for a quick kiss. "Raincheck."

21

LIV

Will called goodnight to various faces on the way to the lobby, but I buzzed with so much energy that I barely noticed. We packed into an elevator down to the garage. His fingers splayed across my waist to pull me against him.

This is happening.

I aimed the fob at my little red Chevy Bolt and glanced over. "It's no Audi."

After an hour in his office, the difference in our financial stations was again apparent. But Will just snorted and buckled up.

This is happening.

"This is happening." The words came out with a giddy laugh.

"What is?"

"You and me. It's a thing."

He reached for my hand and ran his thumb over my knuckles. "Yes. It's a thing. Now drive. We're going to be terribly late if you don't."

"Gah, so bossy." I pulled my hand back to put the car in

reverse. On the short drive to the restaurant, I ventured to ask, "Doesn't that weird you out?"

Will's fingers tapped on his knees. "Weird me out? No."

"Really? You and Olivia Milani are a *thing*. Not weird?"

He inhaled deeply but didn't speak. I wanted to look at him, but traffic was so heavy I had to concentrate on the road. I parked at the restaurant and turned to him with a frown. "You're a man of few words sometimes."

He smiled again. "Olivia Milani and I are a thing."

"Weird, right? At least a little."

He leaned for a gentle kiss. "Weird isn't the word I'd use. Stop worrying. We'll talk more later. I promise."

We walked across the parking lot, but Will slowed at the doors. "Let's not go in together. You go ahead. Say I had to make a call."

With a nod and a deep breath, Family Liv pulled open the door.

"Happy birthday, Mommy!" I wore a huge grin when I found everyone at a table with a round of drinks. Mom squeezed me when I wrapped her in a hug and kissed her cheek.

"Sorry I'm late. Traffic was bad. Hi, Dad." I pecked his cheek, too.

"Did you forget Will?" Mom asked while I sat down beside Tom.

I laughed. "I was tempted, but I knew better than to keep him from your birthday. He had to make a call."

"You look lovely, little one. Simply radiant." Mom gave me an appraising eye.

I tucked my hair behind my ear and simpered a thanks. My phone buzzed, so I snuck a glance.

WL: Watching you smile like that turns me on so fucking bad.

"Happy birthday, Claire." The voice narrating the text in my head was suddenly in my ears. Will bent to kiss my mother, and I shoved my phone deep into my purse.

Not weird? Really?

Once spring rolls were on the table, Tom tapped his knife against his glass. His toast was so heartfelt and grateful that Mom dabbed her eyes with a napkin when he was done.

After we'd sipped, Tom grinned over at me. "While I'm at it, I want to toast Liv, too. She's going to be a teacher at Maddie's daycare. Sis, I am so proud of you for taking this chance at a new career."

Career really threw me, but the smiles on both my parents' faces eased my nerves fast. A tear spilled down Mom's cheek this time. Overwhelmed, I joined the toast and ducked my head.

The family let me hide for a minute, but before long Dad cleared his throat. "What kind of training does the job require? Are you CPR certified?"

Dad, the resident expert on everything, led a gentle interrogation throughout the meal. I hadn't been the object of so much praise since I won first place in a science fair in 5th grade. The more they asked, the warmer I got until I was pretty sure the restaurant could've been powered on the energy I radiated.

After dinner, the wait staff sang and brought cake for Mom, and we commenced with gifts and dessert. When the table was cleared and coffee and scotch were all that remained, Mom sighed and smiled at everyone. "What a fantastic birthday. I'm so happy you all could be here tonight. And yes, Will, that includes you."

"I wouldn't have missed it," he replied.

"That reminds me. My coworker Gail's daughter is back

from Rome. You met her at our Christmas party last year. Remember she was getting her doctorate?"

Will shrugged, and I focused on stirring my coffee.

"Anyway, Gail mentioned she'd returned. I wondered if you'd like me to give her your number? She's a lovely girl."

One drop of coffee splashed out of my cup. The light brown pinprick seeped out steadily on the white tablecloth. I watched it, jaw locked, breath shallow.

"Oh, thanks, but no."

The spoon stopped. My gaze stayed on the stain.

"Are you sure? She's pretty. Blonde, blue eyes, smart as a whip."

"Liv, pass the milk, please." I jumped when Tom spoke in my ear. He took the little pitcher and said, "Why not, man? Go for it."

Will cleared his throat. I didn't look, but I imagined he swirled his scotch around the glass in this unbearable moment. "She sounds lovely, Claire. But I'm seeing someone."

The spoon clattered out of my hand and onto the table, adding another blemish to the linen. "Sorry," I muttered to no one, because that's exactly who was paying attention.

"Oh?" Mom and Dad asked in unison.

Tom's attention snapped to his friend. "Really? You haven't mentioned Stacy in weeks."

"It's not Stacy."

There was no air in my lungs while the table waited on Will to elaborate, but the silence stretched.

Tom tried again. "Who, then? And since when? I don't remember the last time you were officially seeing anyone."

Will's glass thumped on the table. "I'd rather not discuss it. Sorry to disappoint everybody. It's complicated, and I don't want to say much while things are new. Again, thank you for offering, Claire."

"Of course," Mom agreed. "Your business is your business. Offer retracted. I don't like the word complicated, but I hope this girl makes you happy."

"Very."

Oh, my heart.

"She must for you to commit to her." Tom's muttered words slammed my heart against my ribcage again.

"Let's go out sometime then, yeah?" he said to Will.

"What are you guys doing up in the mountains next weekend?" My voice didn't sound like my own as I steered the conversation in a new direction.

In less than half an hour, dinner was over. A sleepy Maddie cried when Tom hugged her goodnight and strapped her into Mom's car. Will stared at his phone beside me while the parents drove away, but energy still snapped between us.

Tom checked the time. "It's already ten. I might as well take off for the hospital and try to catch a nap before my shift."

"Can you drop me at the office on your way?"

Will's question shattered my anticipation. Both Tom and I looked at him in surprise.

"I got a message during dinner. Some contracts were delivered by the courier that have to be reviewed, signed, and in the mail tomorrow morning. Since my car is in the shop, I guess I'll sleep there tonight if you can drop me off."

"It's Friday night." The words came out before I could stop them. I bit my lip, but Tom's agreeing nod let me exhale.

"It's business. I'm sure you'll be devastated to have the house to yourself, won't you Olivia?"

Tom chuckled at his wry tone, but I had to hold back a blush. "Whatever will I do without you? Kick back in the recliner and watch whatever I want on TV? Poor me."

"Sounds rough, sis. Try not to suffer too much." Tom hugged me quickly and went to his car. "Come on, buddy, I'll drop you, no problem."

Will gave me a half-second glance before he followed, but it said enough.

I cranked Arianna Grande's "Into You" all the way home. Windows down, I sang at the top of my lungs as the day sank in a little more.

He turned down a girl with a freaking Ph.D. He told my family he was "very happy" with the girl he was seeing. Seeing, as in dating. As in a relationship.

And he'd meant *me*.

My smile died when I parked at the dark house. This was our day. We were *official*. And what did I have to show for it? A bones deep longing that wouldn't be sated anytime soon.

I flopped on the couch and caught the last half hour of *Casablanca* on TCM, comforted by a relationship more complex than my own. When the fog rolled over the screen, I shut off the TV and went upstairs, picked up a magazine, and perched on the vanity bench to flip through the pages.

By the time I got to makeup tips, I tossed the mag to the floor in a huff, ready for a good pout. *Look at this outfit. Does it deserve to be tossed in the hamper rather than stripped to the floor?*

... You could just go to his office. Maybe finish what we started on the desk earlier?

I chewed on my lip. There were several logistical hurdles to my fantasy of striding into his office unannounced, but who cared? I reached for my keys.

Just then, a car door thumped closed outside. Seconds later, a soft knock tapped at my door. I jolted and tumbled off the bench.

"Come in," I called from the floor.

My pulse rioted when he leaned in my doorway, arms crossed. His brows arched to see me on my ass, peeking over the bench, but I tossed my hair like this was completely normal.

"What are you doing here?"

Will shoved a hand through his hair. "I've been called in late before and always just slept at the office. It was easier."

I got up slowly and straddled the bench. "Uh-huh."

He stood over me. His eyes were hooded as he traced one finger down my cleavage. "There is nothing easy about staying away from you, Olivia."

Will grasped my hand to bring me to my feet. He pulled the tie on my wrap shirt and slid his palm over my bra. "You're blushing," he teased.

"You can be very sweet." I reached for his buttons.

Will grunted. "I'm not sweet. I'm honest."

I pushed his dress shirt off, shook my head, and stepped closer. "No, super sweet. A total sweetie. Made of pure sugar."

With a palm on his cheek to angle him down to me, I sank my teeth into his neck so hard he groaned. "My fucking sweetheart," I murmured, then bit him again.

"Oh, you bastard," I gasped when he fisted my hair. My head bent back when he pulled hard, but pleasure hardened my nipples through the burn.

Will kissed my chin and stripped the shirt off my shoulders. "Not nearly as sweet as you."

My back hit the mattress. Will crawled over me as he unbuckled his trousers, but I was the one who shoved them down his hips. He stripped me too, and teasing gave way to kisses fast.

The wet sounds of our mouths filled the silence and drove us higher. Will's kisses were rough and sweet all at once. One hand drifted to my inner thigh to stroke between my legs.

"I love how your breath stops when I—uh-huh, like that," he breathed when he buried two fingers inside me. "And I *love* how you clench around me."

I clamped on my bottom lip and threw my head back against the bed. He pulsed harder as his thumb teased my clit. Every sound tickled my ears, every detail sexy in its own way: the mattress creaking under us, the rustle of his sleeve as he moved his hand, my broken breath, his short, shallow breath.

"Will... Will, I..."

"You're there. Let go."

I tightened around his fingers as the first fissures of pleasure bubbled up. Just as I blinked to look at him, my orgasm hit hard. I thrashed, eyes falling shut again, and he pulsed steadily until I went limp.

"Oh, god, Liv," he muttered under the sound of foil tearing.

"Fuck, Will." There were no words for the pleasure he gave me. All I knew, all I wanted to know, were our bodies and this bed.

I was still dopey when he put me on my back, closed my hands around the bars of my headboard, and thrust inside of me. My senses returned. First, the scent of his skin and our sex hit my nose. Then the sight of his dark head bent to watch our bodies. My knees pinned his hips. I wrapped my ankles around his back to angle him deeper.

Will clearly didn't see that coming. It sent him over the

edge fast. He pitched forward with a shout, hips flexing into me as his whole body shuddered.

Afterward, I lay with my head on his chest, drowsy beyond belief but reluctant to sleep.

"Say something sweet." I yawned.

"Olivia Milani and I are a thing," he whispered. "And that is *incredible*."

I hid my cheesy grin in his shoulder.

"Your turn. Be sweet."

"When you hold me, my heart bursts," I blurted.

He tensed.

I hid again. "Shit, that was corny."

Will cupped my chin, forcing me up. His voice was ragged, cheeks flushed a deep pink, eyes searching. "Olivia, when I hold you, I forget that there's anything else. Liv, I'm," he broke off, lips bitten into a line. "I'm crazy about you."

All the air left my lungs as I melted into the mattress

"Talk about corny," he muttered when I didn't reply.

I could feel his heart pounding as I lay on his chest. I lifted my head and traced his forehead. If he noticed the tremor in my touch, he didn't let it show. "That is so sweet, Will."

His playful glare had me swallowing a laugh. "Watch it," he growled, and I couldn't hold the giggle anymore. He smiled back as he touched my cheek.

I pressed a kiss on his temple and made myself tell him the truth. "I'm crazy about you, too, Langer."

The words were barely out before he turned for another long, *sweet* kiss.

When he pulled back and yawned, I snuggled him again as he murmured, "I'm going to hold you for a while longer, okay?"

"Very okay," I said, my blood singing with what I could only call total happiness.

22

WILL

I made myself disentangle from her arms once she was sound asleep. For a man who considered himself willing to meet any challenge, that simple action damn near broke me.

The next morning, I sequestered in my room to pack. My ears were tuned to hear when Liv's door opened, and she ambled downstairs. Only after her car started out front did I venture out for coffee.

After a quick breakfast, I hit the road on my bike. It was a later start than I liked for summertime, but I needed to think. I made myself go over the workweek before letting thoughts turn to Liv. By then I was sweaty. My muscles burned with a satisfying level of fatigued. The exercise gave me clarity.

We're a thing. No mistakes. No fluke. No late-night haze of hormones and alcohol like so long ago. This is right.

I squeezed the brakes and planted my feet on the ground before I pitched over the handlebars. According to my watch, my pulse had surged. It had nothing to do with cycling.

We were than mind-blowing hate sex. Liv and I were a *thing*.

"Holy shit." I laughed to use her phrase as I pedaled on.

I got back to the house, showered, and resumed packing with a sense of peace altogether new to me. When Tom woke, we opened some beers and sat on the back porch with Maddie. Liv shouted hello when she returned, but she didn't join us.

For a moment, I considered saying something to Tom. No big announcement. Just something like I was thinking of asking Liv to grab a drink after CrossFit. Before I could open my mouth, a memory shut me up.

Friends for life, but don't go near his sister. My background and subsequent emotional junk are too intense for her.

Besides, I don't think Tom even knows about CrossFit.

I kept my damn mouth shut.

We'd just gone in for dinner when she appeared in jeans and a sexy top, full makeup on. "I'm going out. Jack and some of the band wanted to check out a new venue, so I said it sounded like fun."

The look she cut me was loaded with a message that I had no idea how to interpret.

"Cool, have fun," Tom said with a wave.

"How can you keep up with all her friends' names?" I asked once she'd gone.

He laughed. "That's impossible."

"So, you have no idea what any of that meant?" I wanted to shout my real question at him. *Who the fuck is Jack??*

Another laugh. "Inference tells me she's talking about Jack Spencer and his band, Cellar Door. She got me into their music when they put out an album last year."

"Another pop star? Jesus."

He shook his head. "Nah, this is one of her close friends. I'll share the album with you. You'd like it."

"Yeah, would you?" It couldn't hurt to know what kind of music Liv loved best.

You were telling me it wasn't a date.

The thought came to me out of nowhere, and another piece of "Liv and me" slotted into place. Yet again that dizzy urge to grin like a fool gripped me, but I drowned it in iced tea and put my focus on asking Maddie about *My Little Ponies* instead.

By Sunday afternoon, all of my belongings had been moved back into my condo. I strolled around, inspecting the new appliances and freshly painted walls, and then went out to watch the sunset on the terrace.

"Fuck," I sighed. Being home wasn't supposed to put me in a sulk.

My phone chimed, and my pulse kicked up at the message on the screen.

Liv: What r u doing?

Me: Settling in. You?

Liv: Watching Yellow Submarine w/ Tom & Mads

I toyed with a few replies: "come over," "I wish I was with you," and "how was last night?" None of them worked, so I went with logistics.

Me: Come to Xfit tomorrow.

She didn't reply. I could picture her brow furrowed, trying to be subtle as she stared at her phone. *What did you expect? Dick pics?* I laughed and typed again.

Me: Call me when you're in bed.

Tom must've found some extended version of that film.

It seemed like forever before my ringtone pulled me away from organizing my closet.

"Are you in bed?" No sense in starting with small talk.

"Uh-huh," she breathed. "Are you?"

I threw myself on the mattress and opened my jeans. "Yes. Get your headphones."

"Already done."

I hummed, blood pounding. "Then take off all your clothes, use both hands, and tell me about it."

Liv improved at CrossFit every time. I loved the intensity and variation of the workouts. It didn't surprise me that she was hooked, too. I'd started to notice more muscle definition in her thighs and arms as she hammered through the WODs. Her endurance had improved, too. She'd never admit it, but I was right to push her to sign up.

That said, I think both of us expended a lot of energy staying focused during Monday's class. Liv took every opportunity available to tease me with a covert touch, and I'll admit I returned the favor energetically. By the time the final whistle blew, she and I were staring fire at each other, twin sly grins on our faces.

"Meet me out front," I said before we parted at the locker rooms.

I showered quickly and was waiting at the front when she emerged. Her sweet dress and sandals said she was expecting this to be a date.

I winced.

"Wow. That's the face every girl wants to see." She toyed with the strap of her gym bag.

I lifted it from her hands and splayed one palm on her

back to pull her near. "That's the face of a man who wants what he sees very, very much, and knows he can't have it."

I breathed a laugh, realizing I needed to amend that a bit. "Well, that's one version of that face."

She glanced up as I guided her outside. "What's the other version?"

The one I've given you for eight years. The only way I knew how to keep the wall between us. Except now there's a door, and I don't have to anymore.

I looked away and forced muscle memory to wipe away my smile. When I met her eyes again, my expression was fixed in the flat stare that I'd used on her forever.

My face relaxed, but Liv stumbled over her feet, one hand on her mouth.

"Bullshit. Bull*shit*, Will Langer. That look does *not* mean you want me."

I set our bags beside my car and backed her against it. My lips skimmed her jaw. "You think? Then you've got so much to learn about me."

She trembled when I grazed her mouth, and I forgot that we were in a parking lot. My arms went around her. Her tongue found mine until I pulled back with a groan.

"I don't—"

"Kiss in public. Yeah, yeah." She tugged my hair to summon me for another kiss. "But maybe *you've* got a little to learn about you, too."

Maybe so. "Dear god, then teach me, Olivia."

Her passion morphed into a joyful smile as my request sank in. She hugged me tight. "Yeah, Will, I'll happily teach you. But why not right now? I thought you wanted to see me."

I sighed and took half a step back, my arms still firmly around her. "I have a ten pm flight to Chicago. I'm headed straight to the airport from here, and I won't be home until Friday. I wanted you to know."

She'd asked for me not to vanish. As if I ever could. I would never ghost someone. There was nothing, *nothing*, that would make me disappear on Olivia Milani.

"Oh. Thank you for telling me. So, I guess I'll hear from you sometime?"

Is it too soon? What's the risk here? Ah, fuck it. I scratched the back of my head. "About that."

Her eyes widened, the color draining from her cheeks. "About that?"

My brows went up as I tried to pull her closer. Liv resisted, her shoulders tense.

"You look terrified. What's wrong?"

She closed her eyes. Her jaw flexed. "Just finish your thought."

Do you think that "about that" means I'm about to dump you in this parking lot? What kind of assholes have you been dating?

I waited until she looked at me again. Fear still shimmered in her gaze, but I nodded. "What if you stayed with me next weekend while Tom's gone? Come to my place Friday night. We could have the whole weekend together."

That fear drained away, replaced by the sweetest look of hopeful surprise I'd ever seen. God, for someone so strong and bold, Liv's soft side melted me.

A shiver ran through her body, but her tone was deliberately cool. "I could be into that."

"Into that? You *could* be? Is that the best answer I can get?"

She bit her lip. "Guess that depends on how many times you intend to make me scream, now doesn't it?"

She tried to run for her car, but before she took a step, I

had her in my arms. She groaned every damn time I held her tight like this, and I couldn't fucking get enough.

"Six pm Friday. Do *not* be late," I said with one more quick kiss.

"Not a chance," she promised.

Sweet mercy, what a long week. We didn't talk much, but I did get a text on Wednesday saying her raw score on the exam essentially guaranteed she'd passed. I sent her a screen full of confetti and the silliest celebration gif I could find. She replied with laughing emojis and told me she would be starting full-time at the daycare on Monday, training to take over a class in September.

Then she said she'd missed me at CrossFit. Reading that message gave me that weird dizziness all over again. Liv missed me. How the hell I'd stumbled into this new reality, I could hardly say. For once, it was a question I chose not to over-analyze.

I texted her Friday morning with my address. No sentiment beyond that. I wanted to save everything for when I saw her that night. A thumbs-up bubble appeared, and I went back to packing.

The midday flight was on time, but before we landed, I got an email summoning me to the office to sign off on some final copy. *Please, please don't rope me into the damn Friday wrap-up.*

No such luck. The meeting was on my schedule, even after a week out of town. My phone vibrated while they droned on.

Liv: I'm here.

I stepped out of the conference room and phoned her.

"I'm running late. Go inside, give your name to Gerry at the desk, and he'll unlock for you."

"You're late? How late?"

"I'll be there soon. I swear." I hung up and went back to my seat. Just as I sat, my phone buzzed again.

Liv: I'm not going into that building w/o you. Will be at Sambuca's bar. xoxo

23

LIV

I gazed at the dregs of a whiskey sour, my phone stubbornly dark beside me. The bartender set down another cocktail.

"Here you go," he said with a wink. "It's paid for."

I smiled and looked around, but still no—

"It's my lucky night. Good to see you, Liv."

The unfamiliar voice behind me made me turn. "Oh. Hi, uh, Cam?"

"At least I'm a little more memorable this time. Cheers." He held up his beer.

"Cheers. Thank you." I nudged the glass to his, realizing the drink was from him.

"My pleasure." He took the seat beside me and propped his temple on his fist.

My gaze fixed on his arm while he eyed me up and down. His sleeve hung loosely around the pale skin on his barely-there bicep. It was a douchey thing to think, but I couldn't stop comparing how slim he was to how strong Will was, how tight he could hold me, how no shirt ever dangled from *his* arms.

Cam caught me staring and smirked. "How are you, Liv? You look fantastic, but that's nothing new."

"I'm fine." I crooked a little smile, then glanced at my phone. *Ugh, dude, catch a hint. I'm busy. Thanks for the drink. Now, bye-bye.*

"How are your students? You're back in school, right? A new year?"

"Oh. Yeah. New year this week. They're good. You know, first day jitters and... stuff." No point explaining that I was a daycare teacher to someone I barely knew. *Kind of weird he even remembered that.* I took one more sip and put the glass down. A buzz was the last thing I needed.

"You're good, yeah?" I asked since he was still posted up on that stool.

His hazel eyes lit up. "I was better once I walked in and saw those pink curls of yours."

He smiled, but I looked away, no worthwhile response in mind. When an uncomfortable minute had passed, Cam cleared his throat and tried again. "You're much quieter than my first impression of you. I thought you were more outgoing by the way we, well, first got to know each other."

I winced. Yes, I kind of made out with him the night we'd met, but that was *so* six weeks ago. "Sorry to disappoint."

It's not my fault your kiss left zero impression.

"Oh, it doesn't disappoint. You're cute when you're shy."

Cam's fingers trailed down my arm, and my muscles tensed. He leaned closer and reached to touch my hair. "How about we go get a booth?"

I jerked away and glared at the cherry in my glass with a brisk headshake. Why couldn't I look at him? Why did he creep me out?

Cam laid that wandering hand on my arm, and again I

recoiled. The memory of the last time I'd seen him flared up, when he'd grabbed me as I left the concert. It was an answer to my unspoken questions.

"Aw, come on. You don't have to be *that* shy. We got along so well at that party. Let me buy us another round and get to know each other a little more. It's not a school night."

"No. Thank. You. I'm not shy. I'm waiting for someone."

His fingers grazed me again, this time with a little more pressure. "Cancel."

"She told you no, asshole."

That Girl can handle her own blow-offs, but I literally sagged with relief at Will's voice behind me.

Cam's face darkened. "Not your problem, *asshole*. Mind your business."

Will wrapped one arm around me, and I leaned into his chest. "Even if Olivia wasn't my girlfriend, I'd make it my business. A lady tells you no, the answer is no. Get it?"

I turned my gaze to steel and fixed it on Cam. "Like I said." I shook my head with slow deliberation.

Cam's face was a storm cloud, but I stepped off the stool and turned a tight smile up to Will. He took my bag and my hand, and we hit the door. We held each other tight, our strides long across the street and into his building. I didn't even goggle at the sleek lobby, just power-walked with him to the elevator and watched him violently stab the 15th floor button.

"Who the hell was that?" he grumbled on the ride up.

"Never met him before."

Will snorted. "Bullshit. Can I look forward to creeps hitting on you whenever you're out in public?"

He led me down a hall to a door and stopped with a frown.

I shrugged. "Does it matter? My big, strong *boyfriend* will scare them all away, right?"

Will pressed his lips in a line. "I knew I'd catch hell for that," he muttered. He squinted at me. "Go on, let me have it."

My fingers danced up his shirt. In my valley girl voice, I said, "What do you mean? Just because you, like, have a massive crush on me and you totally called me your GF, like *out loud*."

Will closed his eyes and leaned his head against the door, a little smile on his lips while I continued to tease.

"'S okay, Will. I know you draw my name with hearts around it during meetings." I bopped his nose.

"Are you done?"

"Yeah," I said in my regular voice, and he opened his eyes.

"I was glad you told him off. And if you want to call me your girlfriend, well," I bit my lip, but heat flooded my face until I broke into a huge grin. "I'm definitely into it."

"It's good to see that smile again," he murmured, mostly to himself, but it made me cheese harder.

Will's smile deepened too while he cleared his throat. "Thank you for your generous permission. Perhaps you'd acquiesce to coming inside as well?"

I waved a magnanimous hand, and he unlocked the door.

"*Damn*," I gasped at my first glimpse of his apartment.

The kitchen and living room were one space, decorated tastefully in light gray and navy, with gorgeous tiled floors— masculine but elegant. A sectional couch sat against a wall with a huge TV mounted opposite. Straight ahead of me was a terrace with a sweeping view of downtown, city lights winking on in the evening dusk.

Will hung back while I took a tour. I peeked into the bathroom to find brand-new, super sleek plumbing. The bath was a stone shower with track lighting on dimmers.

Mood lighting for your shower? Damn, this place is a Pinterest board in real life.

"You are a rich—"

The words died on my lips when I glimpsed a bottle of champagne and vase of roses on the kitchen island. I must've missed them in my first view of the room. My eyes widened as I looked to Will and laid a hand on my heart. "Por moi?"

"Oui. They were supposed to be a toast for passing your exam, but I figured they'd double as an apology for running late."

"Wow. That's a serious boyfriend move." I peered at the petals, mumbling under my breath.

"What?"

I shook my head at his question and sniffed the flowers.

"No, what did you say?" he insisted, leaning beside me.

I groaned. "If you must know, no one but my parents bought me flowers before. And no one *ever* bought me a bottle of champagne. So shut up, you romantic geek."

I didn't expect him to frown. "Too corny? I know it's a cliché. Figured I had a fifty-fifty chance that you'd tell me flowers were lame 'AF,' but I didn't have time to be more original."

Will glanced at my wide eyes, and his expression lifted. "Oh, you meant you like them."

"I meant I love them."

God, he made my heart do weird things. How could it race, ache, and melt all at once? Couldn't it just pick one for a second?

His cheeks flushed, but he didn't reach for me. "Excellent. Should I open the bottle?"

"Uh, maybe I should wait for dinner. I already had a cocktail."

We ordered from a Greek place nearby. While Will placed the order, it occurred to me that he'd not really been home in a month. When he set his phone down, I cut him off before he could speak again. "Stop taking care of me. You just got home. You must be tired."

Will leaned against the granite counter. He loosened his tie, unbuttoned his sleeves, and cuffed them to his elbows. "First off, it's no trouble. I like taking care of you. But, yeah, pretty tired. I had to go to the office once I'd landed. Thought it was a quick check-in but got caught up in a meeting. Jesus, this expansion is a pain in the ass. I mean, it's like if something can go wrong—Oh, sorry. You don't care about all that." He chuckled at himself.

I made a face. "How insulting. Of course I care. I just want to talk out there." I pointed to the terrace, and so, with bourbon for him and water for me, we went outside.

"Now, tell me everything," I said while I looked out at the city.

He told me a little about work, then asked about my week. I kept it brief and focused mostly on the huge triumph of crushing that exam. He lifted his glass for me, obviously proud, but it struck me how cautiously he navigated conversations like this. He seemed so unpracticed at it.

I had to ask. "Why is it awkward to talk about work and stuff? Is it because it's me?"

Will shook his head quickly. "No. I'm not used to this kind of conversation with anybody. Who would I tell my day to? I don't even have a cat."

I pictured his tidy, undecorated desk. Not even a single photograph. "Are you lonely?"

He had to think about that. "I don't think so. But I am alone."

"That doesn't bother you? I couldn't imagine."

"I know you couldn't. Your life is full of people. I tell Tom how lucky you guys are with the family you have. I'm lucky to have them, too, but my life is... very different."

Now I pictured Will the first time we met. "Why? When I met you, you were alone. Where is your family, Will?'

His gaze had softened and unfocused. "You remember when we met?"

"Duh. I was in your dorm room."

The look in his eyes trickled to his smile. "Uh-huh. I remember, too."

"How I—"

"Yep," Will said just before he hauled me to him for a kiss.

He was gentle at first, but when his thumb stroked my cheek, he exhaled, hard, and then the tidal wave was back on. We very likely would've given the Gulch a hell of a show if his phone and doorbell hadn't rung all at once.

"Dammit, so many interruptions," he groaned as he broke away and went inside.

I drifted to the kitchen. Will unpacked the takeout bag, but I stopped him with my hand on his arm. His bicep jumped under my touch as I took the cartons from his grasp and wrapped my arms around his waist.

"I don't want you to be lonely."

He hugged me back. "I appreciate that, but I'm not. I swear."

"I don't want you to be alone, either."

Oh, when he smiles like that...

His palm coasted from my shoulder down to the curve of my ass to pull me closer. Will ducked to find my lips. "I'm definitely not alone right now. But I'm touched that you're concerned."

I shivered. "I've missed you this week, Will."

Our lips found each other again and again, each time with a little more urgency until finally, he broke away. "You should eat."

I started to protest, but he pinned me with a wicked look.

"You'll need your energy to withstand everything I plan to do to you. Once we start, we won't stop."

"Well, *that* was the sexiest brush-off I've ever gotten. Fine. Hurry up and feed me then. Gah, you buy me some roses and you think you can call all the shots, huh?"

"I'd never think that. I swear." He laid a solemn hand on his heart, but we were both smiling as we took the food to the table.

He didn't pop the champagne. He opened it carefully under a towel. Barely a hiss escaped when the cork twisted free. That, he explained while he poured, was how to preserve the bubbles. Given the way they exploded on my tongue when I sipped, I was all for preservation over presentation.

When I was stuffed, Will topped off my glass and collected the food. He returned from the fridge and gazed down at me intently. "So," he murmured.

I stood up, my breath surprisingly shallow given that this was hardly our first time. Will held my waist, and I lay back on the table, ankles hooked around his back. His elbows landed by my ears.

"Liv," he breathed. "Oh, baby. You are *all mine* this week-end. Okay?"

I slid my fingers into his hair. "Only if you're mine, too."

It was a night of crisp, cool sheets and hot kisses. Of cold champagne in our mouths and silky roses and wet lips on our skin. It was a night of *I missed you,* and *don't stop,* and *yes, like that,* and *again.* And, from that first kiss on the balcony on, it was electrifying and mind-blowing.

It was *us*.

24

LIV

Sunlight. A shower running. Black sheets that must be a billion-thread count. I blinked, briefly disoriented the next morning. My nose tickled with that lavender-and-pepper scent, and I grinned and snuggled deeper into the covers.

God, my hips were *stiff.*

I stumbled out of bed and dressed in a sports bra and yoga pants, stood firmly on the plush area rug that covered most of the room, and did a couple of sun salutations. The bedroom door clicked open, but Will didn't disturb me.

Ten minutes of stretches had me alert and rejuvenated, but my muscles tensed again when the doorbell chimed just as I finished. Breath held, I strained to hear Will open the door, his deep voice unintelligible from in here. Strange shuffling sounds and a couple soft thumps later, the apartment was silent again. I tiptoed to the door and peeked out.

"No one's here," Will called.

I couldn't see him from my vantage point, so I stepped into the living room. Oh, boy, could I *see* him then. He strolled toward me in nothing but sweatpants, damp hair curled against his temples, every muscle from his abs to *those arms, dear god* on display.

"Good morning," he said when all I could do was ogle him and try to keep the drool in my mouth.

I dragged my gaze up his body, nice and slow, and finally met his eyes. "Hey."

Will cocked his brow and walked his stare over me in return. He slid his hand across my bare waist to pull me close. "Yoga?"

No one had ever made that word sound so sexy. I nodded, on too much sensory overload to talk. He looked like a damn underwear model, he felt warm and powerful as always, and he smelled like a shower.

Will stirred in his pants. "You keep looking at me like that, and I'm going to take you right back to bed."

"I see no problem there."

He grinned. "The milk might. Groceries just got delivered."

I followed his gaze to the boxes on the floor. "Damn milk. Always cock blocking me."

We laughed. With a kiss, he released me and went to open the boxes.

"Can I have a shower?"

He cocked his head. "What kind of question is that? Your towel is the white one on the bar. Use whatever you need."

"Including your toothbrush?"

The line appeared between his brows. "Uh, I guess. If you need to."

I laughed, and he relaxed. "You don't mind my mouth all over your body, but sharing a toothbrush is no bueno?"

He shrugged. "Call it a quirk. But really, whatever you need is yours."

"I like that attitude, Langer." I spun around and hurried to the bathroom to indulge in mood lighting and a spa of a shower.

Clean and dressed in shorts and a tank top, I emerged to find him out on the terrace. He was slouched in a patio chair by a glass-top table, ankle on his knee while he read on his phone. Two coffee mugs, a carafe, and breakfast sat ready. My stomach nearly lurched out of my throat at the tempting spread, so I hurried over to take the empty seat.

"Hungry?"

"Starved."

He smirked. "I'd expect so after last night."

Croissants, fruit, jam, and cheese decorated the table. I took in the spread with wide eyes, but then wrinkled my nose. "Cheese for breakfast?"

"So little faith, Liv. Have I led you astray yet?"

I poked the tip of my tongue out in reply.

He poured from the carafe into my mug. The coffee was so strong and dark that it barely resembled my morning brew. I picked a croissant, but while I reached for the milk, Will swiped the plate away from me.

I whined but hushed fast when he smeared the soft cheese and some strawberry jam on top, then handed it back.

"Aw, such a sweetheart."

"I hope you choke on it."

I laughed and almost did choke on the coffee in the process. "Damn you, Langer. Don't make me spill a drop of this magic. This is my new definition of coffee. God, why is it so much better than usual?"

"French press brewed. You did make it clear you had good taste, so I'd expect you to appreciate it."

I took another drink and fidgeted in my chair. What the

hell brought this question to mind, I couldn't say. Once it was there, I had to get it out. "So, is this little setup de rigueur for your mornings-after?"

Will coughed. "Are you *jealous*?"

"Never. Why would I be jealous of some executive's stilettoes under your bed, her La Perla panties on your sink?" I smirked, but he never did buy my facades.

"How adorable. You are jealous."

"Shut up, William. I was kidding."

A corner of the pastry practically dissolved in a buttery cloud when I popped it in my mouth. The delicious distraction was welcome, so I took a proper bite at last. "Hot damn, this is delicious."

"And you doubted me on the cheese. Don't deflect. You were not kidding, Olivia. What do you want to ask?"

I shrugged. "What kind of women have been in your life before? You know a lot about my past—"

"I don't, actually. I only have a pretty strong impression based on our conversation in my office."

"Well... yeah."

"What makes *you* say yes to a relationship? Why did you say yes to me?"

I crossed my arms in an X and made a buzzer noise. "Nope. I asked first."

Will's smile faded. "Honestly? I usually prefer as casual as possible. I couldn't tell you the last time I was in a relationship. Grad school, maybe? I've been building a career and just haven't, I don't know, met someone who I wanted to... commit to."

He gazed at me a moment while I ate. My insides throbbed with giddy pride that I tried to keep from my face, but, *oh my god*. "What about that Stacy chick? I've heard her name a lot."

"Stacy is my friend. We have sex sometimes. Well, we did. She's an attorney, thus the connection to Erin, and has no time for a relationship, so she and I have worked out." He stole the last piece of food off my plate.

"You douche! Make me another."

"Make it yourself, nosey."

I started for the basket, but he swatted my hand away and built another creation, this time with fig jam. I batted my eyelashes when he set it on my plate, and he laughed.

Between exaggerated yummy sounds, I said, "I still don't get why you wouldn't be interested in a commitment beyond a fuck buddy until *me*."

Will was quiet a long time, then said, "Because it is you."

I wanted to press this, but the guarded look in his eyes told me I wouldn't get far. "Fair enough. You want one of my secrets now, don't you?" I puckered my lips.

"Mm-hmm. I want to know the longest relationship you were ever in."

"Ben. Ten months."

"Besides him."

"High school, I guess. Dated a guy junior year. I'm not... I'm not one for long-term. I guess relationships usually run about a two-month course on average. Probably why no one ever bought me roses before."

Will stirred his coffee. "Why short-term?"

It's easier. That way you don't catch feels. That way it doesn't hurt too bad when he says it's not working out, that you're too busy or bold or bitchy to be his girl for the long haul. Short term means you can just go back to being your badass self without wondering why you are the way you are. Why you're the one who wants to say yes to every opportunity you discover. Why you're the one who says what's on her mind. Why that makes you some kind of weirdo who's a good friend but a terrible girlfriend.

... Yeah, probably shouldn't tell the guy you're dating all that, genius.

I blinked out of my reverie and shrugged. "There's no good answer. It's not ideal, and I guess I don't have a lot of confidence in men as a result, but whatever."

"If it's whatever, then why our agreement?"

That question had an easy answer. "Because I'm tired of whatever. I'd like for what I do—not just relationships, but everything suddenly—to matter more than it has. To be worth more, if that makes sense."

Will spoke slowly. "And so... you would say that *this* is 'worth more'?"

I dropped my gaze. My voice was soft. "Yeah. It sure as hell feels like it."

"Wow. I guess you were right."

"About what?"

"You *do* have good taste."

My head snapped up. Will's teasing smirk made me yelp just before I dissolved into giddy laughter. "You smug jerk," I giggled as I rose and pulled him to his feet.

"Your words, my dear. Your words." He wrapped his arms around me. Immediately our laughter was muted by a kiss.

"We have plans today," he muttered when I kissed across his jaw.

"Damn right."

Will chuckled. "No, I meant plans outside."

"Ugh, *fine*." I touched my nose to his.

Will blinked, then grinned, and I laughed.

"I like silly Will Langer," I finally got to tell him.

"I *love* how you make me silly." Will skimmed his hands down my back and sighed. "Fuck, and I love how you feel against me, Liv."

I gazed at him, glowing all over. *This is worth so much more. This is... incredible.*

The next day and a half passed in a haze of adventures, sex, and laughter—a lot of all three. The plans he'd mentioned were a reservation to blow glass in Franklin, a small town about an hour outside of Nashville. This had been on the top of my "cool stuff to do" wish list for ages, and his smile when I shrieked with excitement made it even cooler.

What literally wasn't cool was the furnace at the shop. "Hotter than the belly of hell" was how the instructor described it, but that didn't stop us from having a blast. Two hours later, I'd created a paperweight and a beer glass, Will had a slightly wobbly looking vase to his credit, and both of us had sweated off half our body weight.

It was a perfect excuse to go have a stealthy skinny-dip in my parents' pool since they were away.

Back at his place, we had sex in the shower, slept, then woke up and did it again before dinner and a movie on his couch that night. On Sunday, we spent the morning in bed before exploring shops in the Gulch all afternoon.

It was like a dream. So simple and happy. So everything we wanted it to be and not a damn thing that we didn't. I'd almost have wondered if it *was* a dream if not for the body-quaking orgasms he gave me at regular intervals.

Sunday evening, I checked my phone while we decided what we wanted to do with the night.

"What's up?" he asked when I began to spin the device on the countertop.

I debated another moment, then went to hug him. "Let's go out."

"Where?"

He's gonna hate this. "Bar Forty, one of my favorite places. Um, my friends are a musical duo called You and I. They're doing a final show tonight before they take off on tour. A lot of people are going to give them support."

Doubt flashed over his features, so I hurried to add, "Swear it'll be fun."

An hour later, I stepped out of the Audi in a little black halter dress. Will gave his keys to the valet and came to rest his fingers on my back. We traded a look, then strode straight to the bouncer. The line out front followed us with their eyes and gave me a tiny thrill of celebrity, especially when my name was all it took to get us inside. David and Kira always put their closest friends on the list. They'd been growing in popularity around town over the past year. At least some of our friend group tried to be at all their major gigs. I was almost always game to scream my head off for my dear friends, so none of this was new.

Will beside me sure made it feel different, though. In the best kind of way.

We wove through the crowded venue. Every time someone shouted, "Hey, Liv!" Will's hand flexed against my spine. I just waved and kept us moving. I thought we might find a seat without actually stopping to talk to anyone, but a wolf whistle brought me up short.

"Hot damn. You two know how to make an entrance," Megan shouted. She waved us over. Will hesitated, but I led us to join her and Adam.

"Don't I know you from CrossFit?" she asked with her hand stuck toward Will.

"I think so."

She laughed. "You know so, Will. This is Adam. Adam, meet Will. He and Liv go *way* back."

I half expected him to bolt, but Will just shook Adam's hand and cocked his jaw. "Megan Riley, it's good to finally meet you. Tell me, how exactly do *you* know Olivia?"

He smirked when Meg's eyes went wide. She shoved my shoulder. "You told him our story?"

In bed this morning, we'd talked about CrossFit, and he'd asked about my friend. Out of nowhere, I'd spun him the yarn of a date who had double booked himself and run late for dinner. My nails had been ready to come out when the hostess showed a smirking blonde to my reserved table, but Megs had just laughed and ordered a drink. By the time the guy showed up bumbling excuses, we were too busy becoming best friends to do more than shoo him away.

"It's epic," I said with a shrug.

"Very true. Fate for sure," Megan said.

Will laughed and motioned for the waitress so he could buy a round for the table.

Megs eyed him while he draped an arm across the back of my chair. "You're alright. I approve."

"I'm honored." He laid his hand on his heart.

The show began, so I scooted my chair a little closer to his and simmered with music and good vibes. When the set ended, Megan and I made a trip to the ladies' room. On the way back, both our gazes snagged on a table near the stage.

"Well, well. Look who's returned from the dead," Megan muttered as our strides slowed.

"I'll see you at the table." Before she could question, I squared my shoulders and headed straight for the party of three.

"Hey, guys," I said when they looked up. "Hello, Nick."

Ben and Celeste nodded, but Nick's hazel eyes darkened behind his glasses. Abruptly, he shoved his chair back and muttered something about a drink. I sighed and wrinkled my nose at the couple.

"He's pissed at you for being such a jerk to Mel," Celeste said flatly.

"Yeah, I caught that, thanks," I snipped right back, then looked toward the bar. "I just thought maybe we should talk."

"You should," Ben said. "He's going through a lot. Clear the air."

"Just be careful. He doesn't need your attitude." Celeste toyed with her necklace.

I pinned a stare on her. "And I need yours?"

She returned the glare with equal frost. Her eyes narrowed as she opened her mouth to reply, but I looked back at Nick.

"Excuse the interruption. See y'all later."

Nick was staring into a whiskey when I approached the bar. "Jesus. Leave me alone," he growled.

I leaned beside him. "No can do, sorry. Came to grovel. Not on my knees, though."

He quirked a brow but refused to smile.

"I'm sorry I was mean to your girl. That was shitty of me, but it threw me how you dicked me over without even bothering to call." I couldn't keep the edge from my voice.

His shoulders tensed. A grunt was my response.

I took a breath and softened my tone. "Still, I shouldn't have taken it out on her. She didn't deserve that any more than I deserved what you did. If it helps, she handled my bitchery like a champion."

"I'm sure she did." Nick covered his face with both hands. He looked like the saddest person in the world. I had never seen playful, funny Nick so completely broken.

When he didn't move, I laid a hand on his shoulder. "You okay?"

"No. Not at all." He rubbed his eyes under his glasses before he turned to me. "I am a total bastard," he said in a hollow voice. "And I'm sorry I dicked you over. You deserve so much better than that. I never meant to—aww, fuck it. Excuses are bullshit. Just rest assured that karma took her revenge."

I shook my head hard. "I never wanted that. Never, Nick."

"Even so."

"Can we go back and be friends again? I don't want to lose you."

He caught my fingers and nodded. "I can't lose anyone else. Certainly not someone like you. We are absolutely still friends." He looked up from my hand and crooked his lips. "That was a mutual grovel. As it should've been."

"I'm satisfied." I held out my arms, and Nick collapsed in a heavy hug. There was no hint of the flirt that sparked all those months ago. There was only my friend, in so much obvious pain that I squeezed him extra tight.

"Good luck with everything, Nicky," I whispered in his ear before I stepped back. He winked, downed the bourbon, and tossed me a wave as the lights began to dim.

Will's curious gaze was on me from the moment I turned from the bar. When I slid into my seat, he tilted his head in a silent question. Applause swelled, but I could only look at him and smile. Impulsively, I pulled on his collar for a kiss and held his hand extra tight through the second set. *I'm so damn glad I'm with you right now, Will Langer.*

The napkins on the table danced from the unending applause when David and Kira took their final bow. They gripped hands and bowed again and again while we screamed like maniacs to show them love. Will looked over after I emitted a particularly powerful shriek. His grin made me duck my head.

At last the duo left the stage, and we all sat down again. "Well, kids, I think we better take off. I've got an early appointment tomorrow," Megs said as she shouldered her purse.

"Do you want to leave?" I asked Will once the other couple had gone.

"Soon. This was fun, but I get one more night of you in my bed, and I want to use it."

"Why are we sitting here then? Let's go." I slammed my glass down and jumped to my feet. Will laughed and followed me to the exit.

In the Audi, I tucked my knees toward him. "You really had fun?"

He swallowed. "I feel like I'm living someone else's life this weekend."

"Will?" I blurted. "Why are you so alone? Where are you *from*?"

The radio filled the silence between us until finally, "A cattle ranch outside of Dallas. Adoptive parents, a rotation of foster siblings, homeschooling, farm work, ascetic discipline, and religion. That's where I'm from. I never knew my mother. Or, if I did, in the church community or whatever, I didn't know she was. Langer was my adoptive parents' last name. I don't even know my background.

"Knoxville was where my life began. My parents gave me two hundred dollars and wished me well, but that was it. I invented myself once I got off that bus."

My eyes burned from lack of blinking. I cleared my throat when he went silent again. "Excuse me while I go find that line I crossed. It's just a couple miles back. I'll let you know when I get there."

He chuckled. "You've been trying to get my biography all weekend."

My fingers knotted. "I just want to know you better."

We pulled into his parking spot. "You do know me, Liv. You just don't think you do. You," he chuckled again, but this was raspy and sexy as hell, "you know how to piss me off and turn me on like no one else. You know how to make me smile *and* think."

"And you know I'm crazy about you. That's the most important thing to remember." He stroked my cheek and then stepped out of the car. I followed.

We weren't off the elevator before my legs were around his back.

The next morning meant work for both of us, so we got up together and made our way through morning preparations. I stepped out of the bathroom dressed in trousers and a button-down top. Will was pouring coffee at the bar, impeccably dressed in a light gray suit. He grabbed the mug I'd been using and set it beside his own.

"Looking very professional today Mr. Langer," I said in greeting as I slid onto the barstool.

"Not bad yourself, Ms. Milani."

"They call me Miss Olivia. It's a little different than your world. Thanks for the coffee." I plucked a banana from the bowl and began to peel. "I'm sad this is over, Will."

"Me too. It'll be weirdly quiet when I come home tonight."

"I still hate that you're alone."

Will gave me a sly look. "Then maybe you should move in."

I laughed, but after the high of the weekend, it didn't sound so bad. "Yeah, that's sure to work out well. We wouldn't be ready to kill each other within a week. Not to mention how surprised my family would be."

Although my tone had been light, those words instantly became the elephant in the room. We eyed each other.

I sipped my coffee. "So, about that. We've both been pretty clear that this is a secret from them so far."

Will shook his head. "I don't like secrets. But."

"But—but we've been so mixed up, not sure what this was, and we've only now figured it out. But it's new. And sometimes when things are new, you need a little private time to acclimate before announcing it to the world." I swallowed hard. "Right?"

Please, please go with me on this. I wasn't ready to tell the family. I couldn't face the shock, the questions, the very likely dismay and doubt. On the first weekend after the daycare, I'd kept that news to myself for the same reason, and it had turned out so well. Will wasn't a "friend" or a fling. I needed to protect this impossibly beautiful connection until I knew for sure that it wasn't a flash in the pan.

Will gazed at me, eyes dark, jaw set. At last, he nodded. "I couldn't agree more."

I slithered off the chair and put my head on his shoulder. "Finally, you admit I'm right."

I smiled when he laughed. With that settled, I pressed a kiss to his cheek and went to get my bag while he put on his jacket. We kissed goodbye at my car, promised to see each other Wednesday at CrossFit and do another weekend soon, and then he was gone.

The whole drive to work, all I could do was fantasize. My

mailroom job would've let me daydream for hours, but now I only had the commute to mull things over before my day was packed.

I didn't fantasize about his kiss or the screaming orgasms or the shower sex. No. My sappy brain just kept inventing scenes of what it'd be like to go home to him tonight. To fix dinner and eat it on the terrace. To watch TV until we dozed on the couch.

To have a life together.

How totally corny.

25

LIV

The rest of August flashed by. Work was a whirlwind as I completed training just in time to take over a classroom on the first day of September.

I almost passed out with nerves the first time I stood in that doorway. My assistant, Emma, was fantastic, and my colleagues were incredibly supportive. After the first week, I no longer thought about vomiting every morning. The kids were cool, and even the rowdy ones seemed to like me pretty well. Parents wanted to know all about me, so I hosted a meet-and-greet, which I think got me huge points with Mrs. Harris. All the parents were smiling by the end of the night.

Labor Day weekend fell at the end of my second full week. I'd just settled at the kitchen table with a beer when my phone rang.

"Yes?" I drawled.

"What are you doing this weekend?"

I grinned at Will's low growl and imagined him seated at his desk. "Well, I'm starting with a beer. After that, my plans are pretty open. What are *you* doing this weekend?"

"You."

My bare toes curled around the rung of the chair my feet were propped on. "Oh, really?"

"Well, it's a tentative plan."

"It sounds like an *excellent* plan." In the past weeks, Wednesday CrossFit and dinner after had been the only time we'd gotten alone together. "Are you suggesting I come over?"

Will hummed. "I had other ideas, actually. How would you feel about a weekend away?"

I almost dropped the phone. "Away? You mean a trip?"

He chuckled. "I'm not sure what else that might mean. Yes, a trip. Be at the airport in an hour and a half."

I *did* drop the phone. When I scooped it back up, Will was laughing. "See you soon," he said, then hung up.

Megan was on the line in five seconds. "The *airport*?" she shrieked. "Girl, you better haul ass to Victoria's Secret and be on time!"

I tripped over my own feet as I ran to find Tom in the yard with Maddie, shouted that I was leaving on an impromptu trip, then ran upstairs and blindly threw every type of outfit I might need into a suitcase. When all that was done, I had an hour to get to the airport. That meant half an hour commute, and half an hour to, yes, go to Victoria's Secret on the way.

I'm a cami and shorts girl when it comes to PJs, but I picked the laciest, silkiest getup I could find. It came complete with a thong and little bows that tied at the hips. Figuring I could wear my heels if the mood struck, I went with black over red. I was almost embarrassed to buy something that was so obviously for sex, but with a shrug I slapped down my credit card and flew back to the car.

By the time I got to the airport, I was a frazzled mess. My hair flowed wild and loose around my too-warm face. I parked and took the shuttle to the terminal. As soon as the bus doors hissed open, I hauled my suitcase off and jogged through the automatic doors—

To find Will standing off to my right, in conversation with a woman. Her smile was wide as her hand fluttered to his arm every few seconds. Since he hadn't seen me yet, I sucked in a deep breath before striding their way. As soon as I moved, Will found me with his eyes. His face creased in a smile that only slightly retracted my claws.

"Thanks again for the ride." The chick giggled just when I got to them.

"Not a problem. June, meet my girlfriend, Olivia. Liv, June works with me. She's in logistics."

Oh, did her face *fall*. June's hand was on Will's arm again. He subtly shifted away. She floated toward again him before she seemed to realize it this time.

My lips curved, brows raised. "Hi, June." *I'm going to take out my earrings and throw down if you touch him again. Hope you catch the message.*

Will's attention stayed solely on me. "Are you ready to—"

His ringtone interrupted. "Dammit," he sighed when he glanced at the screen. "Five minutes, tops. June, safe travels."

He strode to a quiet corner by the window. June didn't move. I fixed my stare on her while she looked me over a couple times, her lemon face deepening with each perusal. *Cue catty remark in three...two...*

"You're Will's girlfriend?"

So damn predictable. "You heard right."

"How... surprising." She simpered a smile and flicked her gaze over my navy sundress and white linen shirt.

My gut clenched, but I didn't flinch. "Why's that?"

"You're not what I expected. I thought he'd go for someone a little more…"

"Like you?" I supplied, pleased when she began to blush.

"That's not what I meant."

Like hell it wasn't.

"I just—he's never mentioned you at work."

"Hmm. He's never mentioned *you* at home." I flipped my hair and stepped forward. "And while I've seen his office, all you'll ever do is dream about his bedroom."

In the corner of my eye, Will pocketed his phone, so I stepped away and left June red-faced and speechless. *Still got it.*

Will took one look at my grin and narrowed his eyes. "What did you do?"

"Moi?" I blinked innocently.

"Yes, you. Did you insult my colleague?"

"Not in the least. We just cleared up a little misconception. So," I hooked his belt loops and tugged. "What are we doing, Langer?"

He palmed my waist and put his forehead against mine, and June became a distant memory. "You drink too much whiskey and beer," he murmured, then dusted my lips with a kiss.

"Glass houses, buddy."

Will just grinned. "Indeed. I thought we should drink some wine instead. Come on."

He took my hand and led me to the ticket counter where the agent slipped two tickets into an envelope. I had to bite my lips to swallow a scream when he said, "Here you are, Mr. Langer. The flight to San Francisco boards soon, so you'll want to head straight to the gate. Your first-class tickets allow you access to the lounge if you have time."

You're not what I expected.

June's words whispered in my head while I followed Will through security. In defiance of the universe and anyone else who might agree with her, I kept my lips pinched tight. That Girl could play it cool anywhere, even in a VIP lounge with a glass of complimentary champagne in her hand. That Girl could act like it's no big deal to settle into her *first freaking class* seat. That Girl could keep her poker face while an airline attendant offered her a hot towel and took her dinner order. That Girl could sneak a peek to figure out that the towel was for her face and use it like she knew what to do all along. She just had to be a little quiet about it is all.

Which, of course, Will noticed.

"Are you okay?" he asked once we were airborne. "You've not said two words."

I took his hand and smiled. "I'm great. Tell me what we're going to do."

Over dinner, he said that we'd spend the night in San Francisco, then drive up to Napa Valley tomorrow and stay there. Sunday we'd return to the city before our flight Monday morning. I picked at my food until Will finished by saying, "It's all a bit last-minute, I know. Feel free to modify anything that doesn't appeal to you."

The cabin lights had dimmed, so I slid my hand along his inner thigh and leaned to whisper, "It all appeals to me, Langer."

Will rumbled and caught me for a kiss before I could withdraw. "Then look a little happier about it and stop making me worry I've chosen the wrong thing, Milani."

So, I did.

We touched down in San Francisco just in time for sunset thanks to the two-hour time difference. A car took us to a gorgeous boutique hotel tucked among rows of colorful houses. We walked into the lobby, and again I had to clamp down on my lips to keep from squealing or gawking.

Will checked us in while I looked around. The clerk caught my attention when he said, "We have you in a room with two double beds—"

"I asked for a king," Will interrupted.

The keyboard clattered. "Ah, yes. Well, unfortunately we had several guests check in this afternoon, and I'm afraid—"

"What else do you have?"

Clatter, clatter. "We have a suite. The upgrade cost would be—"

"We'll take it."

The poor dude was lucky to get out two words in a row. He bumbled an okay, and Will nodded at me. "Please send up a bottle of champagne. Liv, is there anything else you want?"

"Fruit sounds good. Oh, and definitely some ice. I'm really thirsty."

Will's voice was thick when he said, "Fruit and champagne. Do *not* forget that ice."

The room was a mini palace. I didn't bother to hold in the squeak as my heels sank into the carpet. A view of the skyline could be seen from the huge four-poster bed where two plush robes sat waiting.

"Oh, god. How much do I owe you for all this?"

Will turned from the dresser where he'd dropped his wallet. His lip curled in distaste. "That's a joke, right?"

"But—but—you can't pay for the whole thing."

"Can't I?" He laughed, but I plopped on the loveseat and frowned at the cream-colored carpet.

You don't belong here.

That Girl got drinks bought for her, not freaking vacations and luxury hotel rooms. I had never been spoiled in my life. Panic fluttered in the bottom of my heart as I realized I didn't know how to accept this from him, didn't know if I should or even could.

"What's wrong?" He stood in front of me. "Out with it."

I sat back with a sigh. Will's eyebrow quirked, but he mirrored my crossed arms, clearly ready to wait until I spilled.

How to say my thoughts aloud didn't come to me right away, so it was a long stare-off until I fumbled out, "You'll be surprised, but I'd eaten at nice restaurants before you. I'd drunk coffee and wine, too. But damn if everything you do isn't nicer, *better*, somehow."

The line appeared between his eyes. "I like nice things. I want the best. After how I grew up..." He shrugged.

That comment clenched my throat. I imagined young Will, so quiet and stoic. A poor, ranch hand childhood definitely deserved all the luxury he could afford.

"And that's awesome for you. Really. You work hard. You earn your money. Enjoy it. But me..." My hand dropped hard on my lap at the same moment my chin hit my chest. "I don't deserve this. This is too rich for a girl like me."

Long fingers squeezed my shoulders. Will dropped to his knees in front of me, his eyes narrowed. "You don't deserve it? This is exactly your problem, Olivia."

My face pinched in a scowl. "I don't *have* a problem, William."

Why does fighting with him ground me? Just when I'd gotten all thoughtful and moody, snapping at Will brought me back to reality. He squeezed again, and anger and lust flashed through me. I wanted to put my hands on him, but Will had me pinned to the seat.

"Hear me for once when I say this. You have a huge problem, and it's *you*. For years you've sold yourself short, underestimated your tremendous talents, and hidden behind a sharp tongue. I know how you grew up. Your family babied you. But fuck that, Liv. Just because something is difficult doesn't mean you can't handle it. You need to grip the world by the collar, just like you did me in the kitchen that night. Take what you *want*. You deserve it, and I—"

He broke off suddenly, eyes cut down.

My breath was shallow at his impassioned words and the depth with which this man knew me. God, sometimes he knew me better than I did. I wet my lips. "And you?"

Will's left hand glided down to slip off my sandal. He traced the black ink on my instep. "'Not all who wander are lost.' You got this tattoo when you were eighteen. Your mom flipped her shit."

Well, *that* derailed the conversation. "And you were surprised I remembered the first time we met?"

"Did you ever get your passport, Olivia?"

He lifted his gaze, and I tilted my head at the strange wording. "I don't have one, no."

His smile was pure Mona Lisa. Totally enigmatic and unreadable. "I knew you were drunk, but you don't remember anything about that night, do you?"

"That night? Oh. The one at your apartment."

That night had tickled my memory more in the last month than since it happened, but I always pushed the thoughts away. They hurt too much.

"Mm-hmm. We decided you'd get your passport, and we'd go to—"

"Egypt." I sat forward suddenly, hand on my mouth. "Oh, god, yeah. I do remember."

Will's easy grin broke. "Exactly. You wanted to see the world."

"I'd still travel the world if I could," I admitted. "Life—money—kind of got in the way."

Will rose up on his knees, hands on either side of my hips, our faces close. "You deserve precisely what you want from life. Say it, Liv."

I took a deep breath, opened my mouth—and shut it again.

I'd always known how to be myself, give zero fucks, and handle whatever life brought. If my family had indulged me too much, at least it had let me be myself through all my phases and fascinations.

So why is it so hard to say those words? Don't you believe that you deserve what you want? You've always done as you liked. Why is this different?

Because it meant I deserved things I didn't yet know about. It wasn't about impulse. It was about confidence. Rather than careening from whim to adventure, it meant I had to be a woman who possessed her own path.

Not a wanderer.

Will was right. I'd gotten the Tolkien tattoo when I'd wanted to see the world. Over the years, though, the phrase had morphed into a validation of my lack of plans. Declaring that I deserved what I wanted effectively changed my approach to—well, to life.

"I deserve to have what I want." I tested the phrase and glanced around, a little smile on the corners of my lips.

My gaze came back to Will. "I want to be right here with you."

His eyes glinted. "I want you to have everything. And I'll give it to you if I can. You're," he laughed and hung his head. "You're my dream girl, Liv Milani. If you've not figured that out by now, then there it is. I'd do anything for you."

My face melted. "I'm your dream girl?" I whimpered.

He twisted his lips in an obvious yes.

"Since when?"

Will Langer flipped me off.

I yelped and smacked his hand before I grabbed his collar. "Think you're cute, huh boy?"

"No. I think *you're* cute when you're surprised. And I think you're fucking amazing every," he nipped my lip, "single," another nip, "day."

Before I got sucked into the hurricane of his kiss, I locked my knees and stood up. "I'm going to freshen up."

I took my suitcase and left him wide-eyed on the floor. Ten minutes later, I peeked out of the bathroom. Will had one leg over the arm of the loveseat while he read on his phone. He spied my eyes and glared. "I'm falling asleep over here. What the hell—*oh*."

My pulse thundered so hard, I'm pretty sure he could see my heart through my sternum like a cartoon. Or he would've, if his eyes hadn't dislocated from their sockets. I toyed with the hem of the negligee and waited.

Will drank me in forever without speaking. Finally, his gaze lifted to my face. "Well," he croaked. "I didn't think the simple sight of you could turn me on more than that night you barged into my room in your pajamas. As usual, you've blown me away. One second."

I watched him rise and walk toward the door where a room service cart now sat. He filled a glass with ice and water, drank it down, then stalked me across the room. I scuttled to the foot of the bed.

Will bent his head so our lips touched lightly. "I'm still thirsty," he whispered.

My knees shook. Will laughed just before he swooped in and sucked a hard kiss on my neck.

"Hold the post above your head," he commanded, palms already all over my little getup.

I wrapped both hands around the polished wood. Will teased my breasts through the lace until every swish of the fabric made me hiss. He had to remind me twice to hold on when my hands wanted to grip his hair. His lips traveled slowly down, hands too, until he knelt in front of me and kissed my inner thigh.

"So wet already," he said as he ran his nose over my panties.

"You said you were thirsty."

"Indeed I did." He hummed as he inched my underwear down my legs.

My knuckles squeezed the hell out of that poor bedpost while his tongue and lips brought me to climax almost immediately. I threw my head back and screamed his name.

Will pulled away. He swept one arm under my knees, the other behind my back, and threw me onto the bed. I lifted my head just in time to see him drop to his stomach between my legs. Strong hands braced me apart. Two sneaky fingers sank deep inside me while his tongue teased. My body coiled tight again.

I drifted my hands over my breasts. Will's hum of approval when I started to pet myself jolted all the way up my body. The ache in my core reached DEFCON-5. His tongue flicked wickedly over my clit, fingers pulsing steady and deep. I wailed when a tsunami of an orgasm crashed over me, muscles quaking from my thighs to my forehead.

"Shall I continue?"

Will's question rumbled from between my legs. My palms rested on my breasts while I blinked, surprised by blurry vision. A single tear rolled to the quilt.

"Come here." I reached for him and blinked again when

he knelt over me. Another tear trickled down my temple. I ran my finger over his wet mouth. "Jesus, you're a mess."

"And you are the sweetest thing I've ever tasted."

Will slid into me, no friction at all, sighing when I wrapped my legs around him. "I'm going to fuck hard, Liv. You're *so* wet. Just tell me if it's too much."

"It's not too much." *It's never too much with you, Will.*

With his pelvis grinding against me, my body glowed again. I turned a wild-eyed look up to him and sank my nails into his shoulders to brace for another round of ecstasy.

"That's my girl. Come on, baby, let go for me once more."

The sound I made was something like "unnghhhh" when I surrendered *again*. Will didn't give me a chance to recover before he thrust harder than ever. The flush on his cheeks, the shininess of his lips, the crazy mess of his hair mesmerized me.

But then he spoke. "There is *nothing* better than this. You're a dream come true, and I'm never... going to get... enough."

He groaned and pitched forward, so I wrapped my limbs around him tight.

"Since always," I mumbled, brainless and only half aware I'd spoken at all. Sleep claimed me more and more by the second. *You and me. This was always the dream.*

Will lifted his head and gave me a sharp look. "Since always."

He whispered it like a vow, the last thing either of us said that night.

26

WILL

I opened my eyes in the thin gray light of pre-dawn. Liv's dark brown and pink hair swirled in front of me, her back snuggled to my chest as she slept peacefully. I lifted my head and gazed down at her. So fucking beautiful. I could hardly take it all in.

My dream girl indeed. Only her warmth and the taste of her pussy lingering on my tongue kept me certain this was reality.

I rolled out of bed carefully, so she kept sleeping. While the shower warmed, I thumbed through my old photos again. The one I wanted was the last one in my college albums. It was a shot of a Sprite can on a coffee table, taken at almost exactly this same time of the morning.

That Sprite can was the only shot I had from the graduation party night. I didn't have any photos of Liv from that night, but I didn't need any. She wore a halter top and miniskirt. Her hair was long, her heels were high, and she was radiant with excitement from being at a college party. To be fair, all three of us were glowing by the time we'd had a few drinks.

Four years of college had done a lot for me. I grew into my body and developed a sense of self that wasn't prescribed by a strict, ranch hand upbringing. Contact with the people who raised me became minimal. I didn't miss the manure or the sermons. Besides, the Milanis took me in from day one. Holidays were spent with them. Whenever they came up to Knoxville to visit, I was automatically included in family fun.

Every time I saw Liv over those years, there was something different about her. Her hair was longer. Her hair was shorter. Her braces were off. Her legs weren't so skinny anymore. Her laugh was even better. I didn't think about her —she was just a kid, for fuck's sake—but I did notice.

Then came that night. When we got back to the apartment, Tom passed out almost immediately. Liv disappeared to the bathroom while I spaced out on the couch with a Sprite to sober up.

I expected her to go to bed, but she reappeared and sat beside me. As usual, she took control of the conversation. She asked me about my plans post-college, which opened the door for us to talk about life goals.

I remember the way the room was lit by the TV, dim and cozy. I remember exactly how she looked. The way her voice was soft while we talked. She admitted she didn't know what she wanted to be, and I said, "I think you could be anything you want to."

In typical Liv fashion, she started inventing wild career choices that ended with her as a tightrope walker. I watched in amusement as she stood, her back to me, and wobbled a line down the couch. She returned the same way and plopped down. I saw in the breath before it happened how off her aim had been.

Her body crashed into my chest, her ass bumping my

thigh. Dark hair tickled my forearm, and my body went tight as the Sprite sloshed out of the can.

"Oh, sorry," she gasped, turning to look at me.

Oh, god.

Suddenly, little Liv wasn't so little. She was a stunning young woman whose warm, soft body was pressed against mine. I knew I had to get us out of this. I knew it—and totally failed to do it.

I teased her instead. "Good, since you're the one who sat on me."

She gave it back by jostling my shoulder. "I *said* sorry, you ass."

We stared at each other. Her eyelids lowered. Her gaze settled on my mouth. I swallowed hard. She caught her breath.

"Oh, Liv, be careful."

"Okay, Will. I'll be careful," she promised in a low, throaty voice, even as she let her lips dropped open invitingly.

I took that invitation.

I took it, and it changed my life. Everything I'd ever noticed about Olivia Milani solidified the moment I kissed her. Her lips, her scent, and her warm, wet mouth were the sweetest things I'd ever known. In a life of hard work and discipline, sweet was a foreign concept. The other girls I'd kissed—even the ones I'd slept with—were nothing in comparison.

We broke apart before we could get carried away. Although the tension was thick, we somehow managed to keep it in check and returned to talking. The hours passed. Dawn started to creep in as we got lost in plans and dreams of what we would become and where we would go.

Like Egypt. We planned to go that Christmas, knowing all along it was bullshit but loving the idea anyway.

When the birds began chirping, Liv yawned and said she was going to sleep. Another wide-eyed look from her nearly toppled my resolve, but self-control won out. When she'd shut the door and silence fell, I took the photo of the Sprite can in honor of that night.

I darkened my phone and shook myself out of the memories. Abruptly, I shut off the shower and hurried back to bed. Liv hummed in her sleep as I pulled her close to me again, and I buried my nose in her hair.

I never guessed what we started that night would have to wait eight years, but hell yes you are my dream girl, Liv Milani. And I will do anything to protect your heart and watch you shine brighter than ever.

I took photos all weekend for the first time in forever. Wine, redwood trees, the Pacific Ocean, and us. So much us.

My feet touched the ground about half the time. The other half, I was either floating or flat on my back.

27

LIV

"Well, she's a cute little thing. You've met her, right, Liv?"

I grinned at Mom a week later as Tom and Erin walked Maddie up the front lawn of my parents' house. We stood on the porch, waiting for their arrival. This was the first time Tom had brought a woman to meet the family since Jenna passed. My stomach fluttered with excitement for him.

"Oh, yeah. She's great. You'll love her."

Mom hummed. "If she cares for Tom, then that's all that matters."

Will's Audi pulled into the driveway, and my stomach fluttered all over again. I ogled his gray hoodie and jeans, smiling to realize I'd done the same thing last night when he was dressed in nothing but a towel.

Suddenly, I wanted to run over, kiss his cheek, and let everyone aww over us, too. *All Mom and Dad want is for their children to be cared for. Why are we hiding?*

Hang on, princess. This is Tom's moment. You can wait a little longer.

I glanced at Tom. The flutters took on a different kind of tone. I'd been avoiding him a little since returning from

California because I was just so damn happy. For some reason, doubt still nagged at my conscience. Tom had doted on me forever. No matter what, he'd supported and protected me, but that also meant he knew me a little too well. If he decided I was too flighty or too opinionated or too whatever to date his oldest friend, it would break my heart.

We'll tell them soon. It had become a mantra, but it worked.

"Hello, Mr. and Mrs. Milani." Erin shyly shook my parents' hands.

"It's Claire and Anthony, dear. Come on inside!"

Mom's warm demeanor had Erin's shoulders easing quickly. She and I followed Mom into the kitchen to chat. By the time I set the table, she was part of the Milani clan.

Family updates commenced at the end of the prayer. My father spooned mashed potatoes onto Maddie's plate and said, "Liv, tell us about work."

I still marveled at this new respect for my stories. I kept it brief, though, because the cute couple deserved the spotlight that day. Not even Will's upcoming week in Chicago got much airtime. Through most of the meal, questions for Erin and how the two met filled the talk.

Meanwhile, Will and I played a game under the table. Every time he spoke, I rubbed my foot against his calf. My challenge was holding a poker face as he repeated the same sentence twice more than once in the conversation. This would've been great fun if he hadn't done the same damn thing to me every time it was my turn to share.

Will changed the game as the meal wound down. He faced me, his tone bored even as he pressed his knee against mine. "I saw in the news that your friend Jesse Storms had a bit of a day yesterday. Wondered if you'd heard about it."

"What?" It was impressive how snippy my tone to him could still be.

"Oh, I heard that too. He was left at the altar." Mom said, and Erin hummed.

Our little flirtation game was making it hard to concentrate. I looked around, my brows pinched. "What are y'all talking about? Jesse Storms was getting married?"

"Weren't you invited?" Will sneered, clearly enjoying my confusion.

"Yeah, I wondered if you and Nick went. Figured you'd have mentioned it if you were there," Tom said with an evil grin.

"You're still seeing that Nick?" Mom asked at the same time Will said, "Nick?"

I took a deep breath and threw up both hands. "*What* are you people talking about? I'm over here eating meatloaf, and suddenly I'm supposed to know all the celebrity news? Did Jesse Storms get married or not?"

Will rolled his eyes, but I saw his lips twitch. "As you were in his inner circle, I figured you'd know. An hour before the ceremony, his bride ran from the church. It was all over the news. Storms gave a statement this morning. Scripted, but a good show. His album sales are sure to soar."

For celeb drama, that *was* pretty interesting, but I shrugged. "News to me. Maybe I'll give old Jess a call. See if he's looking for a rebound."

I lifted a brow at Will while Mom clucked at me.

Jesus, Sunday dinners were almost too much for my sanity. I pushed back from the table and went to cut the pie. Once everyone had a piece, I retreated to the kitchen to give myself a minute. Will appeared. I tried to glare.

"What was that?" I hissed.

He smirked. "Just keeping you on your toes."

"You'll pay for that one, Langer."

"What, are you going to call up Jesse and make me jealous? Or maybe Nick?"

I rolled my eyes. "Right. As if I give a damn about seeing anyone but you."

His cheeks flushed. "In that case, I'm sorry I have to wait until I'm back in town to learn what my punishment will be."

"Then you better hurry home."

"As soon as I can," he whispered into my ear.

I forgot about the whole Jesse Storms thing pretty fast. I'd never actually met him, and I didn't follow tabloids much. It *was* quite a dramatic story, especially since it all unfolded here in Nashville. But between my kids' Monday anxieties, my intricate plans for just how I would make Will suffer, *and* the text he sent saying that his trip might extend through next week, there was just no time.

The following Saturday, I'd gotten home from yoga and brunch when I got a call from an unfamiliar number. *Please don't be a parent.* Some moms didn't seem to realize that calling the teacher was for emergencies only. I plopped down on the porch step and answered.

"Liv? This is Celeste Greene."

"Celeste? How did you get my number?"

"Ben, of course." Her sigh made it clear she was already annoyed to talk to me.

I rolled my eyes. "Oh, right. Well, what's up?"

Another sigh. *Damn, someone get her a fainting couch.* "I'm on invite duty for a party tonight."

"You and Ben's?"

"No, it's Nick's. He has news, and he wants his closest friends to come out tonight to hear it. I was asked to call you. I guess whatever you said to him last time made him forgive you."

"Yeah, it's a cool little trick I learned called 'an apology.' Works like a charm."

Celeste grunted.

What a wonderful chat. "So, party. When and where?"

"The dueling pianos bar downtown. Eight pm. You're in?"

"Definitely."

"Fine."

"You know, Celeste," I said before I could consider it, "I'm not the beast you think I am. Since you're a permanent part of my circle, it would be nice if we could be a little friendlier."

She was silent for a long moment. "How about lunch in an hour?"

Well, damn.

We met at a café near their apartment. I'm pretty sure we looked like two lionesses circling each other before we sat down. Only after we ordered did I break the silent stare-off. "I didn't expect an invitation to lunch."

She shrugged. "I thought we could talk."

I tilted my head as I looked at her. As usual, her shoulders were squared, chin lifted. Her posture practically dared me to say something to piss her off.

I took the dare. "I bet you and I would get along fine if you'd get off your high horse and give me a chance."

Emerald eyes flashed. "My *high horse*?"

"Mm-hmm. You're always throwing shade at me, but you don't know me at all. You and I have plenty in common, Celeste. And I don't mean Ben."

"Really, Liv? Because when I look at you, I see a smart-mouthed girl who doesn't know when to shut up. "

"And I see a stuck-up pseudo Yankee who doesn't know how to laugh enough."

We glared at each other until I continued. "You're not wrong about me. But that's not all I am. And I have to assume, since Ben loves you so fiercely, that there's more to you, too."

Her auburn eyebrows arched, the lines on her forehead smoothing out. "That's fair. It's hard for me to get past my first impression of you. You were so aggressive, and all I knew was you were Ben's ex. And then that business with Nick, and how you were so nasty to Mel…" she shrugged. "I feel I'm validated in my opinion."

I smiled up at the waiter when he delivered her food and my coffee. It was a good moment to compose a response. "I remember meeting you, too. Gah, you were such a huffy chick."

"You were in my face from the first moment!"

We both started to laugh. "Yeah, I really was. I'm sorry. And about Mel… I'm working on that. You're right, though, about that part of me. It's not my best feature."

Her eyes narrowed. She nodded, clearly interested.

"As for Nick and Ben, my past with them isn't your business. Ben and I ended a long time ago. Nick, well. Messing around wasn't the best decision either of us ever made. But I'm friends with both of them. The rest is nothing to do with you."

Celeste stirred her coffee. "You're right. I guess we just never really got to know each other."

"Yes, and that's too bad because we could be friends. We're both stubborn, and clearly we have similar taste in men."

She laughed, so I winked.

"Better still, we care deeply about the people we love."

Celeste smiled. "This'll be a change, but I agree. Friends."

If this was the craziest moment I'd lived through this year, it would've been a doozy. Compared to the rest of the madness lately, it just made me really, really glad. "Awesome. So, tell me Nick's news."

She gave me a cautionary frown. "It's about Mel."

I caught my breath. "Are they back together?"

Her frown continued, and I realized she didn't know anything Nick and I had said to each other.

"Please tell me it's good news. He looked so sad last time I saw him. I couldn't take it. Is he happy?"

Her shoulders relaxed as she grinned. "He's *so* happy."

My text chimed before I could press for more. I squeaked when I glanced at the screen. "Sorry, hang on."

Celeste's gaze was curious when I finished replying. "Good news?"

I set my phone down. "Yes. I might have a date for the party after all. My... uh, my boyfriend is trying to get on a standby flight from Chicago. I didn't think he was coming home until next week."

She smiled again. "You're glowing."

I waved that away. "Nick. Tell me about Nick."

Celeste wouldn't give me the surprise, but we sat and talked for two full hours and didn't glare at each other once.

God, life was *good*.

I spotted my friends in front of the bar that night, but Nick wasn't there. Kira saw me first. She threw her arms around me and drew the attention of the rest. I gave my hellos and walked straight to where a luminous Mel stood beside Celeste.

Hands clasped behind my back in what I hoped was a contrite stance, I met her gaze. "Hi. I'm Liv."

"I remember." Her lips thinned.

"I'm sorry we got off on the wrong foot. There's no excuse for how I spoke to you, but I'd love a take two if you're willing."

Her blue eyes held me, neither angry nor friendly. She stuck out her hand. "Sounds good. I'm Melody."

I took it with a smile "Olivia. Call me Liv."

"Mel, then."

"Cool. Uh, it's really good to see you again. Apparently, my warning that you and Nick would be history soon was total bullshit."

She laughed, an airy sound that spoke of layers of happiness. "Well, kind of bullshit, kind of not."

My shoulders dropped. Being a peacemaker wasn't so bad.

Ben announced that we should go inside, so I flashed Mel a smile and followed the group. Celeste grabbed my jacket as we began to migrate.

"What's up?" I asked. "And where the heck is Nick?"

"He's inside already. Where's your guy? I thought you had a date."

I stuck out my lip. "Yeah, he couldn't get a flight until late. Sucks."

She gave me a sympathetic frown. *Celeste* gave *me* a sympathetic frown. *How many more stunners can I get in one day?*

One more at least. Inside the bar, Nick himself was screaming out "Hooked on a Feeling" and pounding the piano onstage. I gaped, but Celeste laughed and dragged me to a table.

"What the hell is this?" I screeched. "Was anyone going to tell me?"

A glance around said that everyone but Mel, Ben, and Celeste were just as stunned as me. Once the shock wore off, I couldn't stop grinning. The exuberance with which Nick sang was so wonderfully different than how I'd last seen him. By the time the first round was in hand, our table was the loudest cheering section in the place.

I bent my head toward Celeste. "This is the surprise? He and Mel worked it out and now he's singing here?"

She cut her eyes at me. "Not exactly. He does this for fun, but you've *got* to hear the story of how they got back together—and why they were apart. Liv, I'm telling you. You won't believe it."

"I hate you for the suspense," I complained, but she just grinned and sipped her Jameson.

"It's time to end another show," Nick said an hour later. "I've got people here tonight, so let's make it an extra happy ending. What do you think, Colin? What does the mystical jar of requests call for?"

His partner held up a strip of paper. "'Son of a Preacher Man.'"

Nick howled with laughter. "This might be my favorite song of all time."

Mel burst into giggles. She covered her mouth as a blush painted her cheeks.

"That better be *you* laughing," Nick said into the mic.

I grinned to see Mel slump into her seat, her whole face hidden now.

"Okay, everybody. Get up and dance." Nick began to sing while he and his partner picked up the tune on the piano.

Ben and Celeste hurried to the growing crowd of couples in the center of the floor.

Beside me, David turned to Kira. "Should we dance?" he asked, carefully casual.

I smiled privately when she blushed and followed him. Mel and I were the only ones left in the booth, and she only had eyes for Nick. Her pink cheeks and rapt expression told me everything I needed to know, story or not.

Nick was done. This wasn't a fling. Nick had met his match. *Another huge change.*

"Hey baby. How about a dance?"

The hair on my neck stood up when warm fingers dragged across my shoulder. I whipped around, and the instinct to punch someone's balls morphed into delight.

"Will!" I scrambled to my feet and threw my arms around his neck.

His chest vibrated with a laugh as he pulled me close.

"I thought you weren't—"

"I suspected you'd not checked your phone in a while. I got the six o'clock flight after all."

"Sorry, I guess I missed it with all the noise."

"Just come teach me a dance move before the song ends."

We caught the last verse and mostly swayed, but it was enough to have my face aching from smiling. I took him back to the table and introduced him to the crew, noticing the intrigue on Ben's face to see him again. Heat rushed my cheeks when he quirked a brow at me.

Yeah, yeah, Ben. I remember giving you hell when you introduced Celeste. This isn't the same, buddy.

... Is it?

I shook the thought away as Nick walked up.

"Here are my favorite people in the world," he said in greeting.

Everyone rushed to lift their glass to his performance while he slid into the booth and pressed a kiss to Mel's lips.

"Don't cheer for me. That's what the tip jar is for. Save your exclamations for this story I'm about to tell because, y'all, I swear it's all true."

Half an hour later, the news about Jesse Storms had taken on a whole new depth. *Mel* was his bride, and she'd left him for Nick. She'd walked out of the church, gotten into a cab, and gone straight to Nick's apartment. According to Mel, Jesse was fine. All the drama had indeed been played up for publicity before he set off on an extended tour. According to Nick, he and Mel were living together.

Nick in love. The ultimate holy shit moment.

We talked for a long while. When the tabs were settled, Will leaned over and said in my ear, "Come home with me?"

I turned my head to whisper back and brought us nearly mouth-to-mouth. "Do you even have to ask?"

Nick and Ben fell into step on either side of Will in the time it took for me to grab my purse. He glanced over his shoulder with a raised eyebrow. I started to follow, but Celeste linked our arms.

"Walk with me, Liv. Tell me about Will. What does he do? How do you know him? How long have you been together?"

"I guess you could say we go way back. Why? And what are the guys up to?"

"They're just introducing themselves. Your friends love you."

I stopped walking and faced her, hand on my heart. "*I* love *them*. What's the point?"

Celeste pursed her lips, but her eyes smiled. "You're different. When did you become so mellow?"

I laughed. "Oh, please. I can still kick ass."

"No doubt." She threaded our arms again, but I nudged her shoulder as we walked to let her know the question still stood.

"Ben and Nick wanted Will to know how much you mean to us. Just in case you decide to fall in love with him," she said.

The laugh that welled up came out like a nervous whinny. "Ease up, guys. We've barely been together a month."

Celeste snorted. "I'd *known* Ben for a month before you said to me... what was it? 'You mean you *don't* know he's crazy about you?'"

I smiled at the memory. "I know Will's crazy about me."

"Mm-mm. You two are clearly crazy about each other. I didn't know what you thought you saw that night we met, but I understand when I see you—and Nick—these days."

"You are *way* ahead of yourself," I muttered over my heart in my throat. Celeste just hummed.

We stopped at my car and said goodbye, promised to get together for a girls' night soon, and then laughed at how different that would be. When she'd gone to join Ben, I got in my car and followed Will to the Gulch.

I met him at his front door since I had to park in the guest lot. He pulled me in for a kiss and said, "How about wine on the terrace?"

"Perfect."

We walked in, and I hung my purse on the hook by the door he'd reserved for me. While he uncorked a bottle, I went to the bathroom and pulled my hair into a ponytail, then stashed the brush in "my" drawer and pulled out the bottle of makeup remover that sat there, too. It made me smile every time to notice the little ways he'd made space for me in his home. I wanted to be cool about it, but oh, my god, did it feel *good*.

He handed me a glass when I floated out to the terrace. I sat down and propped my feet on his thigh. Will chuckled as he slipped my shoe off and massaged my arch, like a fucking perfect boyfriend would.

"Is everyone you know in the music business?"

I laughed. "It feels that way sometimes. What can I say? I grew up in Music City USA. Nashville earned her nickname."

"What's your favorite song of all time?"

"'The Rainbow Connection.' My grandma used to sing it to me. It's so beautiful." I smiled, suddenly choked with nostalgia. "What's yours?"

Will shrugged. "I've been deep into Jason Isbell lately. 'Cover Me Up' is a favorite."

"Go you, picking a local artist! That's a love song to his wife, right?"

"Mm-hm. Talk about beautiful."

I knotted my fingers and blurted the question on my mind. "Hey, so, what did the guys say to you?"

He swirled the wine, an amused smirk on his lips. "Oh, just your basic vetting of the new guy. Nothing of note."

My frown made him smile deeper.

"It's fine. I'm glad to know your friends look out for you. It's a bit ironic, though, considering I've known you longer than all of them."

"Celeste said they wanted to get to know you in case we decided to fall in love."

Wow, good work, genius. Yet again, a rewind button on life would be useful. Couldn't keep that train in the station at all, could you? Next stop, awkward town.

But the awkwardness was the least of my problems. The worst part of my free-falling stomach was the reason behind it. Deep, deep in the places of myself I never let show, I desperately wanted him to confirm that we were, in fact, already in love. I wanted to hear I wasn't crazy for thinking my feels were real. I wanted to hear that he got the early flight because he wanted to come home to the person he *loved*.

Will's hand froze on my foot, his face shuttered in that famously guarded expression. "Olivia," he said softly.

Damage control. Play it off. No big deal, nothing to see here.

Before he could say more, I dropped my feet, drained the wine, and gave him a saucy eyebrow. "But that would be absurd, wouldn't it? My friends are great, but dial it down guys, right?"

He leaned too, tracing my jaw. "Liv, maybe we should talk about—"

"Shh." I pressed my finger to his lips. "You've forgotten something, Langer. Your games got you in trouble last weekend. I suggest you stop while you're only this far behind."

His brows lifted, and my stomach tentatively began to find its rightful place again. I stood, hands on hips. "I've had a whole week to plot my revenge. Where do you keep all those pretty ties of yours?"

Will hissed in a breath and loomed over me, fingers sliding into my hair. "Dammit, Olivia. I spent six hours in an airport, almost half of them in lines and on the phone, just to get a flight home. Do you honestly think I endured all that bullshit so you could exact revenge for a little teasing over dinner?"

His voice was dark and deep, but definitely not annoyed. I licked my lips and fisted his shirt. "Yeah, I do, actually."

He tilted my face up with a jerk on my hair. "Damn right. So do your worst. I dare you."

The sun had barely slashed a few streaks of orange across the sky when I shuffled back out to the patio to breathe in the fresh air. Snuggled into the blanket wrapped around my shoulders, I leaned on the rail and gazed at the city.

"I love you, Will Langer," I whispered to the morning.

Alone, it was such an easy thing to say. So delightful to hear. *And besides, if these swollen lips and bite marks don't scream love, what does?* I laughed.

The sliding door's swoosh made me glance over my shoulder. Will yawned and scratched the back of his disheveled head. Even with those curls standing out at every conceivable angle, he defined sexy. He grinned and came to stand behind me, arms hugged around my ribs.

His wrists in the pale light made me hiss. I caressed the red ring of raw skin. "Holy shit, that has to hurt. You shouldn't have strained so hard on that bind."

"Couldn't be helped. You drove me completely wild." He kissed my ear but eased away from my touch.

"Do you have aloe? I'll dress it for you."

"After how filthy you were last night? I'm surprised you'd be so sweet."

His tease made me laugh and turn my gaze up to him.

"Aren't you exhausted?" he asked when I didn't reply. "We haven't slept."

I nodded, but neither of us cared. His lips got closer, and

I leaned in. Then it was just us again, drunk on this need to taste each other and completely unable to stop.

Maybe it was that moment. Maybe it was the cooling weather that made body contact more cozy than sweaty. Possibly it had something to do with how happy every other couple we knew seemed to be. Whatever the reason, after that weekend, Will and I got decidedly greedier about time together. I created a work routine that kept me prepared for each day, and Will's project in Chicago had reached a milestone that meant he would stay in town for now. I started texting him to come over when Tom worked the night shift and endured my brother's teases when I'd announce I was out for the night before skipping off to CrossFit. Things were kind of beautiful, easy and fun, for a good run of time.

But "all good things must come to an end" is a cliché for a reason.

28

LIV

"You're killer at those pull-ups now. How many can you do in a row?" Will said as he escorted me into the restaurant after a Monday CrossFit session. A few paces ahead, Megan spotted Adam waiting for us at a table and hurried on while we followed.

"Eight," I said proudly. "I want to hit ten before Thanksgiving."

He removed my coat and hung it on the peg beside our booth, skimming my shoulders and arms. "CrossFit isn't the only place I've noticed you have more stamina."

I smirked. "Amazing how many benefits exercise has, isn't it?"

"Come on, geeks. You can make out later," Megan called from where she sat snuggled under Adam's arm. I laughed and flipped her off, but her answering grin summed up a shared thought. Double dates were *awesome*.

In the month since I took Will to the You & I show and officially introduced him to Megan, dinner after CrossFit had become a regular event. They got along far better than

I'd have ever predicted. Adam's home remodeling business had begun to take off, which meant he'd cut back on working at the restaurant and was thus freer in the evenings. He still had his Wednesday shift, so the three of us had started going to CrossFit on Monday just to double date.

The guys spent the meal deep in a conversation about hockey while Megs and I discussed our friends. Ben and Celeste were throwing a party on Halloween this coming Saturday, David and Kira were off in L.A. competing on a talent contest, and Nick and Mel were shacked up and too adorable for words. On top of that, Ben and his brother, James, were designing an app that could make them a lot of money. There was plenty to discuss. We chattered until the table was cleared, then traded another smile while our guys split the bill.

"This is so corny," she said.

"Super lame." I grinned back at her. A glance at Will made him cut his eyes my way. He winked, and *god* did my silly heart swell.

We were at the exit when the chilly rush of air made me remember my coat. I insisted Megan and Adam head on. When they left, Will guided me back to the booth. He grabbed the jacket and held it out for me.

I got one arm through before I stopped dead.

"Liv?"

"Um." I swallowed hard. "Will... Erin's here."

I saw his head snap up in my periphery, but my gaze was on her growing smile across the room. We were both statues as she set her martini glass down and scurried over.

"Well, well." She giggled.

I tried to think of something, *anything*, to explain this, but got nowhere.

She clapped and hopped up and down. "I knew it! Oh, my goodness. I *knew* it!"

"You knew what?" Will rumbled in a pretty damn scary pitch.

Erin laughed at him. "I've thought all along that there was something between you two with the way you're always play-fighting. Both of you are so great. There's no way you'd really hate each other. I've wondered since the beer festival if y'all had something going on."

"Since the beer festival? How did you—"

But Will cut me off. He held one palm up as if she were a feral animal. This time, his voice was cautious and soothing. "Erin, Tom doesn't—"

"Have the first clue," she agreed. "It doesn't occur to him. I don't know why. Y'all are so cute together!"

I couldn't appreciate her genuine delight, couldn't accept her compliment. All I could whisper was, "Erin, please, please don't tell him."

Her nose wrinkled. "I'd never meddle like that."

I took a deep breath and nodded in thanks.

She glanced between us. "Could I ask why *you* haven't told him, though?"

"We only—"

"We've been foolish." Will's sigh killed my attempt to explain. He rubbed his eyes and sighed again. "Incredibly foolish."

Erin's brows knitted. "Well, whatever your reason, it won't be me who says anything. I should get back to my colleagues. They'll wonder where I ran off to."

She tried to smile, but the way she looked at Will made me follow her gaze across the room. A table of professionally dressed women sipped colorful cocktails by the bar. Not a hair was out of place among them, even at the end of the workday. They talked and laughed, but my attention hung for a moment on a stylish blonde whose gaze didn't waver from us.

Erin touched our arms. "I'll see y'all soon."

I watched her go and noticed the blonde again, but there was no room in my head to consider anything more at the moment. Will took my hand and hustled us out to his car at top speed. The cool leather seat helped quiet my pulse. I stared out at the night and refused to be the first to speak.

Will finally broke the silence. "We have to tell Tom. It's not fair to ask Erin to keep our secret. God, I can't believe I've been so—"

"Foolish?"

"Yes." He drew a long breath.

"That's what we are? A pair of fools?"

I tried to resist when his fingers cupped my jaw, but Will demanded my gaze. "*Never.* I'm the fool for having avoided this for so long. Tom's not going to like us together, Liv."

My heart twisted. "You don't know that."

His humorless smile made my stomach clench. "I do, actually. I'm not good enough for his sister. Too much baggage. Too many emotional scars. Too withdrawn."

I gripped his jacket. "He didn't say that."

"He didn't have to."

"He never thought that! He'll say it was me. That I'm too—"

Will pressed one finger against my lips. "Not you. Me. He did think it... When I told him I was interested in you."

My heart was ready to leap out of my mouth. "When?"

"Eight years ago."

Check that. My heart stopped. "What?"

He exhaled hard. "Liv, I kissed you that night. And we—"

"I remember."

I turned away as the rest of that night crashed through the barricades my memory had built around it. I'd made myself forget that kiss. How could I bear to remember if I was to protect myself against the humiliation that came after? Talk about foolish.

We'd kissed when I wound up sitting too close to him. I remember leaning against his arm and feeling more turned on from staring into those black-brown eyes than I had in all my short life. I hardly knew what I was doing, but I parted my lips. When he leaned in, I nearly passed out. It wasn't more than a kiss, but good god was it hot. Possibly even more amazing was the fact that he was so sweet to me after. He'd wanted to keep talking to me, had made me feel so interesting as we chatted through that night.

I had gone to bed thinking of nothing but him and the connection I was sure had formed between us. I'd dumped my current boyfriend and floated through the summer, so excited for his and Tom's next visit home that I bought a new dress.

It had red flowers on a white background. I remember staring at it after he walked in, flicked that flat expression on me, and muttered, "Hello, Olivia," before walking past.

Foolish girl.

Tears stung as I looked at my fingers. "I remember, Will."

"What's wrong?" he asked, voice now full of the exact kind of affection I'd wanted so long ago.

I shook my head, sniffling.

"Liv, what?"

"I remember." My voice cracked. "God, I was naïve. I thought... fuck. This is why it's better not to care." I balled my hands into fists. *You're That Girl who doesn't give a damn, remember? Hold onto that.*

I huffed. "Whatever. If Tom likes it, if he doesn't, does it matter? The biggest danger at this point is the fallout when we're over."

Will didn't move or speak, but the air in the car froze over and left no doubt about his reaction. "When we're what?" he asked finally.

"Will, face it. When we end, it'll be messy. You and I aren't the type to hug and agree to be friends. We came together rough and wild. I'm sure the end will be something similar. I hate to think of putting Tom in the middle of that."

"But what if we don't end?"

I shook my head. "That's a fairytale, and I'm no princess."

"You don't have to be a princess to find a good match. We're a good match."

I tried my best to tip my lips into a smile. "We are. But everything ends, and eventually you'll..."

The table of ladies flashed into my mind. Their crisp suits and perfect hair and skeptical eyebrows mocked me.

"I'll what, Olivia?"

"You'll decide that you need..."

Before I could say the ugly truth aloud, my phone went off. The ringtone was garish in the car's dense quiet. Worse, it was Tom. He'd been called in early, so could I get home *now*? Like, five minutes ago now? He was stressed, and all this talk made me even guiltier than usual about leaving him hanging.

By the time I ended the call, I'd lost my nerve and all desire to hash this out. I took Will's hand. "We're not over. I didn't mean we were, and I don't *want* to be."

His shoulders eased a fraction with a heavy exhale. "Good."

He squeezed my fingers. All I wanted was to cling to him until everything else went away. I swallowed hard and seared a kiss on his lips before stepping out and going to my car.

His door slammed just as I fired the engine. Will flung my door open and practically hauled me out. My back pressed against the car as he leaned close.

"I love you, Liv," he breathed. "Fuck it, I *love* you This is the worst moment to tell you, but I don't give a damn. I need to know you know."

For no logical reason, I shoved him. Tears pooled in my eyes as I wailed. "You douche! I have to *leave*. I can't hear that now."

He twisted his lips. "I know. Maybe that's why I said it now."

"I hate you, Langer," I said, but my face split with a goofy grin that made him chuckle.

"I hate you too, Milani. I hate that you have to leave before we can finish this. But I love you more."

"I love..." I bit my lips and scowled. "Take that back. I can't handle it."

His expression collapsed, but he pressed on my heart. "But you know it here, right? Even if I take it back, never say it again, you have to know it here."

He pressed harder as he kissed me. I was dangerously close to falling into hysterical pieces, but abruptly he was gone, headed back to his car.

"Langer?"

He paused. "Yeah, Milani?"

I pointed at him as tears pooled in my eyes. "This isn't done. We'll talk next time."

His lips quirked. "I should hope so."

Every time I replayed that conversation in my head, I noticed another unfinished idea that hung between us. He couldn't possibly understand my train of thought based on what was said, and I still had no clear understanding of why he was so sure about Tom.

But, *Fuck it, I love you*, made effervescent bubbles explode in my heart. Yes, there was the Tom mess, and yes my fears about our future were too real, but—*fuck it, I love you*.

With that in my head, I was unprepared for his phone call just before bed the next night.

"Hey there," I said quietly as I shut my bedroom door.

"Hey."

Three letters carried that many tons of tension. My chest tightened when he skipped all pleasantries and got straight to the point. "I leave for Chicago Sunday night for a month."

I dropped to my vanity bench. "A *month*?"

"I know."

"Do you still want to go to Ben and Celeste's party on Saturday?"

"I can."

Something's off. "Not if it's an inconvenience."

He didn't reply.

"Will? What aren't you saying?"

"We have to tell Tom before I go."

My stomach rolled like a boat on the ocean, but I swallowed hard. "I agree. We can't wait for another month. How about Friday? We could go for a beer or something."

"I was thinking Sunday morning. There's a gala Friday night that I need to attend."

"Gala?" I mentally flipped through my wardrobe. A house party was one thing, but a gala? *Maybe Megs can help me find something.*

"Mm-hm. A lot of schmoozing and small talk. Boring music for boring dancing."

I laughed. "You're selling it well."

"Yes, well, it's not the sort of thing I enjoy. I hadn't planned to go, but Stacy called me today. It's her firm's event, and she gave me a guilt trip about networking and appearances."

Someone pressed my pause button.

"You're... you're going with Stacy?"

"No," he exclaimed. "No, I'm going alone. She just called to remind me."

"You're going alone. To Stacy's party."

"To her *firm's* party. I wouldn't put you through that, Liv. You'd be bored as hell. Believe me, it's the opposite of fun."

But I'd be with you. Don't you get that?

I stared at myself in my mirror, at the thin line of my lips and the pink and brown hair fluffed out around my shoulders. "Will you wear a tuxedo?"

"Yes, it's that kind of function. Why?"

My vision blurred. "Send me a picture, please. I'm sure that's a sight to see."

"Liv? Are you okay?"

A blink and my cheeks were wet. Two streaks turned into a mini-stream before I bit my tongue and wavered, "'Course I'm okay, William."

"Don't do that." His sharp tone made me flinch. "I told you, I'm *going alone.*"

"I heard you."

"Then don't put on a jealous act."

"There's no acting needed," I snarled through the tears, then took a deep breath. "Fine, whatever. Please tell me there's no more to add."

"I'm crazy about you? Can I add that?"

"Sure, Will. Thanks."

I disconnected the call without a goodbye and flopped down on my bed. *Ugh, and we didn't even make a plan for telling Tom. Great. This week can't get better.*

Foolish, foolish girl.

29

WILL

Eight years ago, after a night of talking and a kiss that rocked my world, Liv left the next day without telling me goodbye. For that, I admired her more. How could we look at each other in the daylight after spending the entire night baring our souls to each other? Besides, we had to be logical about this. Figure out how to proceed.

In the fall, I reasoned, she'd be in Knoxville for college. I'd be in grad school. Perfect setup. I let it lie for a while, played it cool—I thought—and waited until the summer was nearly over. Tom was moving home since our lease was up. I would help him move his stuff and go for a visit with the Milanis.

"Got any plans while we're in Nashville next weekend?" I asked one day while we watched TV.

Tom grunted. "Just hanging out."

I kept my eyes on the screen and said, "When does Liv leave for college?"

"I think it's the weekend after," he muttered, mouth full of chips. "What's with you? You bring her up a lot lately."

"Bullshit."

"No, it's not. What's the deal?"

I took a long pull of soda. "Nothing. It's just that the last time she was here we talked about maybe hanging out or something."

His eyes darkened. "You and Liv? Just the two of you? Like, a *date*?"

His spin on the word told me what he thought of that. I shrugged and looked away. "Whatever."

"No, it's fucking not whatever." Tom jumped to his feet, arms crossed.

"Sit down, Thomas. You're getting all pissed over nothing."

"Do you like her? Look at me."

I sighed and met his stare. "She's cool. She's coming up to Knoxville in the fall, and I thought we could hang out. What's your problem?"

"My problem is this. She's eighteen, she's my sister, and I look out for her. It's one thing for geeky high school boys to drool over her. Liv can handle them without batting an eye. But *you*. Don't take this wrong, but I know you, dude. I know your background. It made you intense as fuck. She can't handle all your baggage. Not to mention how I don't want to even *think* that you've got the hots for my baby sis. Got it?"

"I don't have the hots for your baby sis." I arched a brow. "Got it?"

He sat down. "Damn straight," he muttered.

My logical, over-analytical approach to navigating a world I'd been introduced to only four years ago was too much for Tom's precious sister. The brilliant Liv Milani was too good for a boy with dubious heritage and plans to be a self-made success.

End of story.

One week later, we walked into the Milani's house. Liv

stood by the sofa wearing a pretty dress and even prettier smile.

One week later, she put those eyes on me and murmured, "Hi," softer and shier than I'd ever heard her be.

One week later, I clenched my jaw, remembered that the Milanis were the only family I had, and ripped my gaze and my thoughts off Liv Milani the only way I could.

"Hello, Olivia."

30

LIV

"Good morning, Miss Olivia!"

I greeted Mrs. Olsen with a smile while her son Jackson toddled into the classroom Thursday morning. Attempting to get through the week in one piece, I'd been MIA at CrossFit last night with only a brief text to Megan. Will had called after, but I'd let it go to voicemail. Thank goodness for work to keep me focused.

"How is everything?" I asked, taking Jackson's coat.

Mrs. Olsen smiled, but her brow was creased. "We're okay. Jackson's not feeling great, but he doesn't have a fever. He didn't have much appetite and was sleepy this morning, so I gave him some baby aspirin. Hopefully that'll sort him out. I let the front desk know he could have another dose after noon if he needs it."

"Another dose after noon. Got it. Have a great day, Mrs. Walker."

It was a normal morning of playing, counting, and alphabet. Lunch and recess were outside because the day was mild. On the playground, I watched Jackson. He didn't run, but he played with his friends as usual. We trooped back in for story and naptime. My assistant, Emma, and I sat in our chairs as peaceful breathing took over the room.

Everything was fine until the moment it wasn't. Monday was fine until the moment I saw Erin. Tuesday was fine until the moment Will called. Today, that moment began with the telltale sound of a child vomiting.

It was a gross and sad sound all at once, as I'd learned over the past few months. There was the retch and dry heave before the inevitable wet splat, immediately followed by sobs.

I leapt to my feet at the first hack and scanned the room. One of my girls sat up on her little mat. She squealed and pointed even as I moved down the row. "Jackson's sick!"

He was still on his back, which was weird. Kids usually sat up when they were about to puke. A trail of liquid began to seep from his lips, and my strides halted. Except for his jerky stomach, his body was still. Arms lay limp at his sides, face blotched white and red, eyes closed.

This is wrong.

An invisible cold hand clutched my heart as his eyes flickered open. More vomit trickled down. He blinked rapidly, stomach heaving faster.

The seizure started in his hands.

Time lurched into slow-mo. Jackson began to convulse, and I threw myself to the floor beside him. I tugged his collar from his neck with shaking fingers, then tried to keep a grip on his shoulders. *He'll choke on the vomit.*

Somehow, I rolled him to his side. His lips fell open. Puke streamed onto the mat even though he kept thrashing. I held him and looked up at Emma who stood over me, stunned.

"Call 911." I couldn't hear my voice, but I must've said it

coherently because she pivoted and ran for the door, phone in hand.

His tremors subsided, but I held on firmly. Two minutes or an eternity passed before a swarm of people descended. I stared down at him, hearing nothing but my heart in my ears as my arms jerked with his intermittent residual spasms. He began to cough and spew more bile from his lips, face a ghastly gray.

Firm hands closed around *my* shoulders and pulled me back. I resisted but was hauled to my feet. An EMT took my place to check Jackson's vitals. Another EMT still held me, somewhere between a reassuring hug and a restraint. Jackson was moved to a stretcher and wheeled out. I started to follow, but Mrs. Harris, the head of the daycare, blocked my path.

"Olivia. Olivia."

Her voice was the first sound I registered. I blinked hard.

"Olivia, listen to me. They've got him. His parents are on their way. You need to stay here."

"No, I—"

A chorus of wailing stopped me.

"Your children need you. They're scared. Focus where you're needed, okay?"

I nodded. She squeezed my arm and stepped back to follow the stretcher.

I looked around at a swarm of stricken faces, all looking to me for support. With a deep breath and no time to think, I pasted on a brave smile. "Hey everybody, it's okay. Jax got sick, but the doctors will make him all better."

Fourteen four-year-old voices blasted me with questions and sobs. I glanced at Emma, who looked as lost as I felt. "Let's have story time," I announced. "Everyone to the rug!"

We herded them to the corner and passed out juice and

cookies. Little bodies snuggled all around while I read. One picture book took most of the afternoon to get through with all the worried questions popping up after every page.

I was at work over an hour late to answer questions as parents came in. I had no details, but I advised them that their children would be concerned tonight. Gentle support and reassurance to assuage fears was my expert recommendation.

Maddie, I learned, had been collected by Mom. Rachel had heard the commotion from her classroom down the hall and called my parents to help out. I gave my colleague a grateful hug before floating to my car and essentially auto-piloting home.

The moment I parked in the driveway, bottled-up adrenaline broke free in my system. Before I completely crumbled, I fished my phone from my bag. I was shivering by the time he answered.

"H-hey, sorry, but... I..."

"What's wrong?" Will asked.

I couldn't speak. I curled over and put my head on the steering wheel.

"Liv? Are you hurt?"

"Nuh-uh."

"Where are you?"

"Home."

"I'll be there as soon as I can." The line went dead.

I opened the car door and swung my feet to the pavement to lean between my knees and breathe. Images of Jackson's little body wouldn't quit my mind. I shivered under the horrible helplessness. The dread of not knowing his status. The guilt that I didn't do more.

Will's Audi rolled up. I didn't move as his strong footsteps approached. "What happened?"

I glanced up at the sound of his voice. Will's shoulders were squared and even more imposing than usual. His jaw set hard as his gaze swept the scene, clearly ready to spring into action.

"Will."

I reached out my hand. One look at my face made him rush to me. He knelt on the pavement in his pristine suit and gripped my hands, his expression melting into nothing but worry.

"What happened, baby?"

"Will... this little boy..."

I lost it and bawled just like my students. He grasped my elbows to pull me into his arms and walk us inside. In the living room, I broke away and paced while I babbled the story in broken, hiccupping sobs.

"And then he disappeared on the stretcher. I have no idea if he's okay. I should've known he was sick. If I'd..." I covered my face against a fresh bout of weeping.

Will folded me into his arms again, his suit coat cool and crisp against my blazing hot face. "Shh, Liv, breathe. Just breathe. It sounds like you did everything you could. It sounds like you were amazing."

"N-no, I should've known he was sick."

"How could you? You said he was playing. You monitored him, and you cared for him when it got bad."

Nothing helped. I shook my head.

My phone began to sing while Will stroked my hair. He released me, went to my purse which he'd dropped by the door, and looked at the screen. "It's a local number. Should I answer?" I nodded. "Olivia Milani's phone. One moment."

I took it and hummed a hello. "Olivia? This is Susan Harris. I'm at the hospital with the Walkers. Jackson is stable. The seizure was from a fever spike brought on by infection, but the fever broke just a few minutes ago. He's stabilized."

"Oh, my God, Mrs. Harris. Thank you for calling. I was so worried."

"I know, dear. Get some rest. You and I will talk tomorrow."

We said goodbye, and I looked back to Will. "He's stable, thank God."

Will exhaled. "Thank God," he echoed.

We sank on the couch side-by-side. I leaned into his shoulder, and he leaned right back.

"I'm sorry I interrupted you at work," I said after a long silence. "You didn't have to take off."

"Of course I did. You needed me."

"I did." I pressed my face into his sleeve. He was the first —the *only*—person I'd thought to call, dammit.

I got to my feet and pushed my hands into my hair. A harsh laugh burst from me. "Damn you, Langer."

Will cocked his jaw. "Excuse me?"

"I said, *damn you*. Do you have any idea how much I hate that I needed you today?"

"I'm good with you needing me."

"Well, I'm not, especially with the bullshit you're—oh, I'm sorry. I'm not supposed to *play hurt*."

"You're mad about the party," he mumbled. "Liv—"

A messy sludge pumped through my system as I sneered. "I know, how silly. Flighty, temperamental Liv isn't over the fact that you're going on a date with another woman? Gah, girl, let it go. Right?"

Will jumped up. "It's not a date! I told you—"

But I sliced my hand across my throat. "Please don't insult me. You're going to a party with a woman you used to fuck regularly. Don't pretend otherwise."

"It's *business,* Liv."

"Business, sure. Question: was she the blonde at the bar with Erin?"

The realization popped into my head as I spoke. Will inhaled slowly and gave a single nod, which was all I needed to understand the whole thing.

"Of course she was. Business, tuh. Here's the *business.* You're letting that woman make a fool of me, and it says a lot about our relationship. When you accepted her invitation, you told her everything she needed to know about how easily she could come between us if she wants. And based on the timing, I'd say she wants."

"I'm not a sleaze who can't keep his dick in his pants. I'm not even going with her!"

"Sure, sure, and nothing will happen tomorrow. But this opens a door for lunch, drinks, maybe a quick stop by your office one evening... Please, Will. I know how women like that work."

"You're wrong, Liv," he muttered, but the line appeared between his brows.

"Am I? Think about all the women you know, all the professional women you work with. Would any of them ever let their man go solo to a party like this? What if you were married? Would you dream of going to Stacy's gala and telling your *wife,* 'you stay home, sweetheart, while I suit up in a tux and go out for the night'?"

He didn't answer, but his jaw was set and his eyes were wide. I knew I'd made my point.

I answered for him. "No woman who a man took seriously would have to deal with that. I get it, though. A pink-haired daycare worker isn't taken seriously. I completely get it."

Determined not to cry again, I forced a laugh. "This is

why I didn't want to tell Tom. This is why we can't work out."

Will loomed over me. "How can you say I don't take you seriously?"

I shook my head. "It's not just that. I can see you see my point, but what does it matter? It's only time before Stacy or June or whoever wins."

Will Langer had never looked so dumbfounded. I pushed out another laugh. "We both know that eventually you'll need a woman who drinks martinis, drives a BMW, and wears heels to work. A woman who would fit in at a fancy gala. La Perla panties *should* be on your floor, Will. You'll need a woman who matches you—"

"Olivia."

"—And I'll never be her."

There it is. You said it. My head bowed under the weight of those words.

"What in the proper fuck are you talking about?"

Tears slid down my cheeks too fast to hide, but I threw my head back and gripped his coat. "Just kiss me, Will," I wept.

Kiss me as often as you can before it all goes away.

Will put his hands on my shoulders. "This conversation isn't done," he vowed, but he folded me into his arms.

His mouth yielded to mine and absorbed my frustration in equal stride with my fire. The world didn't vanish like usual, but the cold inside me warmed considerably.

"What the *fuck*?"

I jumped out of my skin at my brother's voice. We whirled to see him in the doorway, fists clenched. My hand flew to my mouth as if that would erase the burn of Will's lips.

"What the *fuck* is going on here?" Tom slammed the door so hard the walls shook.

Will met his gaze. "Liv had an emergency at work."

"So you came over to put your tongue down her throat?"

All three of us cringed as the words flew out of Tom's mouth, but Will shook his head. "I came to be with her."

Tom's teeth ground together as his glare turned to me. "Since when do you call *Will* for comfort?"

"S-since we... um..."

"Since when?"

"This summer," I whispered.

"This *summer*?" Tom roared, and I stepped back. "Are you kidding?"

"Tom, listen," Will began.

"Shut up, asshole. You're supposed to be my best friend, and you do this to me? This *summer*? And you," he pointed at me. "How could you?"

"Tom, stop please," I begged. "We never meant to hurt you."

"Oh? Then why didn't you tell me?"

"At first it was just a—or, I mean we didn't..."

I fumbled as Tom flinched and Will inhaled. The implication of my words became too clear too late. "I meant we..."

"You what? Screwed my best friend—in our house, I assume?" He shot a dirty look at Will, but his words were knives with my name on them. "I've never judged you, Liv, but *god*."

"Careful, Tom." Will's stepped forward with a glare. "Liv and I are adults. How we began is our business and not for you to judge."

I snapped at him before I thought it out. "Really? You defend me now, but you let some lawyer make a fool of me?"

Will spun around, surprise written on his face. "Now isn't the time."

"Now seems to be the time for everything we pretended wasn't a problem. Tom, we didn't know how to tell you because we went from kind of hating each other to being crazy about each other so fast. Then we were afraid of... well, I guess of this moment."

Tom sneered. "You lied to me instead. How perfect." He took a breath, then threw his keys at the wall with a shout. "I cannot *believe* this."

"It wasn't about you, Tom," Will said quietly. "We were going to tell you this weekend."

"Oh, sure. What a coincidence."

"No, because we saw Erin..." I nearly severed my tongue to shut up.

"Erin knows?" Tom barked. "Does everyone know?"

"Not... not Mom and Dad." I looked down as tears spilled again. "But Megan and Erin—they figured it out. They could *see* it, Tommy."

"This is my fault?"

"Of course not. The fault is ours. I'm saying we didn't have some kind of debut that we didn't invite you to. It got away from us is all."

Tom rubbed his face and glanced between us. "What the hell is supposed to happen now, a group hug or some bullshit like that? Because I want none of it."

"No. We just want you to understand—" Will tried.

"I understand that you're fucking my sister and I'm supposed to be happy about it, but screw that. You want my blessing? Go to hell. Olivia, I don't even know what to say to you, how I can begin to trust you after this. And as for *you*," Tom pointed at Will. "I want you out of my sight. Twelve years of friendship, man. I thought I knew you."

"Don't do that, Tom," I wailed. "Don't throw away—"

"Shut up, Liv."

Will growled. "Don't talk to her—"

"Don't speak for me," I snapped at him. "You and I aren't good right now, and I don't need your help."

The three of us traded wary glances in a triangle of disaster.

Finally, I shook from head to toe with anger and regret. "Fuck this whole scene. A kid almost died in my arms today, and you two are standing there like total dicks."

I pointed at Will, tears flowing but voice powerful, "Just leave. I don't want to talk to you, with your little lawyer friend and your *function*."

Of all the curses I've ever spewed, none of them were nearly as venomous as the f-word I just dropped. It was so hateful that both men flinched, but I kept my jaw cocked.

"With the mess we've made, maybe you just go on to Chicago and leave me the hell alone to sort out *this*."

I turned to my brother. "As for you, Thomas, you want to take a difficult situation and make it as miserable as possible? Bravo, brother. Mission accomplished. I discover the best relationship of my life. Will makes me happier than anyone ever bothered to even try to. On top of that, he's adored by my family.

"And you're going to take it from me. This was the reason I didn't tell you to begin with. I was afraid you'd be hurt. Then I was afraid you'd say I wasn't right for him. But now I see how dumb both of those worries are, how not your business we are.

"So *both* of you can go fuck yourselves because I don't have the space for any of this right now."

I held up two middle fingers, bowed deeply, and took my exit.

My pillowcase absorbed a flood of tears until wretched misery and a soothing soundtrack of The Beatles pulled me into a fitful sleep. I don't know what happened downstairs, and honestly it didn't matter to me one bit.

I was a total mess at work on Friday. I'd slept terribly, and my worry about Jackson heaped on my own troubles had me jittery from the moment I rolled out of bed.

But Mrs. Harris called me into a meeting early in the day. While I sat with twisted guts and knotted fingers, she reassured me that Jackson had held stable overnight and was due to be released this morning.

And then she told me I'd saved his life. The EMTs said if I hadn't turned him on his side, he likely would have died, either from choking on the vomit or from pneumonia if it got in his lungs. I had been *collected* and *ultimately professional* under great stress. I was to be commended. I was an asset to the school.

Well, damn.

In typical fashion, Megan was a champion bestie when I showed up at her house straight from work. She did my hair and let me pour out my dramas over whiskey, ice cream, and 80s movies. She even got me to laugh as I bemoaned missing the chance to see Will in a tuxedo. By the end of yoga Saturday morning, I was a little more Liv again thanks to her.

31

LIV

Ben and Celeste's party was an engagement/Halloween thing at a trendy spot downtown. I wanted to bow out, but Meg threatened me with violence if I didn't show off my new hair. She'd blended orange and red with the pink to make my ends look like flames. It was perfect for Halloween, so, even though I was in no mood, I dressed in a simple black sheath and knee-high boots with my trademark MAC in Rebel.

Tom was watching TV when I headed out. He didn't look up while I got my coat and keys, but he did say, "I apologize for how I spoke to you."

I nodded.

He still didn't meet my eyes. "That doesn't change how I feel about you and him. God, Liv. Of all the possible people, why'd you have to go for *Will*?"

"I didn't, Tom. We just happened."

He grunted. "You're right that it's your business if you want to be with him, but I don't want to know about it. I *definitely* don't want to see it."

Bile crept up my throat. "You're breaking my heart."

"Broken hearts are life, Liv. Goodnight."

"I love you, Tommy," I said finally, refusing to ruin my makeup.

But I love Will too.

I shut the door and decided it was time to woman up and say it to the person who needed to hear it.

The venue was a restaurant and lounge in SoBro that was known for good food and a hot dance floor on the weekends. By the time I arrived, most of our group had already assembled, and the DJ was starting to set up.

Megan greeted me with a kiss on the cheek. "Gurl, you are stone-cold sexy. Who does your hair? And that dress! Me-oww!"

I laughed, but my stomach clenched as I took a seat. I was the only one flying solo that night. Adam and Megan were on my left, Nick and Mel my right, and Ben and Celeste were cozy and adorable at the opposite end. Across from me, Jack Spencer sat with his lady. Even James Addison had a date. I'd never seen her before and doubted I would again, but still.

The problem wasn't being single. The problem was being without Will. *One beer. Then, off to the Gulch.*

But hanging with my friends was always a favorite place to be. Conversation swept me up through dinner. Appetizers, vegetables, pulled pork, and cornbread were delivered on family-style platters while Mel and I discovered a shared love of music. Since I'd barely eaten all day and everything was delicious, I helped myself to seconds and let a little more time pass while we chatted on.

The lights got low as the music started. Ben and Celeste

grinned and joined hands. "Come on, guys. It's time to dance," Celeste said as they got to their feet.

The rest of the couples were right behind them. Adam asked for my permission to take Megs.

"Go have fun. I'm gonna finish this beer and take off," I said with a wave.

Megs blew me a kiss, and they disappeared. I started to reach for my bottle when the chair to my left me was suddenly occupied.

"Oh. Cam." *You again.*

"Lovely to see you, Olivia. It's been a while. You look fantastic. Different hair, right?"

"Yeah."

I hadn't seen Cam since that awkward encounter in the bar across from Will's, but he showed no hint of recalling how we'd left off. He just winked and sat back to watch the dancers.

Megan's hands landed on my shoulders. She sat in the chair to my right and grinned. "Hey, I just wanted to check on you. You're leaving?"

I nodded. "Yeah, I need to talk to him before he leaves for Chicago. But I'm fine. Go have fun, silly."

She looked over my shoulder. "Who's that? He looks familiar," she whispered.

"Just some Chad." I rolled my eyes, not bothering to turn around.

"You're sure you don't want me to sit with you?"

I pointed to where Adam was waiting and put on my Tennessee twang. "Go on, get!"

Megs laughed and squeezed my shoulder once more as she left. I looked back at the spread on the table and frowned. Two bottles of beer sat close together, angled among plates and napkins.

"Wait. Which beer is mine?"

Cam studied the bottles, then lifted one to the light. "Hmm. I think this is mine. Anyway, if I'm wrong, you know I don't have cooties."

He grinned, but I cringed. *I kissed you four months ago. Let it go already*. My beer was a little flat, but I drained it anyway to get my money's worth.

"So," Cam said as I set the bottle down, "I didn't expect you to be alone tonight."

32

WILL

I stared at the dark TV. No point in putting on something I'd have no interest in watching. Besides, the quiet helped me think. Strategize.

Problem was, no strategy seemed to take me where I wanted to be. I couldn't figure out what path led to my arms wrapped around Liv while we laughed about what a sap I was for being so hopelessly in love with her. No easy road opened that would let me right the colossal fuckups I'd managed to create this week. Stacy and Tom hated me, and I gave not one damn. Liv wasn't here. She wasn't here, and it was my fault.

So how the hell do you fix it? You asked her to trust we were worth it, and she's afraid—

My phone lit up. I jumped to my feet when Liv's name appeared. "Liv? Listen, I—"

Loud music blared behind her. "Will Langer. We are so, *so* wrong for each other. I give up. They all win. Goodbye, William. We're over."

The line went dead.

Dread thundered through my bloodstream. Not from

her words—from the nearly unintelligible slur she'd said them in. I raced through our text history, scanning desperately for the name of the restaurant she'd said we were going to tonight.

You're not there, asshole. Get there. Something's wrong.

33

LIV

Blink. *Focus.*

My phone was in my hand, the screen still lit. *Why? Who did I call?*

Purple dots swirled on the walls in time with a pounding bass. Bodies moved around me. *Right. They're dancing. I'm dancing too.*

Hands held my waist. I moved against him and let my hair swing as we rolled together to the music. *Why can't I see his face? Right. Because my eyes are closed. Open up, silly.*

Hazel eyes gazed at me. His hands slid to my ass. Our bodies ground harder. Something wasn't quite right, but I found it hard to care.

"Liv? You okay?"

Turning my head made me dizzy. I saw Nick beside me. *Why the frown, buddy? This is fun, right?*

I smiled and nodded. "I'm good. I'm great." My tongue was a little thick. "You good, Nicky?"

Nick frowned again. Before he said anything, I was spun away, deeper into the crowd.

I giggled. "Sorry about him."

"I don't care about anything but you, baby." His hands were all over me.

Holy shit, I am so drunk.

The music changed. I tried to step back, but he wouldn't let me go. I pressed my hand into his chest to get some space. "I needta pee."

"Come back quick, okay?"

His face was too close. He smelled like cologne and e-cigarettes. I pushed again. He released me so I could go to the bathroom.

It was small. Two stalls, both full. I waited, washing my hands and staring in the mirror. Except for my eyes, everything in the reflection undulated like a fuzzy old TV. *How many drinks did I have? How long have I been here?*

I touched my cheek, but it was like I'd been shot up with Novocain. I gave myself a little pinch. *Are my hands wet or not?*

A toilet flushed. I bumped the woman who came out. She glared at me. In my mind, I apologized before shutting the door and dropping to the seat. My head swam as I relieved myself. The other toilet flushed, but I just sat with my forehead on the cool metal of the stall wall, even though I could barely feel it. *The Novocain seems to have spread.*

Blink again. *Did I pass out? How long have I been on this toilet?*

All thumbs, I hitched up my panties and stepped out of the stall.

He was leaning against the wall opposite the sink. I did a double-take. *Isn't this the women's room?*

"Got lonely without you, baby. Thought I'd risk it and come see you."

I laughed while I washed my hands. In the mirror, I saw

my eyes and the blur behind me. A paper towel ripped to shreds in my clumsy grip.

His hands caught my waist, his chest against my back. He breathed on my ear. "Sexy Olivia, you know we've got chemistry. Why do you keep turning me down?"

Deep in my fuzzy brain, an alarm went off. I opened my eyes.

Fingers clamped tighter on my hips. Alarm number two blared. I tried to stand up straight, shaking my head no. *Dammit, why is my tongue so thick?*

His fingers moved along my thighs. I was pressed into the counter so hard it hurt.

"N-n-n," I tried to speak again, shaking my head.

"You don't mean no, do you?"

Hell yes, I mean no. I shook my head. It was the wrong answer to the question he'd asked.

"Good. I knew you wanted me after the first time we made out."

His hands were all over me. On the dance floor, that passed as a move. Now, panic began to rise in my throat. In the mirror, my eyes were still the only thing in focus, wide and fearful. I bared my teeth to confirm that my face was still numb, but he spun me around.

"Stop," I tried to say.

He grinned. "What do you want me to do to you, baby? Start with a kiss?"

I swayed backward as he plunged his tongue into my mouth. When he pulled away, he pried one of my hands from the sink and guided me into his jeans. "Touch me. You know you want to."

I deserve to have what I want.

The thought floated up through the murk of my brain. I inhaled deeply to center the hurricane of delirium inside me. My palm closed around his hardness. He started to moan.

Until I squeezed and didn't stop, then twisted my wrist.

"The fuck are you doing?"

He shoved me away so hard I stumbled. I flailed in a pathetic attempt to slap him, but he spun me to face the mirror again. His fingers raked up my thighs. Through fear and fog, I knew I was running out of time.

The dark brown eyes in the mirror screamed at me to sober up. Krav Maga moves began to flip through my head. I focused hard on remembering what I knew.

"Badass boss. In training for life," I whispered to myself. *You're good at what you want to be good at. You've got the moves. You've got the muscles. Fucking use them.*

A fire lit in my gaze.

He continued pawing at me as I raced to remember how to fight off an attack from behind. *Get him to hug you. Then, get ready.*

Relaxing was impossible, but I leaned back into his chest. He paused those icky fingers and took a deep breath. "Good girl. Come here." A kiss landed on my hair as, sure enough, his arms wrapped around my chest.

I rested my hands on his—and then tensed up hard. My grip tightened and pushed down as I rocked my shoulder and hip to the right. Megs and I used to laugh that this was combat dabbing, but there was no time for humor now. I ducked under his hug, pulling him forward with my momentum. My fists slammed down on his back as I brought my knee up into his stomach once, twice.

"Fuck," he shouted.

He twisted away from the attack. I jerked my knee again, forgetting that the right thing to do was back away and put my fists in guard. Bad mistake. He shoved me, and I stumbled against the sink. My ears rang from the backhand he threw to my jaw. Another blow struck my temple by my eye, but the numbness in my face muted the impact. I spun around to escape the assault and found myself in the mirror again.

Take what you want.

I wanted to hurt him. I wanted to *kill* him. But I had to find my center in this mess if I wanted to even escape him.

"Don't turn away from me. Get back here."

He tried to turn me by the waist, but my feet were planted, knees braced. While he kicked at my boots to try and make me yield, I lifted my right arm parallel to the floor, fingers curled into a fist. *Deep breath, girl. This will hurt.*

I rammed my elbow backward. His face stopped the momentum, but I didn't care. My fist flew forward.

My eyes in the mirror disappeared. I drove into the shattered glass, and this pain definitely registered. The shards ground into my skin, just as I'd wanted. My wrist twisted, breath held to grind as hard as I dared before I flew backward, thrown against the opposite wall.

Blood leaked from his busted lip. I must've clipped his mouth with my elbow. He was the angriest monster I'd ever imagined.

"You should've just let me make this nice. I don't like to play rough, but if you insist," he growled.

Brace for impact.

Even though I saw it coming, and even with his pathetic, puny arms, the double punch to my stomach stole my breath. Most of my defense moves had drained out of my head by then, but I curled into myself and ducked away.

"No, no, no. Get back here, Olivia."

He reached for me with his right hand. In the moment before he grabbed me, I knew what to do.

In a flurry of nightmarish seconds, every single ounce of strength I'd been building at CrossFit came into play. I held his wrist and jackknifed his arm, but not to free myself. His elbow bent at a hard angle, which took his attention to that pain. I clamped tighter on his wrist with my left hand and pulled, making him tip downward just enough.

My right fist, the one I'd been saving, arced up by my ear and came down with all my might against his temple. Pain rocketed up my arm as the bits of glass drove deeper into my knuckles, but they ground into him, too. I twisted and dragged my knuckles down his fucking ugly face, imagining I could hear the glass tear his flesh.

His feeble block came far too late. All he could do was bat at my already-retreating strike. He screamed as he recoiled, his hand to his cheek. His head dropped back in pain.

It was the gift I'd counted on.

No hesitation. This was my tenth pull-up. My final burpee. I used all the power I had left to let my fist fly straight to his windpipe.

Cam fell to the floor, eyes glazed. The roaring ocean in my head got quiet. I gulped air until I was lightheaded as I gazed down at him. *You're killer at those pull-ups now... Liv Milani, did you sweep the leg?... Oh, god, get me out of here.*

Finally, I pushed off the wall and straightened my dress. He was still on the floor, semi-conscious, so I buried the heel of my knee-high boot between two ribs for good measure. A wheezy groan was all I heard while I grabbed my purse from the floor and clawed at the lock on the door.

Outside that hell, the party went on like I didn't just fight for my life. The air out here was cooler but stuffy, too, and the music made my head pound. *I'm exhausted. Sleep would be so great. Maybe then I could sober up a little. How did I let this happen?*

"Don't cry," I whispered as I stumbled down the little hallway and out to the main dining room.

Where are my friends? Where is our table? Maybe Megs can call me a cab home. The bar is to my right. Not far. Water would be nice. If my feet wouldn't tangle over each other so much, I'd be there already.

I grabbed a chair to stay upright and spied a flash of red hair—Mel, with Celeste beside her at the bar. *I'll say good-night, congratulations...*

"Celeste," I tried to shout, but my throat was dust and my tongue was still thick.

They heard me, though. Both women's eyes went round as they fixed on me. I cringed in embarrassment to be so fall-down drunk. *Talk fast and get out of here.*

"Hey, ladies, great party. Celeste, I'm so happy for you and Ben. You, too, Mel, you and, um, yeah. Cheers."

"Olivia?" Celeste grabbed my arm. Her voice was strange, full of something I couldn't name.

I winced at her touch. "Yeah, sorry. I know I'm a little..."

I covered my mouth and coughed hard. When I looked down, my hand was coated in blood. I couldn't be sure if it was mine or his.

Keep it together. Don't ruin the party. Jesus, I'm tired.

Hand hidden by my side, I looked at them again and struggled to smile. "Celeste, I need a favor."

I fumbled for my phone and thrust it toward her. "Will... my Will... can you call him? Tell him I'm sorry. So, so sorry." Tears and darkness blurred my vision.

"She's about to pass out," Celeste said. "Keep her talking, Mel. Someone call the cops! Ben! Ben, over here!"

The cops? Who, me? No, I'm just tired.

I forgot about the blood and palmed my eyes. Nothing registered beyond fatigue. "I'm sorry I'm so..."

My tongue stopped working. Celeste disappeared. Mel's lips moved as she gently tapped my cheek, but all I could do was plead silently with her to understand. *Please call Will. Please tell him...*

I stumbled backward into strong arms. Panic surged, but when I forced my eyes open, Ben was holding me. He lifted me, and in his arms where I knew I didn't belong, it made sense that I could rest now.

Blink. *Focus. I'm moving? God, the light. Ow.*

At first, the only sense that worked was sight. Squares of fluorescent light flashed past. A couple breaths later, I could feel, too. I was lying on a moving bed. My hands screamed with pain. My mouth was covered with something hard and plastic. I couldn't talk. Hearing came back. Squeaky wheels and a chorus of chatter filled in the scene.

And the voice I'd prayed for.

"Olivia? Can you hear me? Look at me, Liv. I'm here."

My gaze gravitated toward the dark command of his voice. I blinked back tears of relief. I wasn't sure where I was, but it didn't matter. *He's here.*

"Liv, can you hear me?"

I tried to nod, but it hurt. Tears fell.

"She's awake." He looked from me to—where?

Several people began speaking at once. We turned and slowed down. The words, "Stomach pump," and, "Sutures for her hand," made me tense up in fear. I understood where I was.

Don't leave, Will. My eyes screamed at him. I reached out

with the hand that hurt less, but something restrained my movement.

Will was still there, his face cut with panic and fear. "Baby, what happened?"

I could tell he didn't expect me to talk. I squeezed my eyes to try and make the tears stop, but they wouldn't quit. He reached out and swiped them away with his thumb. It only made more pool up.

"...Toxicology report and rape exam..."

Will's head jerked at those words. He paled and gripped the bedrail. My tears gushed even harder. I wanted to explain so damn bad. He looked at me, and I shook my head no.

It's enough for now. I can tell him later. Once I'm sober and don't hurt so much. Please stay, please be here when I wake up, please, Will...

34

LIV

...Not comfortable with you here.

Your comfort isn't my concern. I have to know what happened. I will tear that fucker to pieces...

You and me both. But consider this: she said she didn't want to see you. Do you think she wants to deal with this conflict while she heals? Please, just go to Chicago and leave our family to get through this.

When at last I took a lazy swim up to consciousness, I looked around. The bed was white. My hand was wrapped in white. My papery gown was white. I turned my head to the window, and a rainbow of flowers blinded me. The only thing on my mind was a monstrous thirst.

"Livi?" Tom was on his feet from a chair in the corner, over me in a flash. He pressed two fingers to my throat, eyes on a monitor above me. "You awake, sis? How many fingers am I holding up?"

"Two," I croaked.

Tom palmed my forehead and lifted my eyelids. He shone a light in each and fussed when I tried to jerk away. I guess he was satisfied because the torture ended quickly.

"Water." I was dying. He put a cup in my hand. I frowned to see ice.

"Eat the ice first," Tom said. "You need to go slow."

I packed my mouth with as much as I could stand. The cold sharpened my senses. The moisture was a lifesaver. Tom brought the chair to the bed and waited to speak while I gobbled the whole cup.

"Better?"

"A little," I said, relieved that my tongue worked properly again at last. My voice was raspy, but at least words came out like I intended them to. I cleared my throat and tried again. "Yeah, a little better."

I tipped the cup for a final droplet. A million questions and worries crept in. I didn't know where to start. Before I could ask him anything, a flock of people arrived. Nurses, three doctors, and my parents, who looked so gray and scared that my heart twisted, crowded around. I tried to smile.

Mom pushed around the lab coats and wrapped me in her arms. Her scent washed over me, and my tears began to soak her shirt. She whispered in my ear, calling me brave and saying how proud she was of me.

"Mom, she shouldn't get her pulse up," Tom said.

Mom hissed. "Let me hold my baby."

No one dared argue.

I was so thoroughly prodded and inspected by the medical team that I felt like tenderized steak. They said I could be released the next morning, but police and a psychiatrist were waiting to talk to me ASAP.

"What time is it?" I asked when they finished.

The doctor checked his watch. "It's sixteen hundred hours—four pm—on November two."

I frowned. "Wait. Yesterday was Halloween."

Yesterday was *not* Halloween. The sedatives they'd given me were pretty powerful. I'd slept almost two days. *Holy shit.*

"Well, now, Ms. Milani, are you up for a little chat?"

The medical team had barely vacated when two policemen strolled in. My family made a little wall of squared shoulders around me, but I leaned forward. "I guess so."

Detectives Carlino and Watts said my family could stay. When they asked me to recount what happened, I clamped my mouth shut and looked at my ghostly mother.

"They need to leave," I said quietly.

Mom wiped a tear, tossed her hair—must be where I got that gesture—and said, "You don't think ignorance is bliss, do you?"

So, I told it all. Mom, bless her heart, had to muffle more than one sob along the way.

The cops seemed pretty impressed, but the interrogation wasn't over. They asked a ton of questions that basically resulted in a second telling. I had to recall everything I'd had to eat in itemized detail. I repeated three times that I wasn't sure how much I'd had to drink. The whole thing was starting to piss me off when they sat back and held up a sheet of paper.

Watts cleared his throat. "*We* know how much you had to drink, Ms. Milani. Roughly twelve ounces of beer. It's the one-point-five grams of Gamma-hydroxybutyrate we're concerned about."

The room went silent.

I gripped the sheet. "What?"

"GHB? Gamma-OH? Georgia Home Boy? It's a popular

narcotic on the club scene. It's also..." Watts trailed off, assessing my reaction.

Don't do drugs. Drugs are bad, m'kay?

I kept that in my head this time. Things started to make more sense, and my teeth clenched along with my fists. "Are you telling me I was roofied?"

"I'm telling you that you ingested GHB. However, it was a very small dose, and you did it on a full stomach. The fact that you're in excellent shape definitely slowed the effects, too. That's probably why you were able to stay conscious enough to fight off your attacker. Are *you* telling *me* you took it involuntarily?"

"Damn right," I growled.

All these years. All the clubs, concerts, and nights out. Never had I been drugged.

I. Was. Furious.

The cops and my family cleared out pretty fast. I guess my story and reaction told them what they needed to know. The therapist arrived right after to find me flushed with rage, still fisting the sheets.

"Roofied?" I barked at her.

Poor woman, she startled and hurried to sit down. "Let's talk, Olivia. Tell me everything, and don't edit. I can handle it."

A stream of profanity mingled with broken thoughts poured out until I could see straight again. When my pulse monitor stopped beeping so loud, I leaned back against the pillows.

"I want him dead," I said simply. "Tell the cops. I don't care. I want him *dead*."

She shook her head. "Only if I feel you're in imminent danger of breaking the law. Wanting and plotting aren't the same things. But I do think you and I should continue talking after you're released tomorrow. Healing is a process."

"Where is he?"

"In another hospital. He's being monitored by the police. They had to hear your story before they knew what to do."

"I hope his fucking windpipe is broken."

She nodded. "Hairline fracture was what it said on my report. Ribs, too."

I smirked.

Dr. Huang put on a serious face. "You'll go through stages as you process this. I encourage you to journal about it and bring those notes to our sessions."

I nodded, but the only stage I could see "going through" anytime soon was revenge on that smarmy fucker.

The rage had ebbed by the time Dr. Huang left, replaced by hunger so great that I wolfed down a whole tray of hospital food. After that, the nurse helped me with a bath.

My appearance hadn't occurred to me until I walked into the bathroom, but my reflection stole my breath. Purple and yellow welts streaked across my hairline and both cheeks. It was worse on the right, where the bruise seeped under my eye, too.

"Oh, my god." With shaking fingers, I disrobed. The sight of my body made me stumble backward in shock. "Oh, my *god*. I'm a mess."

Red and purple marks slashed across the tops of my thighs. The bruise on my abdomen was violet, navy, and green. Deep and angry.

The nurse touched my shoulder gently. "No, Ms. Milani. You have some bruises, but you walked away from an attack on your own."

Her words put me somewhere between pride and guilt. I had walked away. I had fought with all I had to save myself.

But it didn't bring me peace when I thought of all the women who couldn't fight back. Whose battle had to be fought harder afterward when healing and recovery seemed impossible. Why should any woman, *ever*, have to fight for her dignity, for her body?

I'm not special. But, like all women, I am strong.

It was late by the time I'd dried and dressed in another paper gown. Clean at last and with food in my stomach, I felt a lot better, even if I was exhausted again.

I was reading the cards on the flowers when my door opened. Tom came in, still dressed in his scrubs. He stood by me to look at the flowers. "Mom and Dad went home for the night. I just wanted to check in before I left. These flowers started arriving yesterday. Your colleague Rachel volunteered to keep Maddie when we called the daycare. You are loved dearly, sis."

"Yes."

"By me too, you know."

"I know." I perched on the bed.

He leaned against the wall and shut his eyes.

"Tom," I said at last, stomach fluttering. "Where is Will?"

I held my breath while he got still, the muscle in his jaw tight. "Chicago."

Someone must've opened a window because chills crawled down my body. I scrambled into the blankets and pulled them high. "Chicago? He... he just left?"

"He has business to attend to, and you have your family. Speaking of, do you need anything?"

I did not.

"Then Mom and Dad will take you home tomorrow

morning. I work seven-a to seven-p." Tom hesitated, then reached out and touched my hair. "Baby sis, I'm so glad you're so strong."

And with that, he was gone.

I was not to blame. Nothing that happened that night was a result of my carelessness. I did not have this coming because of anything I had done in my life.

Those were the things Dr. Monica Huang wanted me to know. It took two sessions for her to realize that those were things I already knew. No, hell no, I didn't blame myself. I blamed *him*. If anything, I blamed myself for not breaking his fingers the first time he ever put his hand on me.

The good doctor finally got the message that anger, not guilt, continued to be my coping mechanism. She dropped the gentle tones and serious face, threw her pen in the air, and crossed her legs. "Well, hell, Liv. Why don't you fight for the cause, then?"

And with that, I had a new "thing."

Tuesday nights became time to volunteer at a women's shelter. I got involved with Strings for Hope, and I signed up to run a 10K in the spring to raise money and awareness.

That was the best therapy I could've asked for. Having a constructive outlet helped with the anger. It also helped with the frustrations that began to mount as soon as I got home.

Within a week, Cam was charged with assault. I had to give a statement and press formal charges. The cops made me come in and take a billion photos of my wounds. Every trip to the police station made me queasy with horrific memories, but I'd be damned if that dirtbag got to walk.

As I recovered, my family's concern was sweet. After beating the shit out of a grown man, though, it seemed a little absurd that they barely let me feed myself. When I was finally allowed to drive, I went to see Mrs. Harris. Going back to work was all I wanted to do, but no such luck. She gently informed me that my students wouldn't understand why their teacher looked like an MMA fighter. It wasn't all bad, though. My job was waiting for me, *and* my benefits were still in place. Although I ached to return to the routine, I couldn't argue.

Life was a roller coaster of doldrums, frustration, and anger for those first weeks. I wanted my old life back. Even the mess with Tom beat this new reality.

But most of all, I wanted my Will.

35

LIV

The elephant who hung out anytime Tom and I were in a room together didn't detract from the care he took of me. It took two Saturdays for him to approve of yoga again, and then only under my solemn vow to listen to my body and take it slow. Megan offered to pick me up and treat me to a ladies' day out. After two weeks of reality TV, I was delirious with excitement to escape the house.

"Look at you, you fuckin' warrior." Meg flashed a bittersweet grin when I opened the door that morning.

I opened my mouth for a snappy reply and promptly burst into tears.

She was close behind, throwing her arms around me and sobbing. "You are the baddest-ass boss in the world, you know it?"

"I learned from the master." I squeezed her tight before we wiped our eyes and went inside. "But can we skip the waterworks from now on, please?"

She sniffled and sneered. "Definitely. It's gross and you're loud."

My best friend.

In the kitchen, I put a homemade protein bar on a paper towel. "What do you think?" I asked while she chewed.

She wiggled her head in a "Not bad" gesture, and I cut one for myself.

"Yeah, Luna's chocolate coconut is better. Whatever. I was bored as hell."

Tom and Maddie walked in as we finished eating. Megan squealed when Maddie rushed her for a hug, but her smile slipped when she faced my brother. "Good morning," she said, frost in her voice.

"Hey, Megan." Tom avoided her eyes as he poured coffee and checked on me, but Megan's death glare followed him until he collected Mads and retreated outside.

Megan shrugged at my sharp look. "Sorry. I know he's been through a lot too, but he is totally on my shit list. Come on, we'll be late."

"No way in hell is that the end of this story." I picked up my mat and followed to her car.

My inquisitive stare resumed promptly over brunch. Megan ignored me as long as she could but finally spilled.

"I know Tom's pissed about you and Will, but his attitude to his supposed best friend at the hospital was disgusting."

"*What*?"

She scanned my face. "Shit, you're already pale. I'm—"

"Starting at the beginning and not stopping till you reach the end. I can handle it."

Megs sighed. "Let's see... I was dancing with Adam when Will showed up."

"Wait. At the bar? Why?"

"For you. Why else? Anyway, you weren't at the table, so I told him I thought you'd left. Before I could text, blue lights flashed outside and the cops ran in. Then we saw Ben carrying you." She shuddered. "Will and I raced to catch up. They let him ride in the ambulance when we told them he was family. I drove his Audi to the hospital. That was fun."

Her grin was a much-needed break. We both drew a heavy breath before she went on.

"All of us went to the hospital, of course. Will finally came into the waiting room. He said you'd woken up for a few, but they made him leave so they could, um, pump your stomach." She blew out another breath. "Sorry, dude. It's hard to talk about."

"I know," I muttered.

"I called Tom, but he was already on his way. Will had called him. He came in frantic, but as soon as he saw Will, he iced him like he was a stranger. Wouldn't let him go see you when the doctors said family could go back. Wouldn't speak directly to him. All that bullshit. Your mom was the one who insisted Will go with them."

I put my head in my hands.

Megs sighed again. "Like I said. I know Tom's going through it, too. He still shouldn't have been such a dick. Everyone knows you and Will are in deep-end love "

My head snapped up. "Excuse me?"

Megan stared at me a long moment, then threw her head back and laughed. "Olivia Maria Milani, do *not* play yourself. Have you really not admitted that you love each other?"

"He said it once," I mumbled.

"And you dropped your panties and said it back, right?"

I didn't answer.

"Right, Liv? That hot, hot man declared his love, and you..."

"It wasn't like that, okay? And anyway, that was before, and he was nervous because..."

I took a deep breath against the all-too-familiar sting of tears. Crying was so old hat by then. "I think if we were really in love, I'd know it."

She gently gripped my fingers. "You do know it. Babe, it's all over your face. Do you think Will *wants* to be away from you right now?"

"He's gone, Megs," I whispered. "Tom and I *both* sent him away. Why the hell would he still love me?"

"Liv. I'm pretty sure that when you're as in love as y'all are, a little distance doesn't make it stop."

"Everything ends. He'll see what a hot mess I am."

Megan's brows wrinkled. "Hot mess? Hardly. You never were. Now? You've gotten all grown up lately. Committed. It looks good on you."

"Me? A grownup?" I laid a hand on my heart.

"I know, right? And I'm sure Will sees it, too. On the other hand, he's known you through a lot of your life. If he's seen all your ups and downs and still looks at you like that, he's *in*. Question is, are you?"

I twisted my lips. "I hate it when you're a sage."

She flipped her hair and smirked.

"He looks at me like what?"

"He fucking smolders at you. Like this." Megan flared her eyes, then narrowed them tight in a pretty damn good impersonation before she collapsed in laughter.

For the first time in ages, I laughed, too.

According to the internet, vinegar, vitamin C, and sunlight helped heal bruises. Eager to get back to work, I took walks every day, washed my face in vinegar, and ate grapefruit for breakfast. By that Saturday with Megs, I didn't draw as many double-takes from strangers. After a third week, a strong coat of foundation was all I needed to hide the remaining marks.

I damn near danced on the ceiling when Mrs. Harris said I could come in on the Monday before Thanksgiving.

Time still crawled. Friends visited. I played with Maddie. I listened to Jason Isbell a lot. The more I healed, the more the chasm between Tom and me grew. The silence was tight, but I could tell we were both more sad than angry anymore.

Mom held our first family meal in a month the Sunday before Thanksgiving. Thanks to my pleading eyes, we got to eat in the breakfast nook at last. The cozy kitchen chairs did little to ease the weight on everyone, though. Conversation was thin. The usual chitchat and updates were replaced by brief exchanges and forks scraping plates. I wanted so badly to brighten everyone up with stories, but my heart just wasn't in it. The best I could do was promise to bring whipped potatoes and my famous brownies for Thursday's meal.

My phone chimed as Mom cleared dishes. Celeste and Mel wanted me to go to a movie later, so I glanced to confirm the time.

Will: I just need to know you're okay.

I pushed back from the table, stumbled down the hall to my parents' bed, and curled into a ball.

"Liv? What's wrong, love?" The mattress dipped as Mom sat and bundled me into her arms.

I buried my head in her lap. "Mom, what happened while I was unconscious?"

She stroked my hair. "I prayed and prayed."

"No, tell me the story. Please?"

"Oh. Well, we got a call from Tom in the middle of the night. I knew something was wrong as soon as the phone rang. We rushed to the hospital and learned what had happened. They'd sedated you. All we could do was pray and wait with everyone else."

I looked up. "Who?"

Mom furrowed her brow. "Let's see. Benjamin and his fiancée—lovely girl. Megan, of course… There were quite a few others I didn't know."

She paused and then added, "Will was there. *That* was a surprise."

I didn't move. She didn't say more. "Did you talk to him?" I finally asked.

"What kind of question is that? Of course I did."

"What did he, I don't know, say? Do?"

"Do? He did what we all did. He waited. He worried about you. As for what he said, well. I guess he didn't say anything that wasn't obvious from the look on his face."

She scratched my back. "Why didn't you tell us, baby?"

"Didn't know how," I mumbled. "It's a mess now, though."

"Oh, messes can be cleaned up. Don't wallow over that. You saved a child's life and stopped a monster with your bare hands, all in a week. You can deal with a little relationship bump. Now, come have some tea, my darling daughter." She pinched me, and I smiled as I let her pull me up.

Back at the table, I sipped peppermint tea and covertly typed under the table:

Me: I'm okay, thanks.

Good god, you're a douchebag. I stared at my words and knew no reply would come from such a milquetoast sentiment.

"Is Will back from Chicago in time to join us for Thanksgiving? I'd like to know how much turkey to buy."

"I don't know this year, Mom." Tom's voice was flat and hard.

"I wasn't asking you, Thomas," Mom said without hesitation. "Livi?"

I jerked my attention back to the conversation. Tom stared at his plate, but Mom and Dad both smiled at me.

"Uh... honestly, I have no idea."

"Well, try to find out so I can get my groceries by Tuesday. Okay?" Mom winked at me.

Tom growled in the silence that followed. "Really? We're all just acting like Liv and Will together is perfectly normal?"

"What's not normal about it, son?" Dad asked. "They're grown people. If they want to be together, well, we know he's a good man. I'm just glad our girl's happy and in good hands."

Dad smiled at me, and I blushed hard for more than one reason.

Will's hands. Damn, I missed that part.

Dinner ended with hugs and final details for Thursday. I buckled Maddie into the backseat of Tom's SUV, then jumped in the front as he started the engine.

"Olivia, we need to talk," he said on the drive. "Let's have a beer at home."

Déjà vu tickled my neck. "Okay, Tommy," I agreed, but I didn't need to wonder what this was about.

Maddie settled in with crayons and a show while my brother and I yet again gathered at the table and clinked bottles. Dry since Halloween, I took a long gulp, pleased to know that Jackalope IPA tasted as good as ever. At least some things hadn't changed.

Tom put his bottle down and tented his hands on the table. "You go back to work tomorrow, right?"

I nodded. "Mrs. Harris said the short week would be good to ease me in and make sure I was ready."

"Good." He blew out a hard breath. "Look, Liv. I told Will to go to Chicago. He didn't want to leave, but I reminded him that you'd asked for space after our... showdown. I asked that he respect our family's need to get through this. So, he left."

My lips curled into a snarl, but I didn't speak. Tom dropped his gaze.

"That was a mistake," he whispered. "I see how sad you are. How far apart we've become. I misjudged how serious you were about him."

"How serious I *am*."

"Exactly. No man will ever be good enough for my baby sister, and the idea of you two together freaks me the hell out. But all that said, I'd rather deal with it than tear us apart or break your heart. Our family is everything. Livi, I'm sorry, sis. I'm sorry I hurt you, and I'm sorry I sent him away when you needed him most."

I exhaled. "Thank you. I accept your apology, I really do. But it doesn't mean things are better, does it? Our 'showdown' that afternoon came at the worst possible time. Will and I had been fighting about that lawyer's party—"

"Party?"

"What's her face? Stacy."

He shook his head. "Will canceled on that party the morning of. Erin had to listen to Stacy complain all day."

No. More. Crying. I swallowed hard. "Um, anyway. There was that, then you. *Then* my shit went down, and you sent him away. I don't know if we're still together. If we can fix this. I don't even know if he wants to."

His shoulders dropped, expression softening. It was the Tom I used to know.

"Oh, hell, Liv. I can tell you right now he'll want to fix it. I think Will's been crazy about you forever."

Tom closed his eyes and rubbed his temples, so he missed whatever my face did when my stomach hit the floor.

"I hated the way you'd give him those wide eyes when you were in high school. You were too young, and he's got a kind of tough background. It made him really intense and driven."

"I know."

"Of course you do. Anyway, just when it seemed like you'd grown out of it, one summer you were all Will talked about. I told him to knock it off, that you were too young and couldn't handle him. He dropped it. I really believed you both couldn't stand each other after that. I should've known you were too much alike to not realize it eventually."

"One summer?" I croaked.

"Mm-hmm. Right after college."

"And... you told him... so he..."

I leaned back and closed my eyes. *Everything makes so much sense.*

How would life have been different if we'd connected so long ago? I'd never have become That Girl. Never have met my friends through Ben. Never have met Megan Riley on a busted Valentine's date. I'd never have smacked the shit out of Will back then, never ever. Never would've dared to go toe-to-toe with him. He wouldn't have pushed me into CrossFit. We would've grown up—likely apart, too.

I fell out of my chair and stumbled around the table. Tom rose and caught me in a weepy hug. I sobbed and dug my fingers into his shoulders. "Oh god, I hate you so much. Only half as much as I love you, though."

"I'm sorry, sis. I only ever wanted to look out for you."

Tom and I hugged until things got weird, and then we laughed and pushed each other away. I went upstairs to lie down and let my thoughts wander in the dusky light. As I stared at the ceiling, my body grew heavy, muscles still like in yoga. Only when the room was pitch dark did I reach for my phone.

Me: When r u done tomorrow?

Megs: Last appt @5.

Me: Book me for 530. Sharpen those scissors.

Megs: HOLY SHIT.

It's time for a change.

36

WILL

Chicago was fucking frigid, and it was only November. I didn't mind. There was absolution in the biting cold. Every morning before work, I ran along the water. The icy wind burned my lungs until I couldn't bear it and had to turn back. The brutal weather purged me. Banished all the warmth I'd become so accustomed to lately.

Nothing, no miles and no cold, could purge my guilt, though. I would carry that scar for the rest of my selfish fucking life.

Every day was the same cold, gray weather. Same routine. Run, work, bar, work, sleep. Weekends, too. If I didn't work, I had nothing. A man could only drink so much to pass the time. I wouldn't even let myself look at photos. Memories of our time together were a comfort I didn't deserve.

I didn't hear from her. After the first week of silence, I knew I wouldn't. By my final Sunday of exile, I broke down and texted. I had to know something, *anything*.

"I'm okay, thanks."

What the hell, Olivia? What do I do with that?

Like the giant asshole I was, I did absolutely nothing with it. I didn't have the nerve to reply. I itched to push her. I always itched to push Liv Milani. She was the only person I never doubted could take it and give back as good as she got. But this wasn't like before. She deserved the space. If cutting me out helped her heal like Tom had said, then so be it. I was raised to be on my own. I told myself I could accept it and carry on as I had all my life.

I never could lie for shit.

Our project wrapped right on time. The Tennessee crew was excited to fly out the day before Thanksgiving and get home in time for the holiday. As for me, that offhand non-answer only increased my ambivalence about returning to Nashville. I couldn't care less about turkey or days off.

Until Tom called Monday night.

I didn't usually leap for the phone, but I answered this call before the second ring. Silence greeted me at first. Finally, "Hey, man."

"Hey, Tom."

"Uh, listen. Mom wants to know if you'll be at dinner Thursday."

I waited for the punch line, or at least the up yours. Neither came. "I don't think that's a good idea," I said at last.

Tom sighed. "Dude, get your ass home. Come eat my mom's turkey."

We both chuckled, but he continued. "I wouldn't call if I didn't want you to be there. This is my apology. Don't leave me hanging."

Completely unprepared for this conversation, I drew in a breath. "I never meant to disrespect you."

"I know." He paused. "Mom wanted *her* to ask you about dinner. She..."

His tone was light, but it still punched my gut. "What?" I

asked, too anxious to care about subtlety. "Hates me? Wishes I was dead?"

He breathed a laugh. "No. She's scared you hate her. She doesn't know if you want to talk to her, if you still..."

We both knew how that sentence ended. *If I still love her. If I'd still swallow glass for a moment with her.*

My shock wouldn't shake. "If *I* hate *her*?"

"Mm-hmm."

I fell backward on the bed, too stunned to bother with words. Tom wasn't the one who needed them anyway, and he knew it.

He gave me a few moments to reel, then spoke again. "Come fix this. She's miserable. Come make my sister light up again. I give you my fucking blessing."

I chuckled, and it released a literal ton of tension. "What's the plan?"

By the Wednesday wrap-up meeting, I vibrated with nerves so badly that adjusting my tie became a tic. My bouncing knee shook the table and exacerbated the covert glances from colleagues.

Luke Paris, my favorite colleague in the Chicago office, eyed me during a short break. "Jesus, Langer. Did you over-caffeinate or what?"

I shoved a hand through my hair and thought twice about reaching for the carafe. "Must've," I muttered. "Anxious about my flight, maybe."

He hummed as we moseyed back to the table. "Chicago airports the day before Thanksgiving? Don't blame you."

"Do you have plans for the holiday?"

Paris cocked a brow. We'd hung out, grabbed drinks a

few times, and even gone to a Blackhawks game together. But we knew nothing about each other's personal lives. My attempt at civility gave away that there was a lot more on my mind than travel.

He had the decency to keep it cool. "No, I'm here in the city. I usually visit family at Christmas, and I'm... considering a little time off at the new year anyway."

I could tell by his tone that he'd just given me something on him, too. I made a mental note to follow up—after I got my life straightened out, dammit.

As the rest of us settled in for the final leg of this meeting, Paris remained standing. "Okay, ladies and gentlemen, I'll keep it brief." He clicked to a new slide. "We ran three marketing campaigns for this launch. My team..."

Paris's no-bullshit presentation was detailed enough to keep me focused and short enough that handshakes and farewells commenced a little earlier than expected. We nodded across the room before I all but raced to get a cab.

Delayed an hour. But *just* an hour. For the day before Thanksgiving in one of the country's biggest hubs, that wasn't too bad. While I waited on my luggage to come off the carousel at BNA, I looked around at people hugging their loved ones. If not for Tom's call, I wouldn't have noticed. Suddenly, I was really, really glad to be home. Just sleeping in my bed again would be fantastic.

Sleeping in my bed with Liv Milani would be even better.

As I eased my car onto I-40 in the purple dusk, I tapped the Bluetooth and commanded Siri to call Tom. He answered right away, so I said, "Hey, I'm in the car. Are we on for the Five Spot?"

His voice came through the speakers, muffled and hushed. "Change in plans."

My stomach clenched, but he laughed.

"Come to the house instead, and hurry. Liv's got ideas of her own. Big surprise, right?"

The line went dead. I gunned the accelerator and whipped to the far left lane, fingers flexed on the steering wheel.

The twenty-minute drive took exactly twelve.

My palms began to sweat when their house came in sight. I parked at the curb and all but sprinted up the walk. Her bedroom light boxed me into a yellow square as I knocked softly at the door. Fitting. Liv always had been the brightest light in my life. Through all the years and all her phases—even when she did little more than roll her eyes at me—she always was the person who could push my shadows away.

Tom clicked the lock quietly, but stealth didn't matter. Muffled but loud music hit me as soon as the door cracked open. He pulled me in for a hug/back-clap that said we were cool, then waved me inside. Maddie colored on the floor, her pink suitcase acting as a table. She lit up when she saw me. Tom rushed to kneel, his finger to his lips. She instantly mimed him, so I did, too. Before I got too cozy at this scene, the blaring music sank into my brain.

Fuck me. It was "Cover Me Up." I'd wondered if she'd listened. If she would realize that those lyrics spoke to how I felt for her.

Tom rose to give me an update, so I forced my attention to him.

"She was emotional after work today. The kids threw a surprise party to welcome her back. She went upstairs, then reappeared with that look on her face that says watch out."

I had to laugh.

"I stuck to the plan, suggested we go to the bar, but she

gave a flat no. She'd decided to—are you ready for this?—drive to Chicago tonight."

"You're kidding."

Tom rolled his eyes. "You think I'd make it up? This was about an hour ago. I stalled all I could. Got her to talk it out, look up the weather, check oil... I finally resorted to discussing whether I should take Mads to stay with me at Erin's tonight just to slow her down. She's been up there about half an hour, blasting music and packing. I thought I might need to blow the whole thing to stop her."

I scrubbed my face with both hands and blew out a hard breath. Good thing I'd run so much lately. My heart might not have handled all this otherwise.

Her bedroom door opened, and the music got louder. We both jolted hard.

"Tom? Are you about to go to Erin's?"

"We're on our way out, sis. You?"

"Getting my toothbrush and peeing, then I'm ready. I'll call you from the road, okay? Love you, brother!" The bathroom door slammed.

Tom and I traded another *holy shit* look, but then he clapped my shoulder and went to pick up Maddie. "This is your scene. Good luck. I'll see you tomorrow."

I respected the way he looked me in the eye to say that. "Thank you, Tom." *For much more than the good luck.*

Alone in the living room, I looked around as my blood began to thunder. I sank onto the recliner. The vision of her on my lap flashed.

Focus. We need to talk. I'll ask her... tell her... shit. How did you walk into this with no plan?

I raked my hair again. I had no strategy. No game. Never did when it came to Liv. Broken thoughts and points to make drifted through my head.

Every one of them scattered when I heard her footsteps on the stairs.

She thumped down two while I sat frozen in the chair, but then her feet retreated. A second later, the music died. The bedroom door shut as I leapt to my feet and knocked my knee on the coffee table.

Her feet came into view. "Tommy? I thought you left. Erin will—"

My gaze swept over her once, twice, and then again while she stumbled to the bottom step and clutched the banister. She wore black leggings and tank top under a long white jacket made of the softest-looking wool I'd ever seen. A matching white beanie sat on her head. Her dark bangs peeked out by her temple. The red and purple welts that had broken my heart in the hospital were mere shadows on her cheeks. Only someone who looked for them would notice.

She was so herself, strong and yet adorably stunned. The sight of her gripped me with a powerful thirst. It took an enormous amount of restraint not to leap the couch and haul her into my arms.

Wait, asshole.

I'd lost the right to push her. She'd asked me to do one simple thing, and I'd failed. All those runs along the water had trained me to brace for the cold that I absolutely deserved. I didn't get to hold her. Not unless there was no doubt she wanted me to.

Wait.

Wasn't that bag on her shoulder a clear indicator of what she wanted? The music meant a hell of a lot, too.

"Will?" Her voice trembled over my name.

Fuck waiting.

Liv startled when I vaulted the couch and crossed the

floor in two strides. Her hand flew to her mouth, but the second my arm cinched around her back, rose-red lips—no lipstick tonight—appeared again. I dropped my head on the same wave of momentum, dimly registering that her face had already turned up.

Liv Milani's kiss destroyed me every time. Her lips softened as she inhaled, and then her tongue found mine. Her tongue did things to me most men only dreamed. Her sweet-hot flavor, like honey with a kick of cayenne, flooded my system and turned me into a junkie.

Every. Single. Time.

A month without this fix had me out of my mind from withdrawal. Liv whimpered and clutched my hair when I bent her backward and drank her deep. She went limp in my arms, spine arched and body so tight to me that my knees shook. I groaned, and she whimpered again.

Thump.

Her bag hit the floor as she fisted my shirt and pulled, feet scrabbling to stand upright.

Bump.

My shoulder knocked the wall when I turned to lean on it. I spread my legs to fit her hips against mine. Her hat met my touch when I reached blindly for her hair, so I pinched the soft yarn and flicked it away, sliding my fingers to the base of her scalp and down—

My eyes opened because my hands were abruptly empty. Liv withdrew, confused by my confusion.

All I could do was stare.

The pink dye was gone. Her long, sexy locks had been chopped to a sleek style. It layered away from her face and barely touched her shoulders. Her big, dark eyes glittered with the rosy glow on her cheeks. Her plumped lips parted over heavy breaths.

My perfect, electric girl.

Liv fingered her hair but kept one hand wrapped around my arm. "Megs cut it Monday," she whispered, and I realized I'd yet to speak a word. "What do you think?"

"Perfect," seemed to be the best way to break the silence. I stroked her cheek, and her blush deepened. "Always perfect, Olivia."

She fidgeted, eyes darting side to side. "What are you doing here, Langer?"

I smirked. "What are *you* doing with that bag, Milani?"

Her gaze locked on mine, wide and guilty, but she returned my smirk. "Megan invited me to spend the night."

I laughed and pulled her against me again. "Bullshit."

Liv's pupils dilated as my lips grazed hers.

"Kiss me again," I said, somewhere between a command and a plea.

But she pushed my chest, and the well of pain in her eyes twisted my heart. "One more time?"

"Never," I vowed.

37

LIV

Ohgodohgodohgod...

My thoughts were haywire as I kissed Will. I begged him to stay, to understand, to never stop, all without saying a word.

Five minutes ago, I'd buzzed with anxious energy, ready to get on the road, face the music, and figure out where we stood. Now, if I stood on this very spot until I died, I'd be good.

When you hold me, my heart bursts. My words from this summer, back to haunt me. Final detonation began when he jumped the couch. Between our kiss and the sweet power of his embrace, my poor heart had atomized at last.

My heart. Over the years, I'd done a good job of protecting it. Sure, it had some dings and scratches, but That Girl had to learn not to give herself away. People called me sharp and bold, but that was how it had to be. It was how That Girl survived. Guy stopped calling? Fuck him. Another girl came along, and Mr. No-Commitment suddenly settled down? Good luck with that, buddy. My mouth had gotten me in trouble a few times, but it kept me going, too. Repeat *I don't care* enough, whether it's about relationships or dreams or anything, and eventually you don't.

But Will Langer made That Girl break Rule #1. He hadn't dared me or even asked for it. But again and again over so many perfect moments, I had completely, totally, given him my whole heart.

I would never, ever be the same. And I was terrified.

I tore away with a hard shove to Will's chest. "It doesn't get to be this easy. There's no way it's this easy. Why are you even here? That bag is there because I was going to drive to see you tonight. It doesn't work that you just appear and all's well."

"While I'm curious how you'd have worked out the logistics of driving through the night, finding my hotel, and then somehow obtaining my room number, I thought this might be simpler."

"Damn you. That's not the point," I grumbled, although those were indeed valid points.

"I know." The amusement was gone from his voice. Will sighed and leaned on the wall. "I'm here thanks to Tom. That doesn't mean I have the first clue how this goes. I let you down, Liv. The one thing, *the one thing*, you asked me not to do, and I let you down worse than anyone ever could. I can't ask for your trust anymore, and I don't know what you—"

"What are you talking about?"

Will fisted his hair and slid to the floor, eyes bright with more emotion than I'd ever seen from him. "I let you down. It was all you asked of me, and I failed you. I fucked up with Tom, and then that party bullshit. I didn't go, by the way."

"I know."

"If not for all that, I'd have been there when you needed me most."

Megan's story came back to me. "But you *were* there. Why?"

"Because you called and broke up with me. I could tell by your voice that you were out of it, so I came to make sure you were okay." He hung his head. "When I saw Ben carrying you... You'll never know how much I hate myself for not protecting you."

His voice splintered and cracked, and the space in my chest where my heart used to be constricted.

I threw myself to my knees and held his face. "Don't. Don't do that. You didn't let me down. You showed me what I could be. Take what I want, right? I thought of that, and I did. I fought him, Will. Because you taught me to believe in myself. You pushed me to be strong and know what I want. You didn't have to be there to be there for me."

"Oh, *Liv*." Red-rimmed eyes searched mine. He groaned and reached for me, but I recoiled.

"Don't do that, either." A hateful laugh raked my throat. "I broke up with you? God, I fucking knew I'd ruin this. You should've been glad for the out."

Will sat on his knees and caught my shoulders. "Stop. You know I—"

"I'm in love with you, Will."

He smiled. And my heart reassembled itself for the sole purpose of shattering again.

"It's about time," he murmured.

"It's not. It was always true. *Always*." I shut my eyes and shuddered. "Damn you, Will Langer. Don't smile like it's a good thing. I love you too much, you jerk. You've fucked me. Don't you get it?"

"Hmm. I assume you're speaking metaphorically, not literally."

I bit my lip to keep the scowl going. "Hush. This is serious. You should've taken the out when I called. You should've moved on and left me to figure out how the hell I'll survive when you... when you..."

"When I find my BMW-driving, martini-drinking wife?"

I groaned and sank my nails into his biceps. Tears blurred my vision, so the first time I saw his lips twitch, I thought I imagined it. But then he cleared his throat.

I startled. "Are you laughing?"

"Of course not," he rumbled—

Just before he completely lost it.

Tears were forgotten. I slapped his shoulder while he chuckled merrily. "You dick! Deep, dark fears are being shared here. Heartfelt confessions and shit are going down, and you're *laughing*? A bit of decorum, please, douchebag."

I shoved him, but Will was helpless with humor like I'd never seen him before.

"You better stop hitting me," he rumbled at last. "Before it's my turn."

His eyes sparkled when they locked on mine. Knowing full well what I was doing, I punched his arm. It had been minutes since he'd touched me.

Far too long.

Will rumbled a sound somewhere between a laugh and a growl. He launched forward and tumbled me backward to the ground. Knees by my hips, hands by my ears, his scent flooded my nose and all the dark spaces in my soul.

With his lips against mine, Will murmured, "There will be no BMWs. No suits. No Stacy or June. There will be La Perla in my apartment if and only if they belong to you.

There will be you, Olivia Milani, or there will be no one. It's *that* easy. What do I have to do for you to believe me?"

I gripped his collar. "I love you, Will Langer."

His sigh pressed against my chest. "I love you, Liv Milani. I've loved you since always."

The wink he added nearly dissolved my underwear, but I nodded slowly. "I know."

"Oh, yeah? How do you know?"

I shrugged. "I just know it—here." I pressed his heart, and mine began to piece itself together again at last.

His kiss was soft and gentle and only half of what I'd hoped for, but it said everything.

Will lifted his head. We both looked around, seeming to realize at the same moment that we were sprawled on the floor between the living room and the foyer. His eyes swept left, mine right, before we locked gazes again, matching smirks on our lips.

"The agent of my downfall," we whispered together.

My nemesis wasted no time in getting us off the floor and up to my bedroom. By the time the door latched, my cardigan was on the bench, and his shirttails fluttered over his open trousers.

"I brought you to your knees," I teased in his ear, then grinned at his chuckle.

"I brought you to yours. I like the idea of both of us on our knees. Imagine the possibilities."

His fingers threaded in my hair, lips finding mine. I couldn't hold in the whimper as parts of me that had been dark too long lit up.

Will smiled his easy smile before he nibbled my lip. His

hands coasted over my shoulders and curved under my breasts. Thumbs swished, and I went limp.

"Shh, let me give you what you need," he soothed when my shaky hands tugged on his shirt.

I needed slow and gentle. I craved his touch fiercely, but he knew without my saying that we should take it easy. Luckily, Will Langer can do slow just as well as he does rough.

Pleasure had made me dizzy and dreamy when he laid me back on the bed and peeled off my tank top. My hazy eyes opened when his shoulders tensed under my palms. He gazed down at the deep bruise which still stood out starkly on my abdomen.

"Hey," I whispered. "Look at me."

"I want to protect you, Liv. I'm so—"

But I pushed his shoulders and flipped us over. Straddling his lap, I threw my bra to the floor. "Would you rather waste your breath on silly apologies or have hot makeup sex?"

That brought him back. He sat up under me and flicked his tongue across my nipples, and I threw my head back and groaned.

"Good fucking choice."

My orgasm was like finding heaven. Pure bliss washed away any shadow of doubt about us and smoothed all the rough edges of these ugly weeks. They were over.

And we had just begun.

EPILOGUE
LIV

We fell asleep on top of my quilt, woke in the middle of the night, and made love again. I always thought that term was corny, *making love*, but it fit much better than sex or fucking. When we were spent again, we rolled into the sheets and clung to each other until morning.

A gray, late-fall sun filtered into my room when I finally woke, completely wrapped in Will. His arms and legs were around me, my back to his chest, his breath warm on my bare shoulder.

"Happy Thanksgiving," he said with a kiss to my ear.

I snuggled deeper into his arms. "Mmm, you're so *warm*."

"And you're so soft."

I pinched his wrist. "I am not. Badass CrossFit body right here. I'm tough as nails."

He laughed, and I flipped to face him. "Fine. Tough as nails with skin like satin. Better?"

"Better."

"You *were* pretty docile last night, though," he teased.

"Just you wait. I'll be raiding your ties again in no time.

Consider that a warning to behave yourself at dinner today, FYI."

"Oh, you're in for it now." He laughed.

We dozed and petted each other in easy silence. Somewhere between asleep and awake, I mumbled, "My parents know about us. How weird."

"Weird indeed."

"What did you say to Mom? She didn't really tell me."

He yawned and groaned, one arm over his eyes. "That was easily one of the most awkward moments of my life. Well, it would've been if I had given a damn about anything other than you."

"Tell me the story." I put my head on his chest and listened to his heartbeat.

"Things were crazy and tense when they first came in. I was with Megan and Adam, waiting like everyone else. After several hours, your friends went home when it was clear you were being admitted. Tom and your dad went for coffee, and your mom looked over at me. She asked if I'd come with Tom. I didn't answer, but she hugged me, and I guess she just knew. Her eyes got big, brows up, all that. She said something like, 'Oh. You're not here for Tom.' And I said, 'No, Claire, I'm here for Liv.'"

"What did she say then?"

He laughed. "She said, 'Just say it so we can move on.' So, I told her I was in love with you—and I was flattened with guilt over this. She smiled, folded me into a forever kind of hug, and whispered, 'It's about time you two saw it.'"

I didn't need to hear any more. I jerked his boxers down his hips and climbed on top of him. My hair brushed his jaw as I bent for a kiss.

"I love you."

God, it was so easy to say. Why had I ever thought otherwise? Especially when I got his broadest, most perfect grin every time the words left my mouth.

Eventually, we got up, showered, and went to make breakfast. I refilled the coffee and found a good playlist, then began the potatoes and brownies I'd promised to bring for dinner. Will sat at the kitchen table and watched until I made him peel spuds while I did the batter.

"Aren't we cute?" I teased, bumping his hip.

"Precious."

"Aren't you glad you're here instead of all alone today?"

He smiled at his hands. "Yeah, pretty glad."

We fell silent and let the music fill the room while we worked. Once the brownies were in the oven and the potatoes were whipped, I wandered to the living room to watch TV. Will disappeared.

He came into the room and leaned on the top of the recliner, gazing at me while I lounged on the sofa. "I've been thinking. I don't want to be alone anymore."

I smiled and wiggled my feet. "I'm right here, silly."

"Well, exactly. You're here, which means I have to miss you and wonder when you'll be free next. I'd like to know your thoughts on this."

He reached into his pocket and tossed me something. I lifted a hand to intercept before it beaned me in the forehead. It was a key ring with a little pyramid on it, a single key on the loop. I looked at it, then up to him.

Will sat on the couch, so I tucked my legs and sat up. "Move in with me. I was serious the first time I said it. I'm more serious now."

I yelped. "You're crazy. We'll—we'll—we'll never get out of bed. We'll annoy the hell out of each other. We'll... drink coffee on Sundays. We'll make dinner together and talk about our workdays. We'll *not* share a toothbrush."

My eyes got wide. "You're insane."

"We established that long ago. But I'd be a damn fool not to want all I can get with you. Come on, Liv. What do you think?"

I spun the little pyramid between my fingers. That Girl didn't move in with guys. She only stayed the night after a month had passed. More rules from the book.

But That Girl wasn't me anymore. I'd been through too much. Changed too much. I still had whims, still liked my bourbon straight, and would never, ever shy from being myself.

But I'd become someone new.

This girl, Liv, *I*, looked up at the man I loved and smiled. Just before we tumbled to the couch in a kiss, I shrugged and bopped his nose.

"I could be into that."

SNEAK PEEK: JUST YOUR TYPE
ANTI-BELLE BOOK 4

Aren't Megan & Adam cute in *Nemesis?* Wonder what's next for Liv's bestie? Take a peek now, then go buy JUST YOUR TYPE and find out more.

The song "Don't Go Breaking My Heart" blasted from my bedroom stereo. I kicked off my heels and sang along, taking a few spins across the room so my skirt billowed up. "Hey, can you see my panties if I do this?" I asked as I spun again.

Adam laughed from where he sat in the chair in the corner. "Yep."

"Then I guess I'm glad I didn't do it on the dance floor."

"No one would've cared. They were too busy having fun."

I flopped down on the bed and grinned at the ceiling. "It was a perfect wedding, huh? Ben's song he wrote for Celeste was so beautiful. I almost shed a tear."

"You? Crying?" Adam chuckled, and I flipped my middle finger at him. "Celeste's hair was impeccable."

The man knew how to flatter me. My middle finger shifted into a thumbs-up. "Why, thank you for noticing."

Doing wedding hair was always fun. Today's job had been special, though. Having a full-on party in my salon for one of the crew was a blast. Celeste and I hadn't known each other for long, but she was cool. My bestie, Liv, had done her makeup after I did her hair. We both laughed at how she squirmed to be the center of attention. Celeste's mom, grandmother, and aunts were all there, plus the other crew ladies, Melody and Kira. There was no denying it was a special day for her.

I sat up on the bed and crossed my legs, letting the skirt flash my undies again as I smiled at my boyfriend. "It's that time of life, I guess. Everyone's pairing off and settling down."

Adam scratched the back of his head, but he didn't smile. He let his gaze drop to the floor. "Seems like it. Um, babe? Can we talk? I don't know if this is the right time, but... I don't think it's the wrong time, either."

My stomach hit the mattress. I sat up straight and folded my hands in my lap. *Oh, oh my gosh, he's about to... And I'll have to finally tell him about... Shut up, Megs. He's talking.*

I swallowed hard and nodded, biting my lips together.

His gaze stayed on the floor as he spoke. "Megan Riley, you are so special. Since we met last summer, I don't have to tell you what a great time we've had together. I was so pumped when you gave me your number at the restaurant. This hot, badass blonde actually smiled when I said I'd switched tables to wait on her. I felt like I'd freaking *won*."

He finally looked up, and we traded a smile. Adam and I met last year when Liv and I started Crossfit. We'd stumbled into a nearby pub afterward, and Adam waited on us. He and I had chemistry from our first meeting. We'd started dating after a couple of weeks. In the almost year since then, Adam's home contracting business with his brother had taken off.

The anonymous investor who'd gifted them $500,000 at the end of last year vaulted them into a full-fledged company. He quit the restaurant in January to focus solely on growing the business.

Almost a year together. A flourishing business. A wedding today. My heart kept pounding in anticipation of where this was going. I knew if I spoke that I would ruin the moment. So I flashed another grin and tried not to mind that his gaze went back to the carpet.

He took a deep breath and continued. "Anyway, a lot has happened this past year. And with everything going on, I just can't help but think..."

I held my breath.

"That we should take a break."

GET IT NOW.

MORE BOOKS TO BINGE

Click to Get on Skye's Newsletter Now!

The Connecticut Commodores Series

Book 1: Scoreless

Book 2: Scored On

Book 3: In the Crease

The Anti-Belle Series

Prequel: The Not So Nice Girl

Book 1: Not Suitable for Work

Book 2: Off the Record

Book 3: Nemesis

Book 4: Just Your Type

Book 5: What Happens At the Beach

As Sarah Skye

The Unlikely Pairings Series

ACKNOWLEDGMENTS

Sarah, Lily, Jess, and Lauren, your feedback was invaluable as I rounded out Liv and brought *Nemesis* into the world. Avery, as ever, your artistry on the cover is incredible.

Brian, you were an amazing resource on Will's character. Will is the right kind of stylish (fancy) thanks to you. Here's to glass blowing, inflection points, and the Madness.

Readers, you are making this series grow! So thank you for your support, your reviews, and for being your perfect, Anti-Belle selves!

ABOUT THE AUTHOR

Skye McDonald writes books that will make you laugh, cry, and swoon. She believes that falling in love with yourself is the real path to happily ever after.

Skye's first novel, *Not Suitable for Work*, won the Linda Howard Award for Romance in 2019. Her co-authored Unlikely Pairings series (written with Sarah Smith) have been Amazon bestsellers and #1 New Releases. Skye writes about living life with your heart open in her "A Bit Much" Substack.

Born in Nashville, Tennessee, Skye spent years teaching English in Brooklyn, New York. Now, she lives in Montclair, New Jersey, where she writes and facilitates a women's group. In her free time, she hikes with her dogs, runs Spartan races, travels, Scuba dives, and is learning to ski. Someday she'll take a break and chill out, preferably on a beach. But not yet. There's so much life to live first.

www.ingramcontent.com/pod-product-compliance
Lightning Source LLC
Chambersburg PA
CBHW051952240626
47153CB00005B/1729